Echoes in the Cotswolds

Echoes in the Cotswolds

REBECCA TOPE

Allison & Busby Limited
11 Wardour Mews
London W1F 8AN
allisonandbusby.com

First published in Great Britain by Allison & Busby in 2021.
This paperback edition published by Allison & Busby in 2022.

A CIP catalogue record for this book is available from
the British Library.

10 9 8 7 6 5 4 3 2 1

ISBN 978-0-7490-2732-2

Typeset in 10.5/15.5 pt Sabon LT Pro by
Allison & Busby Ltd.

FSC
www.fsc.org
MIX
Paper from
responsible sources
FSC® C171272

Printed and bound by
CPI Group (UK) Ltd, Croydon, CR0 4YY

*Dedicated to friendship in the abstract,
and Liz, Margot, Sally and Flo in the particular.
They've all stuck with me for over fifty years.*

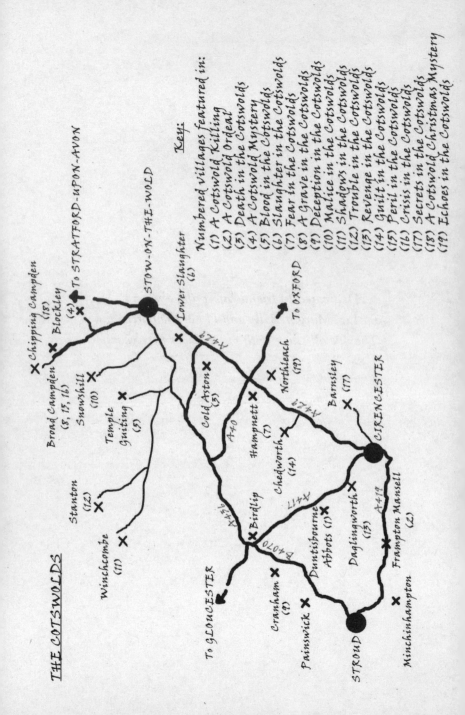

THE COTSWOLDS

Key:

Numbered villages featured in:
(1) A Cotswold Killing
(2) A Cotswold Ordeal
(3) Death in the Cotswolds
(4) A Cotswold Mystery
(5) Blood in the Cotswolds
(6) Slaughter in the Cotswolds
(7) Fear in the Cotswolds
(8) A Grave in the Cotswolds
(9) Deception in the Cotswolds
(10) Malice in the Cotswolds
(11) Shadows in the Cotswolds
(12) Trouble in the Cotswolds
(13) Revenge in the Cotswolds
(14) Guilt in the Cotswolds
(15) Peril in the Cotswolds
(16) Crisis in the Cotswolds
(17) Secrets in the Cotswolds
(18) A Cotswold Christmas Mystery
(19) Echoes in the Cotswolds

TO STRATFORD-UPON-AVON

Chipping Campden (18)
Blockley (4)
Broad Campden (8, 15, 16)
Snowshill (10)
Stanton (12)
Temple Guiting (5)
Winchcombe (11)
Birdlip
Cranham (7)
Painswick
Minchinhampton
Duntisbourne Abbots (1)
Daglingworth (13)
Frampton Mansell (2)
STROUD
TO GLOUCESTER
B4070
A417
A436
A40
Cold Aston (3)
Hampnett (7)
Chedworth (14)
Barnsley (17)
CIRENCESTER
A419
A429
Northleach (19)
TO OXFORD
STOW-ON-THE-WOLD
Lower Slaughter (6)
A429

Author's Note

As with all titles in this series, the action is set in a real village. But the houses and characters are my own invention. The Updike sonnet 'Iowa' is well worth looking up, as are his other poems.

Chapter One

Drew was busy. Beyond busy, in fact. Seven funerals in one week was almost too much for a very small alternative undertaker with limited storage space and an assistant who could hardly move thanks to a vicious bout of lumbago, with the added woes of sciatica for good measure.

'I'll have to turn at least two of them away,' he wailed, whilst knowing the idea was unthinkable. It was five to eight on a Monday morning and already the week was looking impossible. The weekend had bristled with phone calls about dead people.

'You can't,' said Thea firmly. 'We'll get somebody else to help. Call Maggs and Den.'

'They're too far away and we need somebody *now*. This afternoon. There's a man to be removed from the nursing home at Stow, and somebody from the hospice. And nowhere to put either of them. We'll have the council onto us at this rate. Somebody's going to complain. We can't hope to keep it discreet if there are bodies lying around the garden.'

'Calm down. Can Andrew drive at all? If he goes to Stow, there'll be people at the care home who'll do the heavy lifting. That'd be a start. If tomorrow morning's is coffined-up, he can spend the night in the hall.' Thea looked at Drew's children, who were very much involved in the conversation, to the point where Stephanie was liable to be late for school. 'Just don't tell anybody, okay?'

Stephanie had already suggested they ask Mike, the window cleaner, if he had any free time for digging graves. He came every two months to do the windows, and the twelve-year-old had taken to chatting to him. It had, however, come as a surprise to Thea that her stepdaughter had his mobile number. Mike was over thirty with a wife and three children and was not at first sight a threat – but you never knew, as people would insist. 'He left his card here, remember,' said the child patiently. 'And last time he came he said he was worried about losing some customers.'

'So what did he say about digging graves?' asked Drew.

'I think he thought I was joking. You'll have to call him.'

'It's an idea,' said Thea. 'Think how much time that would save. Get him to do all seven.'

'Five. We only need five. I've done the first two already.'

'So *can* Andrew drive?' Stephanie asked.

'Barely. But he might struggle as far as Stow, I suppose. I don't want him to do anything that makes him worse. It was lifting that big coffin ten days ago that set it all off in the first place. The man weighed sixteen stone, Lord help us.'

'Well, just being able to drive is better than nothing,' said Thea, who had her own reasons for wanting everything settled. 'And has tomorrow's person got some sturdy relatives who can do the lowering?'

'Luckily, yes. A sister and two daughters, all pretty well-muscled.' The whole family giggled at the picture this conjured – Timmy loudest of all.

'Don't laugh,' said Drew. 'None of this is funny.'

'It is, though,' said Thea, with a glance at Stephanie. Her stepdaughter generally shared her subversive sense of humour. 'So long as we can laugh about it, it'll all work out fine.'

'At least tomorrow seems to be okay,' Drew conceded. 'But on Wednesday I've got another two, and on Friday there are *three*. Not to mention the big one on Thursday.'

'Big in what sense?'

'Thirty mourners at least, most of them wanting to say something. It'll last for ages.'

'But not really any extra work,' Thea pointed out. 'Just a bit time-consuming.'

Drew was in no mood to be mollified. 'I just can't see how it's all going to be possible.'

'You must have thought it would be when you arranged them all,' Thea said, with dwindling patience. 'Couldn't some of them have waited a bit longer?'

11

'The two o'clock on Friday isn't definite, but I did say I'd pencil it in. She only died on Saturday.' One of Drew's selling points was that families did not have to endure the excessively long hiatuses that mainstream undertakers inflicted on them. A week without embalming fluid could be a long time. 'But they'd be very disappointed if we moved it. Plus, I thought I'd have Andrew. He said he was getting better. And all three families really do want it to be Friday. It's always the favourite day.'

'Yes, I know. Which leaves you quite a lot of Thursday to get everything sorted. Think positive – think of how it's going to boost the coffers. I'm already planning a celebratory trip to Waitrose with the proceeds.'

Timmy laughed again, but nobody else did. It was a somewhat anxious laugh, revealing the child's unease at a situation he couldn't trust to turn out well. Timmy, more than anyone, remembered all too clearly that his stepmother was planning to go away in the middle of the week, taking the dog with her, and would very likely be gone all weekend as well. This, he knew, was why she was so eager for Drew to get his funerals under control, so she wouldn't feel too guilty about going. Not that she was ever much use with Drew's work – and there wouldn't be any actual funerals at the weekend. So she wouldn't really be missed. There had been a full-scale family discussion about it, back in February, and everybody had agreed that there wouldn't be a problem. Now it was almost April, with only a week left of the school term, and Thea's person in Northleach was going for her operation on Wednesday. Probably. 'You can never say anything

12

for definite when it comes to medical matters,' said Thea cynically. 'She wants me to keep it flexible.'

The person in question was called Lucy, and Thea had worked for her before when she'd looked after an assortment of animals in a remote barn conversion and it had snowed. 'I went to a children's party,' she reminisced. 'And there was a very sad dog. Lucy says he's dead now, and all the rabbits have gone, but she still wants a house-sitter.'

'Rabbits?' queried Timmy.

'They were very sweet. Baby ones. Gladwin helped me with them.'

Gladwin was a detective superintendent, who had first befriended Thea years ago in Temple Guiting, during her – Gladwin's – very first murder investigation in her new role. She came from Teesside and had an unorthodox streak that appealed greatly to Thea.

'*Why* does she want a house-sitter?' Timmy had persisted. It unsettled him when Thea went away, mainly because something awful always happened, and everybody ended up scared and cross.

Thea had rolled her eyes and sighed. 'She just does, okay. She's got some nice things and doesn't want to get burgled. Anyway, I won't be there all the time. Just enough to make it look as if the house is still lived in. I told you – I'll pop back here at least once over the weekend.'

Drew had noticed something in her tone and took over from Tim. 'There's more to it than that, isn't there?' he said with a frown. This was after the initial discussion, during which he had been characteristically resigned, and

13

Thea was sorry to have the subject raised again.

'There really isn't,' she promised. 'Some people just hate to leave an empty house.' She wasn't exactly hiding anything, she told herself. There were no hard facts to be concealed – just an impression that all was not well with Lucy Sinclair, regarding not just her physical health, but her mental welfare. She had been restless and distracted when Thea had visited her in February. She left sentences unfinished and constantly threw worried glances out of the window. 'Are you expecting someone?' Thea had finally asked.

'What? No – I hope not. I was just wondering about the neighbours . . .' She had tailed off with a shrug.

The Northleach house was semi-detached, its partner being a smaller dwelling than Lucy's. Thea had conscientiously described it to Drew as being a considerable change from Lucy's Hampnett home. 'Talk about downsizing,' she said. 'The rooms are about a quarter the size of the ones she had before.'

'Easier to heat,' said her husband absently.

'Right.' In fact, the converted barn had boasted a highly efficient heating system that had kept Thea perfectly warm throughout the snowy and icy time she was there. 'I think it's her bad back that's forced her to move,' she added. When she had known Lucy before, there'd been nothing wrong with her back, as far as she could tell. The main detail she recalled was that the woman was freshly divorced and determined to celebrate.

But the funerals were the only topic that Drew currently wanted to think about. He had roamed around

14

the house muttering about schedules and removals and giving a decent service, since seven o'clock that morning. Only Stephanie gave him any attention, remembering names and making suggestions. And then, at eight-fifteen, the phone rang.

All the funeral business was conducted on the landline, unless everybody was out, when calls were diverted to Drew's mobile. If he was at home, only he would answer it – at least in theory. Now he visibly tensed, clearly afraid that here was a final feather that would break his back.

'Shall I get it?' asked Thea, on the third peal. She had been standing on the doorstep watching her stepson trotting up the lane to the bus stop, thinking how much better it was now the mornings were getting lighter. Timmy was still at primary school, entitled to a seat on a bus. Stephanie's transport arrangements were more complicated, generally requiring Drew or Thea to take her there and back in the car.

'No, no.' Drew answered the one in the hall, rather than going into his office at the back of the house. Automatically he switched into his professional voice: kind and approachable, while also businesslike and reassuring. Thea always relished the sound of him soothing a newly bereaved person, remembering why she loved him and what was so exceptional about him.

'Of course,' he was saying. 'Would four o'clock be all right? Sorry I can't manage anything sooner, but . . .' Clearly the person at the other end found this quite acceptable, with no call for excuses. 'All right, then. I'll be here . . .

15

Don't worry about that. It's all part of the service.'

He put the phone down and looked at Thea. 'It's the husband from Saturday. The Friday woman at the hospice. He sounds nice.'

Thea had no difficulty in interpreting the shorthand. A woman had died at the hospice – and was to be removed that afternoon, if at all possible, by the suffering Andrew. Her husband would be coming in at four o'clock to make arrangements for the funeral, which had already been booked for Friday of that week. 'Will Andrew have her back by then?' she wondered. 'If so, where's he going to put her?'

'Good question. I think she'll have to stay in the vehicle till he's gone. Otherwise, there'll be coffins in the passageway and we don't want that. Actually – there'll be people coming tomorrow as well, about the other Friday ones.' He looked harder at Thea, as if trying to summon courage to ask a favour. She knew what he wanted to say – *Can't you do something practical to help? Like sitting down with a family and arranging the funeral?* She had only done that once and found it far beyond her comfort zone. She didn't have the right skills for it and didn't think she ever would have. Stephanie would do a better job.

'I could probably do a removal if you're desperate,' she said with a little laugh. 'So long as I don't have to actually carry anyone.' She was five feet one, and not especially strong. The well-muscled females detailed to lower their relative into his grave the next day were a very different species from Thea Slocombe.

16

'Don't be silly,' said Drew with a sigh.

'Listen – we've already figured out how it can all work. People will understand if you tell them how busy you are. They'll be glad to step up and do more themselves. Didn't you say one of them's already got their own coffin? Things like that. You can make a virtue of it – which is all part of your ethos, anyway. Holding back so the families can be really hands-on. You might even find one or two of them would be happy to dig the grave as well.' She looked at him hopefully, waiting to see if she was saying the right things.

'Thanks,' he smiled, much to her relief. 'I needed that.' He pulled her into his arms and rubbed his face against the top of her head. 'There's nobody in the world who could have made me pull myself together like you've just done,' he mumbled.

She squeezed him tight, thinking that his former partner Maggs would have done just as good a job, and probably Stephanie too. But it was nice that he said it. They'd been married less than two years, having met right here in Broad Campden. They had all too short a history for the kind of risks she had been taking with the marriage. She had forced Drew to be supremely tolerant at times, frightening him and then neglecting him. This time she was going to be a lot more careful. 'Mmm,' she said.

'But what about you?' he asked, pulling back to meet her eyes. 'Going off to Northleach, I mean.'

'Well,' she began, 'it's not for a few more days. I've got time to make sure everything's okay here. I'll take the dog with me, and I'm probably only staying two or three nights. If you need me here, I can come home – I told Lucy that.'

'I know. I didn't mean . . . at least . . .'

'What? What are you trying to say?'

He was starting to look wretched. 'Thea – darling – I keep getting the feeling I'm in your way. That you'd be having a far more interesting life if it wasn't for me and the kids. All this agonising about burying people is hardly thrilling, is it? The Frowse business at Christmas seems ages ago now, and I was pretty boring about it, I know. I'm just a hopelessly dull person.'

She had heard this, or variations of it, before, and felt just as miserable as usual on hearing it again. 'I wish you'd understand how awful that makes me feel,' she said. 'What sort of horrible person wants constant excitement? It's childish. And honestly, Drew, it isn't true. I'm *perfectly* happy here with you, ninety per cent of the time. At least ninety per cent. We've got the best two kids in the world, and just about everything we could wish for. If I get a bit antsy now and then, that's not your fault, and it's not important. Think of it as a sort of psychic malaria that strikes me down three or four times a year. It doesn't do any permanent damage. Not if we don't let it.'

He obviously felt a similar self-reproach to hers. 'Are you sure?' he asked. 'Really really sure?'

She took a deep breath. 'What do I have to do to prove it? Other than break the speed limit to get Stephanie to school on time.' The child was waiting on the doorstep pretending not to notice the adult intimacies going on in the kitchen.

'I don't know. Maybe if you came back saying that Northleach is even duller than Broad Campden, that would be a start.'

'Right then,' she said recklessly. 'I'll do exactly that.' She grabbed the car keys. 'Come on, Steph.'

Chapter Two

But almost immediately the brief harmony was disrupted. Shortly before midday, Thea got a call on her mobile from Lucy Sinclair. 'Just to confirm that the hospital say I'm definitely on the list for Wednesday. There was a risk that I'd be bumped off until Friday, but that's been sorted. I'm assuming Mr High-Up Surgeon wants to play golf or something instead of hacking into my lumbar region.'

Thea had only the most slender grasp of Lucy's medical arrangements. She was going private to have an operation on her back – that was the whole story as far as Thea knew. She would be in a private section of the John Radcliffe Hospital in Oxford, and had hoped to be in control of the schedule as a result. But even private surgeons had constraints and conflicting calls on their time, it seemed. 'Oh,' she said, feeling an entirely inexplicable rush of apprehension flood through her. 'So what does that entail, exactly?'

'It entails me going in either last thing Tuesday or first thing Wednesday – if I go on Tuesday it'll cost more for the extra night, so I decided to make it Wednesday. I might not be home until next Monday. They keep telling me, all reproachful, that I'm making it worse for myself by insisting on general anaesthetic. Slower recovery and all that. They don't believe me when I say it would take even longer to recover my sanity if I had to listen to them chiselling away at my poor bones. And it strikes me that the site for an epidural is dangerously close to the area he'll be operating on. You'd think he'd be glad to have me completely out of it.'

'Mm,' said Thea, thinking there would probably be headphones available to block any gruesome sounds and that the surgeon would already have considered the implications of the proximity of an epidural. 'So – when would you want me, then?'

'Well – would it be out of the question to be here for Wednesday night? And stay till Saturday? Then if I'm not home until the middle of next week, maybe come back on Monday for a night or two?'

'Three nights,' Thea calculated. 'They can probably spare me for that long – although poor Drew's got a terribly busy workload this week.'

'I would be eternally grateful. I realise I sound stupidly paranoid – but the way things are . . . Honestly, Thea, if I couldn't find somebody to be here, I'd never be able to have this operation at all.'

There are other house-sitters available, thought Thea. But Lucy was paying handsomely, and Thea did feel a certain degree of obligation, given how badly she had managed the previous commission in Hampnett. The surprise was that Lucy would even consider using her again. 'None of it was your fault,' she had insisted generously. 'I think you coped magnificently. Anybody else would have run away screaming after the first night.'

When Lucy hesitantly explained precisely why she wanted a guard for her empty house in a peaceful little town, Thea understood that she had very probably been stitched up.

But by then it was too late to change her mind.

She sat down with Drew after lunch and gave him her full attention. Over the washing-up she had been struck by the idea of asking Andrew's wife, Fiona, if she had any spare time to help with the burials, which she immediately conveyed to Drew.

'She works,' he said dismissively.

'Not full time.'

'What were you thinking she could do?'

'Some heavy lifting,' said Thea without hesitation. 'Like Maggs always did. Fiona's used to it, after all.' The Emersons had been farmers until very recently, with all the hay bales and feed bags and floppy newborn calves that had to be routinely shouldered by everyone, male or female. 'She could probably do a removal, if it came to it.'

'My head's all over the place,' Drew complained, passing a dramatic hand across his brow. 'I can't think straight.'

'Come on, then,' she ordered, leading him into the office that had originally been a dining room. 'We'll write everything down, starting from this afternoon. One funeral tomorrow, two on Wednesday and three on Friday. Is that right? And a man coming today to make all the arrangements for one of the Friday people.'

'One on Thursday as well. The biggest one of them all. Seven altogether.' He groaned. 'It can't possibly be doable. What on earth was I thinking?'

'It's absolutely doable. Don't be so pathetic.' She sat down next to him, in the seat designated for relatives who came to arrange a burial. 'Can I write on this?' She tapped a lined notepad lying on the desk. Without waiting for an answer, she wrote 'Monday' at the top and underlined it. 'Somebody has to go to Stow this afternoon. That's the first thing. What's the person's name?'

'Adrian Waters.' He consulted a page of notes. 'Two o'clock tomorrow. The relatives are carrying and lowering.'

'Great. That's him sorted, then. And you've got one of the graves dug for Wednesday, did you say?'

'Penelope Allen,' he nodded. 'Half past ten.'

Rapidly Thea filled the page and moved onto a second and then a third one for Thursday and Friday. She listed the tasks to be fulfilled and likely people to be doing them. At several points she wrote 'family?' as possible participants.

Drew watched her, half amused, half impatient. 'This is my job,' he protested. 'I shouldn't need you to do it.'

'I know. But another pair of eyes can't hurt. You were getting all overwhelmed and panicked. You would have forgotten something. Writing it out like this makes us feel we've got it all under control.'

'Thank you,' he said. 'I must admit it does feel much better now. Although it's never that simple. The families always want to talk. They expect me to be available most of the day of the funeral. You know what they're like. Somebody phones at seven in the morning to tell me they can't find their husband's favourite tie. And afterwards they call to thank me and talk for an hour. I won't have time for any of that this week.'

'Let Andrew do it,' she said decisively. 'He doesn't need his back to take phone calls.'

'Good idea – but they won't have his number, and once I answer the phone, I won't be able to just pass them over to him.'

'Get him over here, then. Sit him down with the phone and let him be useful. It'll take his mind off his bad back. He can arrange any new funerals for next week as well, come to that. He's always saying he'd like to do more of that.'

'While I'm out in the rain and wind doing the dirty work.'

'Precisely.'

'The forecast is horrible for Friday – did you see?'

'I never bother to look more than two days ahead. It won't be right, anyway. Friday is *ages* away.'

'You sound like Timmy,' said Drew with a smile.

'Do I?' She paused, holding her breath. 'Actually, there's something I haven't got round to telling you.'

'About Timmy?' Alarm filled his face.

'No, no. About me. And Northleach. Nothing drastic –

24

just that Lucy's had definite confirmation that she'll be done on Wednesday. There was a chance it would have to wait till Friday. She's going in very early that day, and wants me to be there overnight for three nights.'

'I always did think you'd be going on Wednesday. You make it sound like new news.'

'Do I? I wasn't sure you'd heard it as definite before. And knowing what hospitals are like, it's still not a hundred per cent. The uncertainty must be awful for poor Lucy.'

Any other husband would have drawn suspicious conclusions long before this point. Any other husband would think she had been so unusually helpful and attentive as a way of compensating for a very inconvenient absence. But not Drew. He merely looked at her and asked, 'So when are you going?'

'She wants me on Wednesday evening. She says I can come back here on Saturday night, but I don't think she's very keen on me doing that. She's hoping to be home on Monday. That leaves the house unguarded on Sunday, but it seems she's less worried about weekends.'

'Am I right in thinking she's a very anxious person? That's the impression I've been getting. What can possibly happen to her house for a few days, anyway? People go off on holidays, lock the door, cancel the milk and everything's fine.'

'I know. I expect it's mostly the worry over the operation. She's been agonising about a whole lot of "what-ifs" and got herself in a stew. After all, it's quite a big thing she's having done, and they're not sure exactly what they'll find once she's on the table. Nobody's going to feel very relaxed about something like that, are they? It's all very scary, by any standards.'

'Poor woman,' said Drew. He sat back in his chair. 'You know something? I've a nasty feeling that I ought to feel more sympathetic towards people with problems like that. All I can do is think – well, nobody's dead, what are you so upset about?'

'It's your job,' she reassured him. 'And you're brilliantly good at it. Almost everybody shies away from death, and won't let anybody talk about it. I mean – remember that marvellous woman who kept saying how glad she was her husband had finally died? I bet you were the only person she knew who she could talk to honestly. Everybody else would have expected her to pretend to be grief-stricken. And you help them to *understand* the whole business. The way death's at the absolute heart of everything, even if nobody will ever admit that to themselves. I heard you just the other day saying that to somebody. That girl whose granny had just died. Wasn't she doing philosophy at college or something? You sat down with her for about an hour in here, just letting her try to work it all out. Honestly, Drew, you're much better than any vicar – or doctor or *anyone*.'

'Blimey!' he said. 'That's twice in one day you've told me what's what. It'll get to be a habit at this rate.'

'Don't worry. It's not the sort of thing a person says very often. I guess we both needed a bit of reminding, that's all.'

'That girl reminded me of Stephanie – if "reminded" is the right word. She's how I hope Steph will be when she's twenty. I had no idea she and I were in here so long. It felt like a real privilege to be talking to her, oddly enough.'

'Well, at least you left the door open. We could all hear you. I think Stephanie was even more impressed than I was, actually.'

'Isn't it her chess day today?' he asked, in a fairly obvious association of ideas. 'We're still all right about that, are we?'

'Oh yes, I think so,' said Thea. 'I think they're good for each other.'

Ever since Christmas Stephanie had gone across the lane to play chess with a male neighbour in his sixties. They all called him 'Mr Shipley' and treated him with a degree of deference. Drew had buried his sister, and Thea had invited him to a Sunday lunch many months earlier. He collected antique glass and seemed to have independent means. Regular trips to London were assumed to have a romantic purpose – probably with another man. Information concerning his private life remained in very short supply. Stephanie's eager anticipation every Monday afternoon convinced Drew and Thea that the friendship was perfectly wholesome. 'We talk about philosophy mostly,' the child reported.

'Although they can hardly leave the door open, can they?' Drew's expression suggested that he hadn't liked the implication behind Thea's earlier remark. 'Which I did not do deliberately, let me tell you. The office was cold, and I was hoping to get some warmer air coming in if the door was open.'

'It's okay,' she smiled. 'I feel just the same as you about that sort of thing. It's no way to live, expecting everybody to have lascivious motives all the time. Even so, it did cross my mind that Stephanie could be developing feelings for Mr Shipley that need to be acknowledged. You know what it's like when you're twelve.'

'Not really. I have a feeling it's different for boys.'

'Everything's incredibly *intense*. You can't imagine how passionately I adored my French teacher – though I think that was fourteen, actually. Anyone who takes you seriously at that age is liable to become an object of worship. When the French teacher left, I instantly transferred my affections to Mr Clarke.'

'History,' Drew remembered. 'Yes, you told me about him.'

'It all seems a thousand years ago now,' she sighed. 'Just a faint echo somewhere at the back of my head. I can't properly remember what it was like. I just know it felt terribly important.'

'But she can still go and play chess with him?'

'So long as it's all right with him, I suppose. I did wonder if we should have a little talk to him about it. It might be awkward being the object of adoration.'

Drew said nothing, but tapped his fingers on the desk as if waiting for a change of subject. Thea fell quiet for a moment and then said, 'Your customers must fall for you sometimes. All that heightened emotion and you so sweet and sympathetic with them. It's obvious, really.'

'Luckily it doesn't last very long.'

'Unless it's Greta Simmonds.'

Drew laughed uneasily. Greta Simmonds had fallen for his charms to such an extent that she'd left him her house. He and Thea were living in it now. If they were entertaining echoes from the past, then Greta had to be one of the primary ones.

'So it's all right for me to go to Northleach, then?'

'You aren't really asking for my permission, are you? I thought we decided we weren't that sort of couple. And I thought it was all settled months ago.'

'I'm consulting your wishes, and your convenience. It's not the same thing. And I'm trying to avoid making the same mistakes again as I made last year. We are a couple, after all – of whatever sort.'

'We're being ever so serious today, aren't we? Checking that things are all right, and working as a team. It's nice,' he added hurriedly. 'Very nice, in fact.'

'That's all right, then. And listen – I'm going to keep in better touch this time. I won't just disappear and leave you to make the best of it.'

'If I remember rightly, it was more a case of me not wanting to give you the full story, if we're talking about when you went to Barnsley. I never did understand why you felt so guilty about it.'

She shook her head, feeling suddenly too weak to attempt any further soul-searching. She had done her best, and Drew showed no signs of annoyance or wounded feelings. His funerals would all get accomplished somehow, of course. After this hectic week, it was almost certain there'd be a period of inactivity and scanty income to balance it out.

'I've got to collect one of the Friday people from Cheltenham,' he said glumly. 'Did I mention that? I hate Cheltenham – I always get hopelessly lost.'

'So do I. And no, you didn't specify that it was there. I

29

thought they were all local. When would you have to go?'

'It'll have to be Wednesday afternoon, I suppose.'

Thea consulted her untidy list of tasks. 'What's the name? Which one is it?'

'Julia Edwards,' he said automatically. The names of his customers fixed themselves firmly in his mind from the first time he heard them. 'She's ninety-eight and lives with her granddaughter, who is sixty or so. They're keeping her at home until I arrive to remove her.'

'Ah,' said Thea, tapping the relevant line on her pad. 'And making their own coffin. Good for them. So you don't really need to go until Thursday, do you? When did she die?'

'Saturday night. It's iffy leaving her till Thursday, although the weather's not particularly warm.'

Thea could not repress the thought that any aroma of decomposition might just as well haunt Mrs Edwards' granddaughter's house as her own here in Broad Campden. Once in a while she wondered if any taint of the all-too-distinctive smell clung to the clothes of the Slocombes. Did the children go to school trailing clouds of mortality, thereby repelling potential little friends?

'Well, that's up to you,' she said. 'The satnav should be able to get you to the house, surely?'

'Mm,' said Drew. They had an elderly TomTom, which was not au fait with recent alterations to road layouts, and which seemed to find Cheltenham particularly challenging. 'Sometimes it drops the signal at the crucial moment,' he added.

'Stephanie would tell you to use the phone, like

30

somebody living in the twenty-first century.'

'I would if she was there to hold it and tap it and stop it constantly switching itself off,' he snapped, finally giving way to the stresses of the day. 'When I'm by myself, the thing sets out to torment me. I'll print out a map before I go – the old-fashioned way.'

'It's two o'clock,' she observed with alarm. 'Aren't you supposed to be somewhere?' Again she consulted her list, having forgotten what they'd decided. 'Adrian Waters has to be removed from Stow. And then you've got to coffin him up and check that everything's all right with the family. And you've got that man coming at four. Right?'

The phone rang before he could reply. And while he was still speaking to someone who sounded like a bereaved relative, there was a knock on the door. Hepzie the spaniel barked. Thea opened the door to find Lucy Sinclair standing there, very white-faced.

Chapter Three

'Oh!' said Thea. 'It's you. Come in. What's the matter?' It was only a matter of hours since they'd been speaking on the phone. Seeing the woman here in the flesh was unnerving. She could not recall an instance when one of her house-sitting employers had visited her in her own home and she realised that she did not like it. The two aspects of her life had always been kept as separate as possible, although she could not exactly say why.

Lucy walked in carefully, as if expecting an ambush. For the second time in the past week Thea was struck by the change in the woman she had known a few years earlier. Quite what had brought about the transformation remained unclear. From the confident, affluent owner of a large barn conversion surrounded by fields, Lucy was now transformed into the nervous inhabitant of a small ancient house in a row, with hardly a glimpse of a field to be had. All her pets had disappeared, too. In the process she had aged and now looked to be in her mid fifties, where before she could have passed for ten years younger. She was only an inch or so taller than Thea, with grey hair that looked as if it had been returned to the wild, with none of the dye so common in women her age. Her work had been as a computer fixer, with legions of desperate customers wanting instant rescue. Thea presumed that Lucy still did this work in Northleach, although she had not observed a comparable computer-filled space to the one in the previous house.

'I had to speak to you face-to-face,' Lucy said. 'I couldn't explain properly on the phone.' She looked around. 'Is your husband here? Oh – I recognise the dog.' She bent down awkwardly to pat the spaniel's head. 'Do you remember poor old Jimmy?'

'Very much so,' said Thea, who had the dog slightly on her conscience, even after so much time. The rescued lurcher had shown more spirit than expected, and asserted his ancestral instincts to a fatal degree. Thea had not taken it well. 'You told me he'd died.'

'Yes,' sighed Lucy. 'Not long after you were there, actually. I had him put down in the end. He was an absolute wreck – not enjoying life at all.'

Thea's conscience twanged like a piano string. 'Oh dear,' she said. 'I hope it wasn't my fault. I don't think he and I ever really understood each other.'

Lucy worked her shoulders in a half-shrug. 'Never mind that now. The thing is—'

'Come in here,' Thea interrupted, indicating the kitchen. 'Drew's on the phone in the office. It's all rather hectic here this week.'

Lucy settled at the kitchen table and started again. 'The thing is, I came to the conclusion I should tell you more about what's been going on with my neighbours. I was hoping I needn't explain – that just having you in the house would be enough to keep everything – well, to prevent anything bad happening. It's my own fault, I know. I've never found it easy to get along with people like them. To begin with I thought they probably meant well, but the truth is, they really don't.'

'What have they done?' Thea asked impatiently.

'Nothing specific. It was me, really, if I'm honest. I said the wrong thing, and caused offence without meaning to.'

'All too easy these days,' Thea sympathised.

'I suppose so. But it wasn't anything like that – none of the usual sensitive areas. It's a long story and will sound very silly, I expect. But the fact is, I'm actually quite scared. There's a man called Hunter, who preaches free speech and personal liberty and then doesn't like it if somebody says the wrong thing.' She wrinkled her nose in disgust. 'It's fine as long as it stays in the abstract, but try telling him anything about himself, and all hell breaks loose.'

'So you're scared he'll actually do something violent?'

'Not exactly. It's just the whole *atmosphere*. The women next door are always spying on me, and even the girl over the road is terribly intrusive. They all tell me what to do and what to think, and try to drag me into their pathetic societies.' She looked miserably at Thea, with wide blue

34

eyes. 'I should never have moved. It was a huge mistake.'

'Oh.' Thea was briefly transported to the weeks she spent in Lucy's barn, snowed in and frightened. The absence of colour or sound or human company had shown her new areas of vulnerability that she had mainly avoided up to then. It seemed to her that living in a quiet village street had to be preferable. 'Are you trying to warn me about something in particular?'

'In a way, yes. After last time, I'm surprised you even agreed to come, although everything's completely different this time, because I'm not doing the same work now. And I know it all seems back to front. Nobody could think of Northleach as threatening. But they probably won't leave you alone, once they see you're in the house. Although you won't be bothered by people with broken computers, like last time, because I'm not doing that any more.' She sighed. 'That's sort of the problem, really.'

'Oh?' said Thea again.

'I make websites for people now. They do still phone or come knocking on the door, at odd times, but nothing like so much as before. The thing is, I've been doing some work for a group in Northleach. All to do with old songs and broadsheets and the wool industry.'

Thea laughed in bewilderment.

'Honestly – it does all link up. But there are some very strong characters, and they get very passionate about it all. My crime was in not taking them seriously enough. I stupidly hurt some feelings and put some backs up, and now they seem to want to kill me.'

Thea held her breath for a moment. Not only was she

the wife of an undertaker, but she had personal experience of far too many violent deaths. Lucy obviously didn't mean it literally, but it was still a statement not to be taken lightly. 'Why?' she asked, thinking she must be missing something.

'Oh, it's too silly to explain in detail. You know how committees can be. There are factions and vendettas and all that sort of thing that matter terribly at the time, but sound ridiculous to an outsider. There are these two women next door, Faith and Livia, not to mention Bobby. They live together but make a great point of insisting they're not a couple, as if anybody cares. And Hunter, who thinks about sex at least ninety per cent of the time. Everything he says is innuendo and can be incredibly offensive. That was my mistake – trying to get him to back off. I dare say he doesn't really mean it, but it's very annoying. I guess he's done it all his life and can't change now. He's an utter fool, believe me.' Lucy's expression suggested that she might have some personal history in connection with Hunter, but Thea didn't ask.

'I've never been on a committee,' she said irrelevantly. 'They sound awful.'

'They are,' Lucy confirmed. 'Anyway, the point is, Faith and Livia are right next door, with our gardens adjoining at the back. They'll talk to you over the fence every time you go outside, all chummy and interested. But really they'll be wanting to ferret out how long I'm away and whether there've been any phone calls, and did the book I ordered ever arrive. All sorts of stuff like that.'

'Doesn't sound too bad,' said Thea cautiously.

'They've taken over my *life*,' Lucy wailed. 'It's a

nightmare. Believe it or not, this is the first time I've ever lived with neighbours, and it's absolute hell. I feel watched and judged the whole time. Honestly – in the *Cotswolds*, where everybody's usually too busy or too rich or just too stand-offish to bother with the people next door. Why did I have to land up with neighbours who think my house is just an extension of theirs? If I don't keep the back door locked, they think nothing of hopping over the fence and coming in without even knocking.'

'Put up a bigger fence,' Thea advised.

'I can't. They're responsible for the one on that side.'

'And what about Hunter? Where does he live?'

'The other end of town, on the high street. Five minutes' walk away. But he does at least wait to be invited.'

'And Bobby? Who's he?'

Lucy looked blank for a moment. 'Oh – Bobby's a she. The one across the road. Her name's Bobine, apparently. American. That's a whole different story.' She reached for a biscuit that Thea had placed on the table. 'And then there's Kevin,' she said, as if keen to complete the picture. 'He's my ex. He keeps turning up in Northleach, for some reason.'

Despite herself Thea was intrigued. She liked meeting new people, learning as much as she could about the undercurrents in a village or small town. Northleach was inescapably lovely, as so many Cotswolds settlements were. No two were the same, and yet they almost all achieved the effortless appeal of old stone and colourful gardens. In an undulating landscape, many of them seemed to have perversely chosen to perch on a hillside or nestle discreetly in a valley, giving their streets odd angles and elevations that led to the need for flights of steps or sudden little alleyways. Footpaths ran in all directions, and stone walls required stiles of every description for people to gain access to the other side.

Lucy's little house was in a row that formed part of a street called West End. It was indeed the western end of Northleach, albeit barely two minutes' walk from the centre, where there were a dozen or so shops and the big famous church. The houses opened directly onto a wide pavement, their front windows mostly blanked out by thick curtains or internal shutters. Why, Thea wondered now, had Lucy elected such a conspicuous site, when she clearly hated to be seen? The front rooms inside the houses must be sadly deprived of natural light, where the inhabitants were so keen to elude observation. Many of them probably contained valuables, which had to be concealed from aspiring burglars.

Closer to the centre of town the houses were set well back from the pavement, with intervening gardens. They were bigger and far more expensive, Thea presumed. And a great deal more private. There were gates into the gardens and hedges or fences. All this she had observed on her preliminary visit some weeks earlier. She had described it all to Drew.

'So – you've come here now to warn me not to fraternise with the neighbours? Is that right?' She frowned at Lucy, trying to assess the exact level of difficulty in what she had heard.

'In a way, yes. If I've understood you as I think I have, you won't be any keener than I am on being interrogated by people with too much time on their hands. I don't want you to get in a state about any of it, if it comes as a surprise. But believe me, you'd be wise not to encourage any of them.' Lucy mirrored Thea's frown. 'That sounds garbled. I probably shouldn't have come, but you can see why I couldn't say all that over the phone. But I did want to ask you one more favour.' She took a breath. 'Do you think you could drive me to the hospital early on Wednesday?'

'What – all the way to Oxford? No, sorry. I can't possibly.' The refusal came readily, with no need for thought. She made no attempt to find excuses. The idea was preposterous.

Lucy was startled, but refrained from begging. 'I suppose I'll have to get a taxi, then,' she said.

'There must be somebody that can do it. What about taking your own car? You'll be all right to drive when they discharge you, surely?'

Lucy shook her head in exasperation. 'No, I won't. They can't say for sure how I'll be, but I might have to have weeks of physiotherapy before I can even walk properly.' She put a hand to her back, and seemed to press hard enough to make herself flinch. Thea was reminded of Andrew Emerson and his lumbago. And before that, her sister-in-law, Rosie, whose back had not been right through her entire adult life. And yet Lucy showed none of the same signs of chronic pain that the others did. A slight stiffness, a bit of hesitancy, were all she revealed as reason for needing surgery.

'Is it a dangerous operation?' Thea asked baldly, thinking she ought to have asked this sooner. 'Is there any chance that it won't work?'

'Some. I haven't told you the full story about that, either. It's an old injury that's flared up. Two of my vertebrae are crooked and getting worse, and they're pressing on nerves. We thought it would come right with a lot of physio and a horrible corset thing, but it hasn't. So they've got to try and fuse them together. Right in the middle of my back.' Again she put a hand to the place. 'It's started to get quite painful, and it's an awful place to try to get at. I end up rubbing myself against doors and corners of walls to try and ease it.'

'It sounds as if they know what to do to fix it,' said Thea bracingly. She was getting the impression that there was nothing unduly alarming or even urgent about the woman's condition.

'Let's hope so. I still wouldn't trust them to get an epidural right.'

Thea heard the front door opening, and Hepzie gave a yap. 'Gosh – what time is it?' Thea said in alarm. 'Is that Timmy home already? I'm going to be late for Stephanie, if so.'

'It's three-fifteen,' said Lucy.

'Heavens! Sorry – I'll have to go. She'll be waiting. I'd better send her a text.'

Timmy came slowly into the kitchen, looking tired and somewhat grubby. 'Was it games today?' Thea asked him in puzzlement.

He shook his head. 'No. I fell over.' He looked down at his knees, and the muddy stains on his trousers. 'Sorry.'

'Oh, Tim. Do you want to come with me to get Stephanie, and tell me about it in the car?'

He shook his head again. 'Is Dad here?'

'Yes. He's busy. There's somebody coming at four. This is Mrs Sinclair, whose house I'm looking after this week.'

'Hello,' said Tim listlessly.

'Hi,' said Lucy. 'If you ask me, there's been a bit of fighting going on – am I right? I can see the signs.'

Thea was texting Stephanie and gathering up car keys and coat. 'Fighting?' she echoed, absently.

Lucy stood up. 'I've got three boy cousins, all younger than me. I remember that look.'

'I've got to go,' said Thea urgently. 'Tim – tell Dad about it, if you like. And show Mrs Sinclair out. I won't be long.'

And she was gone, leaving a trail of unfinished stories and unconfirmed plans behind her. In the car she thought about Northleach and new people, and tourists passing by outside. She wondered about the references to old songs and local history, and what any of it had to do with anything.

Chapter Four

Stephanie was sitting on a wall outside the school gate, staring into space, apparently unconcerned at being left uncollected for twenty minutes. But when she saw Thea her expression changed. 'Why are you late? Is Dad all right?' she demanded, before she was fully inside the car.

'Yes, he's fine. We had a good long talk at lunchtime and now he's feeling much better about getting everything done. The families are going to have to do more for themselves, but that won't matter. They'll probably be glad. I expect he's phoned them all by now, to see what they can work out.'

'Good,' said Stephanie thoughtfully. 'Was that your idea?'

'Not really. I might have had to remind him of a few things. I think he'd got into a bit of a rut, and needed a nudge. He hasn't done one of his talks to the Women's Institute or wherever for ages now – they were always useful for getting him back on track.'

'Andrew should do that. Like Maggs did. She was always telling him what the families really wanted, and how he should try not to be such an undertaker.'

Thea laughed. The young girl had pinpointed precisely the crucial issue.

'So why were you late, then?' Stephanie persisted.

Thea told her some of Lucy Sinclair's worries, trying to make it sound amusing. 'Sounds as if we're lucky with our neighbours,' she concluded.

'Right. And now I'll be late for Mr Shipley. That's not being a very good neighbour, is it?'

'I forgot all about him,' Thea admitted.

'You forgot about *me*,' Stephanie pointed out.

'And there I was thinking I was doing rather well these days,' sighed Thea. 'But at least I've kept your father happy. I should get a star for that.'

'Mm,' said Stephanie, clearly thinking that a wife ought to do that sort of thing automatically, without expecting praise for it. Then she changed the subject. 'We did something about Northleach at school,' she said. 'All that wool making so much money – it was corrupt, you know.'

'Enclosures,' said Thea vaguely.

'Partly. I can't remember exactly, but we had to look at history websites, and there was more about Northleach than almost anywhere else. Can I go there with you one day?'

'Absolutely. Maybe at the weekend. If the house is as

43

quiet and safe as I expect, I can come home for Saturday night – and then maybe pop back on Sunday with you. I still don't properly understand what she wants me for, anyway. She just seems to think that everybody hates her, and they might burn her house down or something. Then you could come at the weekend.'

'Great,' said Stephanie. Then they were home, and Drew was looking drained, and Timmy said he had a headache. The girl ran upstairs to change and then over the lane for her promised chess game.

Lucy had left a note, with the house key and her mobile number, saying she was sorry Thea had rushed off, as there was more she'd wanted to say.

'Oh dear,' said Thea. 'I suppose it was a bit rude of me.'

'She wasn't cross,' said Timmy. 'Not until Dad made her go, anyway.'

'I didn't!' Drew protested. 'I just told her we had quite a lot to do and there wouldn't be any time for further discussion.'

'The phone kept ringing,' Tim added.

'Has anybody been to Stow yet?' Thea asked. 'And where's your four o'clock person?'

'Andrew said he could manage so he's going off now. He'll be back by five. Actually, I doubt if he'll be able to do any lifting, so . . . ?'

'You want me to carry a dead body into the back room with you,' Thea supplied, with only the slightest shiver. 'I hope he's not very big.'

'Not carry – just lift him onto the trolley. Andrew might say he can do it, after all. He seemed a little bit easier today when I saw him. He thinks it's mostly sciatica now, and not so much lumbago. And the four o'clock is only a couple of minutes late.'

'Somebody's here now,' reported Timmy, a fact confirmed by a yap from the spaniel. Drew and his client disappeared into the office, and Thea began preparations for the evening meal. An hour passed with people coming and going in a predictable pattern. Stephanie and Andrew were both in the house before five, talking together in the kitchen with Drew, who had made a pot of tea. Thea and Timmy were idly listening.

Stephanie was tapping her phone – a habit she had recently acquired and which Thea found irritating. 'Sciatica . . . Lower back, with sharp shooting pains down one leg, which is often worse when sitting down,' she reported. 'Although painful, most cases resolve with non-operative treatments in a few weeks. That's good, isn't it!' She beamed at the adults. 'Although it sounds as if driving must be nasty.'

'No mention of lifting or bending, then?' asked Drew.

Stephanie flicked and tapped for a moment, and found that lifting heavy loads could be a contributory cause, and that sudden movements were a bad idea. 'Nothing about bending,' she concluded.

'Sounds as if you don't believe me,' Andrew challenged jokingly. 'Are you trying to say I ought to be out there getting Mr Waters into the cold room on my own?'

'Absolutely not,' Drew assured him. 'I'm just curious, and Stephanie likes to look things up.'

Thea was still thinking mainly of Lucy and her little

house. The story had been ruthlessly interrupted, she realised, with a lack of a proper explanation for the woman's neurotic anxieties. Perhaps that was just as well; perhaps it would be best to find out for herself just how troublesome the neighbours really were. The list of names was already growing fainter in her memory, and she went in search of a notepad to jot them down before they vanished completely. 'Faith, Livia, Bobby and Kevin,' she murmured, as she wrote. 'And somebody else on the committee, who lives in the high street . . . a surname . . . Hunter! Got it.' And she wrote that down as well.

Andrew had arrived at four-fifty with the body of Adrian Waters, looking pale but determined. When Thea asked how his back was, he muttered that it was about the same, through gritted teeth. 'Turns out driving doesn't do it any favours,' he added. Watching him, Thea thought he had a very different look from that of Lucy Sinclair. Both middle-aged and suffering from spinal issues, there was little of Andrew's dogged stoicism laced with apprehension in the woman. She seemed to pay very little attention to her physical self.

'Did anybody help you?' asked Drew, who now went outside to help him. 'Are you all right to back in?' The van needed to be carefully reversed around the side of the house to the door into the cool room that had been constructed for the storage of bodies.

'No,' said Andrew decisively. 'It's agony if I twist. I'm not going to try and lift him, either.'

'Let me, then.'

Andrew and Thea both watched as Drew took his place in the driving seat. Thea was waiting to see if she would be needed. A wheeled trolley stood beside her to receive the body. The whole process was practised and efficient, the need to be quick and inconspicuous taken for granted. Whilst there had never been any direct complaints from the neighbours on either side, there was every reason to maintain discretion. The hearse was tucked further down the garden, out of sight until in use. Recently Drew had asked himself why he'd ever needed such a striking vehicle anyway. A large van would have been a lot more economical, used for all stages of the business, and probably more in keeping with his preferred way of doing things. But somehow a funeral seemed to demand at least some of the traditional accoutrements. A van would lack the side windows or the purpose-built platform for the coffin and the flowers. While it might be suitably adapted, there would still be an air of casualness and lack of dignity that offended Drew's sense of rightness. There was a deep-seated need to celebrate the person's last journey, to give it an element of display and ensure that there was no hint of secrecy about it. A proper hearse provided a defiant counter to the abiding taboos around death with its generous windows and Drew was foolishly fond of the big black thing.

It was only the second time Thea had been actively involved in transferring a body and she found herself flinching more than expected. She had the feet, invisible in the dark green body bag, but still very tangible. 'Hold him under the knees,' Drew instructed. 'His legs aren't stiff any more.'

The weight was considerable, and Thea was small. The whole operation was cumbersome, though blessedly fast. It had only been a matter of swivelling the body around at ninety degrees to be dropped onto the waiting trolley, once Drew had slid it out of the van. 'Urghh!' she said when it was done.

'Sorry,' came Andrew's voice behind her. 'I'll make sure you don't have to do that again.'

'Don't worry. I don't mind really,' she assured him. 'It's just that I'm not built for this sort of work. We've got a whole lot more to come this week, haven't we?' The details that she had worked out so carefully with Drew that morning had grown as hazy as the names of Lucy Sinclair's adversaries. 'But the families are going to do most of the heavy lifting,' she finished optimistically.

The day ended with all four of them feeling exhausted. Timmy had admitted that there had been a scuffle at school, but insisted it was nothing to worry about. Nobody had picked on him specifically, just the usual pushing and punching. Drew was obviously unhappy about it, not least because he already knew that he would consign the whole episode to the very bottom of his list of priorities.

Stephanie was in full diplomatic mode, pleased to see the adults in such harmony, and teasing Thea lightly for her enforced participation in funeral matters.

'I'm only waiting until you grow a bit more, and then you can do it,' her stepmother told her.

'I'm looking forward to it,' said Stephanie calmly.

'Poor girl was born to it,' said Drew. And he recounted

yet again the story of his daughter's early years, which were largely spent with him in his office, or following him and Maggs up to the burial ground just outside their house.

Tuesday passed much more smoothly than either Thea or Drew had expected. Mr Waters was buried with the exact right level of ceremony, his relatives enthusiastically participating. Afterwards they clustered around Drew with shining faces and told him how *real* it had been, and how enormously much they appreciated his style. They had no aversion to seeing the open grave waiting for Penelope Allen next morning, asking with genuine interest about schedules and procedures and workloads. When they'd gone, Drew dug the second grave for Wednesday and spoke at length to the family of Susan Westcott who was to be buried there.

'So far so good,' he puffed, when he finally joined the family for the evening meal at six. 'And you know what? One of the Waters daughters said I charged much too little, and they were adding two hundred pounds because it was all so wonderful.'

'Well done,' said Thea. 'That's fantastic.'

'Did you ask Mike if he could help?' Stephanie enquired.

'I left a message on his phone,' Drew told her. 'But he hasn't come back to me.'

Thea's thoughts turned increasingly to Northleach and the new cast of characters she was hoping to meet. A brief exchange with Lucy during the day had resulted in a decision to go over there early next morning and stay at least two nights. 'It won't hurt to change the plan if you want to. It might be a good idea to keep everyone guessing,' said Lucy ominously.

When Thea had looked after Lucy's house in Hampnett, she had been paid seventy pounds a day for a month, which had been very generous. 'I got a good divorce settlement,' Lucy had said. The husband was still around some years later, although on what basis remained entirely obscure.

Timmy had come home from school with a bruised elbow after what had obviously been another scuffle. When Thea examined it, she could see it must have taken an exceptionally hard knock. 'What happened?' she asked. This time, Timmy revealed a more worrying situation, with two Year Six boys throwing their weight about, and mocking the undersized son of the undertaker.

'Don't tell anybody,' he begged her. 'That'll only make it worse.'

Thea sighed. For all the pious words about bullying, with study days and earnest homilies and mantras delivered constantly, little had actually changed. Adults could never hope to monitor the subtle cruelties and tortures that went on right under their noses. For some reason, it seemed to Thea that teachers more than most people had forgotten what it was like to be a child. The terror that could be inflicted by a big sister or even an enraged smaller brother was beyond description. If you were born into a big family, every day could be a war, with deep scars and real fear. Blackmail, extortion, malicious teasing and extreme mind control could all emanate from curly-haired little cherubs. Quite how anyone made it through to adulthood without serious damage seemed quite miraculous at times.

'I hate to say it, Tim, but your only hope is to fight back,' Thea told her stepson. 'Maybe you could try scaring them with stories about dead bodies. Make them think you know all sorts of dark secrets about what happens when you die. Give them some good nightmares and see how they like that.'

'Thea!' Drew protested. 'What are you saying?'

'It's good practice for adulthood,' said Thea, who had begun to understand that this was precisely true. People with siblings were better equipped to deal with conflict in later life. Arguments amongst committee members would always feel trivial in comparison with childhood battles. Lucy Sinclair had all the signs of an only child, it seemed to Thea.

'She's right,' said Stephanie, to everyone's surprise. 'Come on, Tim – I'll help you think of what to say.'

'If the teachers hear about it, we'll be even worse social outcasts than we are now,' worried Drew.

'The teachers won't hear about it,' said Stephanie. 'Teachers are idiots.'

'My thoughts exactly,' said Thea.

But Drew had the last word. 'It's wrong to generalise,' he argued. 'I've known some magnificent teachers in my time.'

Later, with the children in bed, he reproached her again. 'I'm all for a bit of healthy scepticism,' he said mildly, 'but deliberate undermining of authority can't be good, surely?'

'You're right, I know. And I don't really think all

teachers are idiots, exactly. It's the system. And all the impossible efforts not to offend anybody. That must be paralysing for the poor things.'

'Let's not get started on that,' said Drew and fell instantly asleep.

Chapter Five

Thea left for Northleach before nine next morning, having first delivered Stephanie to school and given Timmy some bolstering remarks about dealing with his unpleasant schoolmates. No way could she have taken Lucy to Oxford, she assured herself. She was far too indispensable at home for a dawn drive of that sort. The fact that the family would have to manage without her the following two school mornings had entailed considerable forward planning as it was.

The route took her through an estate called Sezincote, the name alone enough to fascinate her. It was part of a short cut from the A424 to Stow-on-the-Wold, which had become popular thanks to GPS systems seeking the shortest route regardless of conditions. In fact, the road was reasonably good, with an added bonus of sudden immense vistas over the eastern stretches of the Cotswolds. Great trees clustered here and there beside the road, adding to the beauty of the landscape in exactly the right measure. At the centre of the estate was a grand house built in the Mughal style two centuries ago. Thea had never gone through the gates for a look, even though the gardens were open to the public. Tours of the house were impossibly expensive. She knew there were statues of elephants and snakes and Brahman bulls, the whole property a shameless folly, as bonkers in its own way as the ridiculous-but-fascinating Snowshill. There were numerous eccentric properties scattered around the region, many of which she had encountered in her house-sitting days. From Winchcombe to Bibury they survived, protected by the National Trust and admired by Americans.

Sezincote had thousands of acres of farmland, with outbuildings and cottages, and a similar secretive atmosphere to many other large estates, despite the public road running through it. She never saw any signs of life there.

Northleach was some distance to the south of Broad Campden, the drive taking a good half-hour. From Stow she took the familiar A429, redolent with memories from recent years. She passed turnings to Cold Aston and the Slaughters where she had become embroiled in troubles that had touched her closely. Not far beyond them lay Temple Guiting where another crisis had drawn her in. The very road itself carried echoes and associations that filled her head, even in the short stretch between Bourton-on-the-Water and Northleach. She characterised it as 'Roman-straight' when describing it to herself, along with other highways which also gave witness to the invaders of two thousand years ago.

Lucy's house appeared entirely unmolested as Thea parked in the street outside and unlocked the front door, feeling very conspicuous. There were no sheltering trees or walls to conceal her from observers in the houses opposite or passing cars. It was dramatically different to her own home in Broad Campden, which was down a dead-end track where hardly anyone passed. Already she had a glimmer of comprehension about Lucy's paranoia. Anyone would feel edgy in such a situation.

Inside it was shadowy, but warm. The thick walls kept out any cold winds, as well as virtually all external sounds. The rooms were small, but well proportioned, with little sense of being cramped. Even in her converted barn, Lucy had erected several walls, avoiding too many of the huge rooms that many people favoured. There had been one big central space, and several much smaller ones on either side. She had been frugal in this current home, with minimal furniture, but had hung pictures everywhere. There were rugs and skins on the floors. Upstairs Thea found two bedrooms and a tiny third room made even tinier by shelving covering two of the walls. Here was a version of the office Thea remembered from the Hampnett days – smaller but every bit as busy. There was evidently work to be had as a website designer. 'Nice,' Thea murmured to her dog, who had come with her as much-needed company.

The spaniel sniffed a few corners and then jumped onto the sofa in the front room. The window onto the street was behind and above her, covered in a gauzy material that was the contemporary version of a net curtain. It admitted a yellowish light from the street outside that was just enough to obviate any need for further illumination.

There was no sign of a landline phone, and only a very small television was tucked onto a corner shelf. Beside it was a sound system that was evidently of greater importance. The kitchen was at the rear of the house; a narrow space with nowhere to sit. Behind the living room was a dining area that opened onto the further end of the hallway that began inside the front door. Everything was neat and economical, tidy and efficient. A very persistent and observant detective might have concluded that the same person had designed this interior as had done the Hampnett barn conversion.

'So what are we going to do?' Thea asked Hepzibah. 'It's too cold to sit in the garden.' She had brought a book with her, as well as her phone and a small bag of mending. Buttons to be reattached and a torn hem on Stephanie's favourite top. Thea's grandmother had talked a lot about mending and darning and patching, but only in very recent times had people begun to relearn these ancient skills. Thea found it remarkably satisfying, to the point of actively seeking out garments in need of repair.

As had happened many times before, a knock at the door sent everything in a whole new direction. A young woman stood there on the wide pavement, her face full of urgency and excitement. 'Hi! You're the house-sitter, right? Well, I'm here to tell you that Lucy's got trouble. She's in a coma. The hospital just called me.'

American. It had to be Bobby, according to Thea's

calculations. Just how and why she had become the harbinger of awful news was yet to be understood – probably quite a long way down the line of explanations. 'Come in,' she said. 'Or the dog's going to escape.'

It was a calumny against poor Hepzie, who hardly ever felt any need to escape from anything. But it worked and her visitor stepped hurriedly into the hall, and then turned left into the living room with no further invitation. 'Explain,' Thea ordered.

'Right. Fine. They never started the surgery this morning because Lucy had some kind of reaction to the medication – the stuff they give you to get you woozy before the real thing kicks in.'

'Pre-med,' said Thea.

'Okay.' The woman sat down in a chair beside the fireplace. 'Sorry. I'm Bobby Latimer. I live just over the street, a couple of doors from the pub. I've got two kids. Lucy gave my number to the hospital – as well as yours, I guess. She's more my husband's friend than mine, as it happens.'

Aha! Thea seized this detail with her habitual relish.

'Not that I ever thought she'd have them call me. Must be a mix-up. I mean, if she's unconscious, she wouldn't be able to tell them it was best to call you, not me – right? Because there's no way I can drop everything and go visiting. I *told* Lucy I could only manage one or two evenings, if that. Why, hell – it's all the way to Oxford.'

It crossed Thea's mind that an American could be expected to find a thirty-five-mile drive little more than a moment's work. 'Have you left the kids on their own?' she asked.

'Yeah. Just for a couple of minutes. They'll be okay. Millie's five now, going on twenty-two. And Buster's asleep.'

Not Buster! Thea's inner voice protested. *That's too much.*

Bobby read her thoughts and grinned. 'He's actually called Burgess, but that's no name for a baby, let's face it. *Anyway,*' she said again with emphasis, 'someone's got to go over there and check out what's what. I couldn't work out if they think she's likely to die, or what. I mean – it sounded pretty bad. The woman said "She's quite poorly, Mrs Latimer", which wouldn't mean too much in the States, but I guess it's different here. British understatement and so forth.'

'It doesn't sound good,' Thea agreed, her mind whirling. All of a sudden she recalled Lucy saying, 'Now they seem to want to kill me.' Had somebody somehow invaded the hospital and tampered with the medication? Was that even remotely possible? And if so, where did it leave her, Thea Slocombe? 'But I'm just the house-sitter. Nobody's going to tell me anything, are they? She must have some relations.' Knowing as she spoke that the only people Lucy had mentioned were three male cousins and an ex-husband.

'She hasn't. You could pretend to be me,' said Bobby Latimer carelessly.

Thea loved this girl from that moment on. How rare, how delicious, to have somebody actually voice such a transgressive idea. She ought to have known already, of course, from the neglectful parenting and the easy grin. Here was a kindred spirit, unbowed by being in a foreign land with two small children and an invisible husband.

And what's more, Detective Superintendent Sonia Gladwin would love her too, if they ever chanced to meet.

'I doubt it,' she said with regret. 'They probably check ID before they even let you in the building, the way things are these days.'

'Hm,' said Bobby Latimer. 'I guess I should get back to my kids. Do you want to come over and meet them? No sense in staying here.'

There never had been very much sense in staying in Lucy's cottage, Thea decided. Whatever dangers lurked in the shadows, they had directed their malice at the Radcliffe in Oxford, and not in Northleach at all. 'Can I bring the dog?' she said.

'No problem. What's his name?'

'It's a she, called Hepzibah. Hepzie for short. She goes everywhere with me.'

'Like a daemon,' said Bobby. 'You know – in the Philip Pullman books.'

Luckily, Thea had become familiar with the concept of a daemon, thanks to Stephanie. 'She is a bit like that, yes,' she agreed. 'We've had some exciting times together.'

They crossed the street to a cottage similar to Lucy's in age and colour, but larger. Inside it seemed impossibly spacious. Essentially it had been transformed into one enormous room with expensive wooden flooring and very little colour. In no way did it match the character of Thea's new friend. 'I know – it's awful. Bunch had it done before Millie was born, without even coming over to see it.'

'Did you say "Bunch"?'

'Yeah. He's my stepfather, lousy with money. Lives in

Atlanta. This was his gift to me when I was meant to be getting married. Long story.'

But you've had five years or more to change it, Thea silently protested. 'Couldn't you at least put down some bright rugs, and get a bit of decent furniture?' she asked, unable to stop herself.

'I tried that, but every time he got me on FaceTime he spotted another change and went ape about it. Upstairs is better.'

A small girl appeared through an archway, holding a slice of bread. 'Buster's still asleep,' she reported, looking at Thea. 'Are you the house-sitter?'

'That's right. My name's Thea.' She realised she had not introduced herself to Bobby. 'Sorry – I should have said that before.'

'And there's a dog!'

Thea watched as child and spaniel took the measure of each other. Each appeared to be unnaturally wary, slow to make physical contact. 'She won't hurt you,' Thea said irritably. She hated having to reassure people about a perfectly harmless little spaniel.

'I'm allergic,' said Millie ruefully. 'Dogs make me wheeze.'

'Oh, Millie – that's just a bit of nonsense, as you well know,' her mother chastised. 'The world is full of dogs – you've just got to get over it. If you ask me, it's all a story concocted by your father to make sure we don't get a dog of our own.'

Thea was still watching her pet. Hepzie seemed aware of some reason for caution. Where she would normally jump up, lick, pant and generally manifest great enthusiasm, she simply sat a foot away from the little girl and slowly wagged her plumy tail. 'Maybe there is something,' she said. 'She's not usually as careful as this. She must have sensed it somehow.'

'Oh well,' shrugged Bobby. 'I'd better go and wake the baby. He won't sleep this afternoon at this rate.' She ran up the stairs that were open to the big room, and footsteps were heard overhead.

'He's not really a baby now,' said Millie. 'He's one year and two months.'

'Can he walk yet?'

'Nearly. Then he'll be a toddler.'

Thea looked around for toys or baby equipment. Shouldn't there be something to push along, and bricks, and teddy bears and picture books and trains? 'Where are all your toys?' she asked.

'In the playroom,' said Millie, eyebrows raised as if to say *Where else would they be?*

'Is that upstairs?'

'No.' She waved towards the archway. 'Out there.'

Thea went to look, realising that the house had been extended into the garden, with a flat-roofed addition that contained all the mess and colour and humanity that the big living room lacked. This was more like it. She sighed with relief. 'That's more like it,' she said, coming back into the living area. She looked at Millie. 'Why aren't you at school?' she asked suddenly.

'It's the Easter holidays. Today is the first day.'

'No, but you're in the same county as me, and my kids don't finish until Friday.'

Millie tilted up her chin. 'I go to a private school,' she said with dignity.

Bobby was halfway down the stairs, carrying a red-faced infant who looked as if he could do with another hour of sleep. She was bent over, in order to see through the uncurtained window at the foot of the stairs. Only then did Thea notice that neither of the two windows had any sort of covering. 'Uh-oh,' said Bobby. 'Here comes the Dynamic Duo.'

Millie giggled and went to the other window. Thea was torn between curiosity and a desire not to appear nosy. All she could see were two women wearing respectable Cotswolds outfits.

'That's another reason for keeping this room as it is,' said Bobby in a low voice. 'People can stare in and admire it as much as they like. It gives them a thrill. But it's frustrating for them, because they've got to keep walking. Give them a wave, Mills.'

Was life just one long social game for this family then, wondered Thea. Teasing passers-by and stepfather alike and living their real lives in the kitchen and playroom where nobody could see them?

'They're coming to the door,' said Millie.

'Bottoms!' said Bobby and her daughter giggled again. 'They can't possibly have heard about Lucy already.'

The knock on the door was superfluous, since Millie was already reaching up to turn the handle and let them in. Bobby handed the dopey Buster to Thea without any ceremony and went to add reinforcements to her daughter.

Thea had time to register that this could well be the first

male child of such a young age that she had dandled for ten years or more. Drew's Timmy had been seven before she met him. Her sisters both had boys, but they were now in their teens. This youngster was something inescapably different from Maggs's Meredith and Damien's Kim. The little man did not nestle or burrow into her as the girls did. He pulled back his head and studied her face with acute concentration. 'Hello, Buster,' said Thea. 'Pleased to meet you.' He smiled then and Thea told herself she was being ridiculous.

Within moments the big room felt a lot smaller, with four women, a dog and two children filling it. The newcomers were both large and one was loud. 'Oh, hello!' she gushed in a rich contralto. 'I'm Faith and this is Livia. We're next door to Lucy. We wanted to ask you how she was getting on, and then we saw you coming over here, and thought we might pop over to ask.'

'I'm Thea,' said Thea, 'and this is Hepzie.' The spaniel was standing politely, tail slowly wagging, jaws parted in a doggy smile.

'A cocker!' Faith approached eagerly and bent to fondle the irresistible ears. 'Aren't you a lovely girl, then!'

The other woman hung back, a tight expression on her face that was barely short of a sneer. She had a long nose and close-together eyes, which arrangement was already halfway towards an expression of superiority and disdain. 'For heaven's sake!' she muttered.

'Lucy's in a coma,' blurted Bobby, effectively silencing the whole room. In Thea's arms, Buster was still not fully awake, but sensing that he was being thoroughly upstaged by both the dog and his very own mother, he made a tentative intervention. 'Goggy!' he said. 'Goggy, goggy, goggy.'

'He means dog,' his patronising sister explained.

'Sweet,' said Faith with a smile that revealed a decided preference for dogs over babies. Then she turned to Bobby. 'What do you mean – in a coma? How in the world . . . ?' She had rather prominent blue eyes, and a small chin.

'I don't know the details. The hospital called me less than an hour ago. They hadn't started the surgery. We guess it must be an allergy of some kind.'

'Probably to the pre-med,' Thea contributed.

Faith and Livia looked at each other, in a silent exchange that made Thea doubt their famous denials of being a couple, as reported by Lucy. Thea was rapidly putting faces to the names she had already noted down. All that remained were the two men – one called Hunter and the other Lucy's former husband.

Livia's eyes widened and her mouth puckered. Several interpretations came to mind: *What did I tell you?* was one of them. A flickering hint of satisfaction or confirmation could be discerned. Faith's face was less visible, partly turned away from Thea's line of sight, but she was convinced she detected a tiny nod.

Already she had labelled both women as typical Cotswolds types. Moneyed, educated, confident and secure; impervious to the buffeting fortunes and fears of lesser mortals. Aged somewhere around sixty, expensively but casually dressed and under no observable pressure, they conjured echoes of others in other villages and small towns – Cranham, Chedworth, Blockley and Winchcombe had all produced similar examples of the type. So had Temple Guiting and Duntisbourne Abbots. The list was a long one. Only when given closer inspection had these people revealed distinctly individual characters, with a wide array of personal quirks. One or two had proved capable of murder. Others had shameful secrets. And they all had history.

'Somebody ought to go and see what's going on,' Bobby continued. 'It ought to be me, I know, but with these two . . .' she shrugged. 'It ain't gonna happen.' The American accent was deliberately caricatured, Thea realised. It had the effect of making Bobby seem more detached and less easy to control. Nobody gave any sign that Lucy Sinclair's fate mattered enough to cause serious upset.

'But poor Lucy!' she burst out, before clamping her lips together. None of the things she wanted to say would sound sincere or even relevant. The absence of information, the unexpectedness, the sheer confusion of the situation all meant that really there was nothing worth saying.

'Have you known her long?' asked the woman named Livia, speaking for the first time. Her voice was breathy and constricted as if she had something wrong with her throat.

'I first met her some years ago,' Thea replied cautiously. 'I can't say I know her very well, if I'm honest.'

'Well, I hope you *are* honest,' said Faith with a smile.

Thea was silenced by this, trying to process the wealth of information the few words had provided. Here, then, was one of those people who took words literally, who listened with unusual attention to what was said, while perhaps ignoring the undercurrents and backgrounds. One of the symptoms of autism, she recalled, was that kind of response to what was said. Even if it was far too soon to make such a diagnosis, she resolved to monitor her utterances closely in Faith's presence.

Or perhaps she had leapt to quite the wrong conclusion. Perhaps Faith was intensely clever, probing this new acquaintance for sensitive spots, shifting from one mode to another in a game that nobody else understood was being played. 'I hope so too,' she said lightly.

'Well, will one of you go over there and see what's what?' Bobby persisted, eager for action. 'Lucy's got nobody else but us, you know.'

'She's got that son,' said Livia. 'We need to get hold of him.'

'Oh no,' Faith argued. 'She won't want him, will she? He's not her real son, is he? Just a stepson. They hardly ever even see each other.'

'Son?' said Thea, halfway through this exchange. 'Why didn't she give the hospital his details, then?' Before anybody could reply, she put the increasingly burdensome Buster down on the floor. He immediately began a rapid but ungainly progress across the room, sitting upright and using one leg as a kind of propeller. Thea watched in fascination.

'He does that,' said Millie. 'It's quicker than walking or crawling.'

'Lucy wouldn't want that son of Kevin's anywhere near her,' said Bobby, gazing fondly at her own little boy who was determinedly making for her. 'She said so.'

'You do know, I hope, that if an infant never crawls properly, it's liable to have difficulties in reading later,' said Faith. 'I'm sure I've mentioned it before.'

Nobody paid this any attention, perceiving it to be a wholly irrelevant distraction. 'Well, what about Kevin, then?' said Livia. 'I mean – there's got to be some blood relative that needs to be informed.'

'Kevin's not a blood relative, is he?' Again Faith sounded pedantic and excessively literal.

'Next of kin,' said Thea automatically. The undertaking business entailed a clear understanding of the legal pecking order of contending relatives.

'They're divorced,' said Bobby. 'That cancels out any rights he might have had.'

'True,' Thea agreed, wishing she had remained silent. Her role in this strange situation was at best peripheral. She could make no claim of any sort. If Lucy was incapacitated, that very probably also cancelled out any responsibility Thea might have towards the house. She could hardly guard it indefinitely, with no idea of what the outcome for Lucy might be.

'I think you should be the one to go to Oxford,' Bobby said. 'You can go as my deputy. I hereby authorise you. Maybe I should put it in writing.'

Faith and Livia made small sounds of concern, but soon realised they had no choice but to keep quiet. Short of offering to go themselves, they had no helpful contribution to make. And there appeared to be no chance of their doing that. These, Thea recollected, were the hellishly inquisitive neighbours that Lucy disliked so much.

'I'm not sure I want to dash off to Oxford,' said Thea with a frown, only then remembering that she had refused to do that very journey, earlier on that very morning. There was a whiff of nemesis attached to the thought. 'What about my dog?'

'Leave her here,' said Bobby blithely. 'She seems to like us.' Millie and Hepzie had gravitated towards each other while the adults stood around agonising. Now they were closely entwined on the only rug in the room – a pale grey piece of elegance in front of the boarded-up fireplace.

It would be dishonest to claim that the spaniel would pine or even protest if abandoned by her mistress. As a breed, spaniels were promiscuous, moving seamlessly from one household to another if so required. Loyalty was barely even skin-deep in a spaniel.

'I don't know,' Thea dithered. As far as she could recall, this was an unprecedented turn of events. People had been found dead a number of times during her years of house-sitting and Thea had marched into homes to conduct her own amateur investigations. She had accosted people in the street and put herself in harm's way. She had spied and accused and risked and insulted – but not once had she been asked to go to the bedside of someone who was apparently struck down by entirely natural causes. 'What good can it do?'

Faith spoke up. 'Ask them who they think needs to be informed. Ask them what the prognosis is. See if you can establish just how deep the coma is – she might be able to hear a voice and respond.'

Livia's hoarse voice interrupted. 'They might be worried

68

about litigation, if they gave her the wrong drugs. Don't you think that's the most likely explanation?'

'Oh!' said Thea, feeling foolish. 'I never thought of that.' They all looked at her, their faces confirming the feeling. 'I suppose that must be what happened.'

'What else could it be?' said Faith.

Chapter Six

Before anyone could reply, a noise outside sent every head turning to the window. 'There's a commotion,' said Faith superfluously. 'Someone's banging on Lucy's door.'

The street was sufficiently wide and busy for ordinary knocking on the opposite side to be inaudible – especially through Bobby's double glazing. 'That's not what we're hearing,' said Livia. 'Look!'

A face was seen at the window, shamelessly staring in, one hand tapping the glass. Quite how Faith had managed to focus on the person several yards away was unclear, when this much more prominent person was only two or three feet from them. It was a woman with a sharp nose and badly dyed purple hair. 'It's a witch!' cried Millie in genuine alarm.

'Better let her in,' said Bobby calmly. 'It's just an ordinary woman, Mill. Nothing to get scared about.'

Nobody moved for a moment, hypnotised by the insistent tapping at the window. 'Why didn't she just knock at the door?' wondered Faith.

'Because she could see us all in here,' said Bobby, adding a silent *obviously*. She went to the door and invited the woman in. 'The more the merrier – I guess,' Thea heard her say. Bobby's calm was starting to feel unnatural, given the circumstances.

'Sorry, sorry,' jabbered the newcomer. 'I'm Tessa – I'm with Kevin. He's just heard that Lucy's gone in for her op, and he wanted to come and ask about visiting. He always does that, even when he knows perfectly well he isn't wanted. I told him it was no sense going to her house if she was in hospital, but he said she might have somebody staying. Then I could see all of you, right over the road, so I came to ask if you know how she is, and if there's any news, seeing as how you're neighbours. She'll have told you not to speak to Kev, of course. But he still cares, you know. She's been very shabby towards him, if you ask me.' She paused for breath and looked around at the circle of faces. Thea realised how odd it was that they were all still standing, after at least twenty minutes. Bobby had not invited anyone to sit on her spotless furniture. It gave the proceedings an awkward temporary feeling. Nobody – except Bobby – was relaxed; any of them could make a sudden move. Tessa faltered, belatedly aware of the atmosphere. 'Is something going on?'

'Quite a lot, actually,' said Faith. 'Perhaps you should call Mr Sinclair over here as well.'

The suggestion was unnecessary as it turned out. The man was already at the window, waving an arm, but not tapping. 'Let me in,' he mouthed.

The intrusion of a man into their midst changed everything. He brought cool air and a loud display of anger. Buster whimpered and tried to climb up his mother. Hepzie tucked her tail in and sat on it. Garments stirred as if in a breeze. Livia in particular, who was wearing a long, loose, dark blue top, appeared to be quivering.

'This is getting silly,' said Bobby, who appeared to be counting heads. 'Faith, Livia, perhaps you could go now. I'm not really sure why you're here anyhow. It's not as if you and Lucy are exactly on good terms, is it? If you just wanted to check up on the latest news, you've done that, haven't you?'

'She's right,' said Livia, with impressive dignity somehow enhanced by her husky voice. 'We should go.' And she led the way without a backward glance, Faith one step behind her. They closed the door quietly behind themselves.

It was still quite a roomful and Thea found herself torn between her inborn curiosity and a wish to walk away from the increasing sense of Northleach as a hotbed of ill feeling and hidden histories. Her anomalous position was causing her increasing anxiety the longer she stood there. Bobby was a poor hostess by any standards. Her children would surely start to make demands at any moment, once the strangeness of the unexpected gathering faded enough to give them the courage to assert themselves. The man who had been married to Lucy had opted for anger over suspicion or bewilderment, his appearance in the street a powerful twist to the growing mystery of what was going on.

'Who told you Lucy was in hospital?' Thea asked him, since no one else seemed inclined to speak first.

'That Hunter bloke from the committee,' said Kevin Sinclair impatiently. 'Just seen him in the bread shop.'

'Do you live in Northleach, then? Are you on the committee as well?' Already Thea felt better for having slipped into her familiar questioning role. Somehow or other she was going to get at least the outline of the story. She heard herself say *the Committee* as if capitalised. Almost as if it was some kind of soviet apparatus for surveillance of all that went on in the town.

'We live in Stroud, actually,' said Tessa. 'But we know people here.'

It was a Wednesday, Thea remembered. Normal people should be at work. Even those in their sixties like these two generally had gainful occupations these days. Unless, of course, they were patently idle and affluent like Faith and Livia.

'Have you got a business or something? I mean – most people would be at work,' she said boldly.

'Oh yes?' said Tessa, jutting her beaky nose forward and giving Thea a challenging look. 'Wouldn't that go for you too, then?'

'I am working,' Thea flashed back. 'I'm working for Lucy, as it happens.'

'She's the house-sitter,' said Bobby in a weak-sounding voice. 'And, to put it as nicely as I can, I've had about enough of all this. I never signed up for a houseful of friends and relations arguing about what happens now. I've got children to think about.'

'Nobody's arguing,' said Kevin Sinclair. 'We just hoped for a bit of information. If this lady's the house-sitter, she'll be the one we want. She can fill us in on what the excitement's about. Can't she?'

Again, Thea found herself attaching labels. The man was tall and well-covered, with broad shoulders and a fleshy neck. His hands looked muscular, the nails short and not especially clean. A builder, she hazarded, or something along those lines. Perhaps he had done Lucy's barn conversion, before their marriage collapsed. Lucy's replacement was just the sort of woman who might take up with a builder, Thea thought, while knowing her judgement to be outrageous.

'I understand you have a son?' she prevaricated. 'If you're divorced, then he must be her next of kin.' She knew as she spoke that she'd got it wrong, but she enjoyed the sense of provoking the man into correcting her. He did just as she'd hoped.

'He isn't anything of the sort. He's not *her* son. They're nothing to each other.'

'Oh. I just thought she might have given his contact details to the hospital – but they called Bobby this morning, not him.'

'Why did they call *anyone*? Did something happen? Why's everyone just standing around like this if there's some trouble?'

'Maybe you should both come over the road and we can talk about it there,' said Thea, with a questioning look at Bobby. Wasn't she overstepping a mark, usurping the American woman's role? 'If that's okay,' she added.

'It's more than okay,' said Bobby. 'It would be doing me a huge favour. Look – this is the ward, and the phone number.' She opened a drawer and took out a sheet of paper that Thea supposed had been provided by Lucy. It struck her that she had been given no such information. Bobby thrust it at her. 'Call them and say you're the contact person now, not me. Lord, it's practically eleven o'clock already. Buster must be starving.' Only then did everyone notice that the child had been complaining more and more loudly ever since the last two people had entered the room.

'Sorry, baby,' Bobby crooned. 'What an awful mother.'

'I'm thirsty,' said Millie, getting up from the rug. 'When's Daddy coming home?'

'Don't start that,' said Bobby, and instigated a wholesale exodus that successfully saw Thea, Hepzibah, Sinclair and Tessa all on the pavement in under a minute.

She saw no alternative but to let them into Lucy's house and offer them a drink. It felt completely wrong, and completely inevitable. They all sat down in the living room, Tessa unable to resist a thorough inspection. 'Never been in here before,' she said.

'Nor me,' said Kevin. 'Best not tell her we were here. She won't take it kindly.' Then he looked hard at Thea. 'You'll visit her, then?'

'I doubt it,' said Thea impatiently. She felt there was a lot to be explained before she took any impulsive action. 'You didn't answer my question about your son. Where is he?'

'No idea. I don't keep track of him. Neither does Lucy. He's a grown man, lives his own degenerate life.'

'Degenerate!' Thea repeated the word incredulously. It sounded old-fashioned and horribly condemnatory. 'How old is he?'

'Twenty-something. I lose track.'

'He's twenty-eight,' said Tessa. 'His name's Ollie.'

Thea was burning to hear the story, to fill in the gaping holes left by this all-too-brief account. Lucy had never said anything about her married life, with or without a stepson. Frustratingly, it was no use expecting any of these people to come to the rescue now, she realised. Although perhaps it was worth one last try. 'So why did you come rushing over here when you heard she was in hospital? It's all been planned for months – it's funny you only just heard about it today, when she's had a collapse. You're the nearest thing she's got to family – shouldn't you go and see what's happened?'

'Collapse?' the man repeated. 'Is that what happened. Why can't you just tell me?'

'Because I hardly know any more than that myself. The hospital phoned Bobby and said the operation didn't go ahead because Lucy was unconscious or in a coma or something. We were all trying to guess what exactly happened when you showed up. Why don't you just go there and find out for yourself? Rather you than me, anyway.'

'Nice try, love,' said Kevin, holding up his hands. 'But if you knew Lucy, you'd know better than suggest such a thing. Even if she's at death's door, she'd not want me near her.'

Thea just nodded and shrugged, unable to think of anything more to say. There was nothing so murky and rancorous as the aftermath of a messy divorce. And nothing so mysterious, either. The real reason for the split was seldom disclosed to outsiders. 'Okay,' she muttered. Then another thought struck her: 'I wonder how she got to the hospital this morning?'

'Oh – Hunter took her,' said Kevin carelessly. 'He wasn't long back when I saw him. Said he could hardly say no when she asked him outright, and he'd managed to combine it with a bit of business. Great man for business, is old Hunter.'

'But Lucy doesn't like him,' Thea blurted without thinking.

'Lucy doesn't really like anybody,' said Tessa confidentially, hugging Kevin's arm as she sat beside him on the sofa. 'But she'll make use of them when it suits her. Right, Kev?'

'Right,' said Lucy's former husband. He drained his coffee and gently disengaged his arm. 'Best be off. Things to do. First on the list is phone that hospital and find out what's what.'

Thea watched the couple as they got ready to leave and tried to assemble her thoughts. There were still several areas of bafflement. Too much information had been flung at her, making a far from coherent picture. Apart from Bobby, all the new people she'd met that morning had been of roughly the same age. They would have been at their most active, sexually, financially, socially, in the 1990s, she supposed.

'So will you go and see Lucy or not?' Kevin urged.

'Because as much as I'd like to, I'd only open old wounds and set the old girl back. That's if she's compos mentis. If I phone them, they'll just fob me off with some bland bit of nonsense. Sounds as if somebody ought to be going there in person.' He looked at the spaniel. 'You can leave that with Mrs Thing over there.'

'Latimer,' Thea remembered with an effort. 'But I've no intention of going – haven't I said that enough times?'

'Stalemate, then,' said Kevin.

Tessa laughed and neatly sidestepped the argument. 'Latimer's a nice name,' she said. 'Don't you think? Sort of *solid*.'

'It is nice,' Thea agreed, rather glad to introduce something light and irrelevant. 'So is Livia. I always think three syllables work best in a name. Like my daughter – she's Jessica.'

Kevin just stared as if they'd both lost their wits, but Tessa kept it going. 'Imagine if she was Livia Latimer. Wouldn't that be nice!'

Thea knew, deep down, that she was merely trying to postpone a final decision about what to do next. She was hoping, probably, that Bobby would emerge from her front door waving her phone and reporting a change in Lucy's condition – whether for better or worse, it could well excuse Thea from having to go to Oxford. Apart from anything else, she very much disliked Oxford. It had disagreeable associations.

'So you do at least accept that I can't go anywhere right away,' she told Kevin. 'I'll have to speak to my husband. And he'll say it's not my job to take orders

78

from anybody but Lucy herself.'

'Oh?' Scepticism beamed brightly from his eyes. 'Where's he, then?'

'At home. Miles away. He might be needing me.'

'What if Lucy *dies*?' said Tessa, with relish. 'Who'd get her house?'

'Not us,' said Kevin. 'And not Ollie. Most likely she'll leave it to this lady here. She seems the sort of person that could happen to.'

Thea winced at the accidental accuracy of this remark. The house she lived in with Drew and his children had in fact been an inheritance from a grateful customer. 'I don't think so,' she said. All three of them had moved to the front door. As Thea opened it two people were passing on the pavement, giving them curious glances.

'Bit of a comedown, all the same,' said Kevin. 'After that great barn.'

'Did you do the conversion?' asked Thea, following her earlier hunch.

'Who – me?' He guffawed. 'Do I look like a builder?'

Tessa joined in the laughter. 'You do, Kev. I've always said so.' She turned to Thea. 'He's mostly a feed merchant,' she explained. 'Animal feed. And he drives his own lorry – huge great thing. Deals in hay and straw. Lends a hand with other stuff sometimes – transporting sheep, when it's busy. There's never enough people for that these days.'

'Poor sheep,' said Thea, thinking of the lorries she had seen crammed with woolly bodies, often on three levels. The creatures always seemed so hopeless, too sunk in despair even to feel frightened.

Both women had let Lucy slip yet again from the front of their minds. But Kevin was more tenacious. 'Well, say hello to my ex-wife if you ever get to see her,' he said heavily. 'We should be getting on.' He eyed the cottage again. 'Pokey little place. Not like hers over the road. Can't think what Luce was doing, moving over here.'

Thea and her spaniel went back into the house. Then she stood with her phone in her hand, wondering what in the world she was supposed to do next.

Chapter Seven

Drew would be conducting Penelope Allen's funeral, by Thea's calculations. He had another burial that afternoon, for a person whose name escaped her. She had said she would try to be back on Saturday, but would let him know if that changed. The painful contrast between her expected boredom, doing nothing but guard a house against unlikely marauders, and his hectic schedule gave her frequent surges of guilt and frustration. She ought never to have accepted such a nebulous commission. Lucy had not provided any convincing reasons for her anxiety, and now everything was thrown into total confusion by her bizarre collapse in the private wing of the John Radcliffe.

She should at least tell Drew what had happened and prepare him for a range of possible developments. But she must time it carefully, or the call would interrupt a delicate stage of one of his funerals. Probably, she told herself, he was so focused on his work that he wouldn't notice whether his wife was at home or not.

The most striking factor in the whole scenario was the absence of any sense of urgency. Kevin Sinclair had pressed her to go and see Lucy, but it had not seemed to emanate from any undue concern for his ex-wife's welfare. A person in a coma could wait, of course. Lucy wasn't going anywhere, didn't need anything that Thea could provide, was in a safe place and whatever happened next was beyond anyone's control. She definitely did not want to go and sit by the bedside for uneventful hours at a time. She had no expectation that the medical people would tell her anything meaningful, given that she was no relation, and barely even a friend. Lucy's life was looking very sparsely peopled – something that should have been apparent already from the mere fact of needing a paid house-sitter to do something any friend would cheerfully undertake. The whole business hardly involved Thea at all, in fact. Except that if somebody *did* break into the house, or rubbish the garden, or pour petrol through the letter box, Thea would feel she had betrayed a trust. She certainly couldn't just walk away as if the whole thing was out of her hands. That would be morally untenable, and she wasn't sure she could cope with any more guilt. Which meant she was trapped there until Lucy either recovered or died, and she would simply have to put up with it.

There was one person on Lucy's brief list of Northleach acquaintances she had yet to meet: the man called Hunter, who was on the committee. The man who had told

Kevin about Lucy's operation that very morning. She supposed she would never encounter him now. Lunch was looming – a modest snack that she had brought with her from home – and then she would have to start making some decisions. The lack of any real information about Lucy was tantalising, and felt unnecessary. Modern regulations about revealing personal information meant that such situations were all too common. Unless Lucy had left precise written instructions that a certain Thea Slocombe was authorised to receive details of her condition, treatment and prognosis, she would have to remain in ignorance.

Except that Bobby Latimer, who was at least to some extent so authorised, had handed the baton to Thea. *Pretend you're me*, she had said, and there was every chance that such a ruse would work, despite Thea's instant assumption that it would not. Surely hospitals had not yet reached the point of demanding passwords or actual physical thumbprints before they would let a person in or disclose any information. It probably wouldn't be long, Thea thought crossly. Meanwhile, she decided to at least try a phone call.

The hospital switchboard was slow to respond, but then put her through to the relevant ward without delay. 'Oh hello, I'm enquiring about Lucy Sinclair, who's on your ward. You called me earlier today to say she's in a coma.' Too late Thea remembered Bobby's American accent. If she was speaking to the same person who phoned that morning, that could give the game away.

'Oh. Can you give me your name, please?'

'Latimer.' What was Bobby short for? Lucy had told

her and she'd forgotten. Roberta, Robina, or some weird made-up American name? And did she call herself Mrs, Ms or Miss?

Luckily it didn't matter. 'Oh yes. Well, she's slightly better now. It was never really a coma, you know. I don't know who would have told you that. She lost consciousness for a little while, which meant the surgery had to be postponed – cancelled, actually – but she's not in any danger.'

'Thank goodness for that. Is it possible to visit her?'

'Best leave it till tomorrow, dear,' said the nurse, or whatever she was. 'Give her time to get over it. She's very incoherent just now. You wouldn't get any sense out of her.'

'All right. That's a great relief. Thank you very much.'

Which was some sort of progress, she supposed, but it was of very little help in the decision as to what to do next. Lucy could be home again by Friday, the way hospitals discharged people these days. She would have lost her place in the schedule for operations, and until they worked out what had caused her collapse, they wouldn't dare try again.

Perhaps, then, it would make sense to go and visit the next day, if nothing changed in the meantime. Until then she could loiter here in Northleach, staying until about three o'clock, switching lights on and off, turning the radio on, and generally making it look as if the house was being comprehensively lived in. At that point she could make the decision whether or not to stay. On the face of it, she knew she ought to – the house was just as empty and vulnerable whether Lucy had surgery or not. But somehow that was not how it felt. Everything was standing on shifting sands, the whole exercise undermined by Lucy's strange descent into a brief semi-coma.

She ate her sausage roll and apple and looked to the dog for stimulation. 'Well?' she said. 'Maybe we could take a turn around the town square for half an hour.' Hepzie wagged in wholesale agreement.

Taking care to lock the front door and checking to ensure her car was where she'd left it, Thea and spaniel headed eastwards. There was a feeble attempt at sunshine, and the air felt mild and springlike. Loud laughter was coming from the door of The Wheatsheaf over the road. As a pub it struck Thea as being at the more pretentious end of the spectrum, with an eye to American tourists rather than unreconstructed locals. It offered lavish accommodation and equally lavish cuisine. In short, it was typical Cotswolds – and most visitors would look no further. They might well ignore the more modest Sherborne Arms, despite it being right in the town square, leaving it for less affluent locals. For the moment, Thea was not tempted by either of them.

The laughter was prolonged; most likely the result of a coachload of tourists enjoying a pre-booked lunch before exploring the famous church. Far too big for the little town, St Peter and St Paul's had been financed by plutocratic wool merchants, who had enjoyed enormous prosperity over the centuries. Six or seven centuries, in fact, if Thea remembered rightly. Northleach had been a sort of 'hub' for the wool industry in the Middle Ages, with an important road running right through it. There had been numerous inns and taverns and handsome houses. Snippets from a guidebook came back to her as she strolled along.

A handful of buildings could trace themselves back to 1260-something, while plenty more could provide plentiful detail of their erection in the 1500s. Cotswold stone was nothing if not long-lasting. No wonder, she acknowledged to herself, that people from younger countries liked to come for a look.

She walked past the town square and carried on along High Street, which was pleasingly varied with a mixture of houses from all those centuries. One or two appeared to be barely twenty years old, their stone still buttery and fresh. But for sheer exuberant variety it fell somewhat short of Winchcombe, which was Thea's personal favourite. Having sampled close to twenty Cotswold villages over the past few years, she had developed prejudices and sudden judgements that were difficult to shake.

Nobody took much notice of her. The locals were inured to strange faces, smiling vaguely at the visitors but seeing little more than necessary nuisance. Those who ran shops or offered accommodation were glad of the business. Actual permanent residents – like the Latimer family and Faith-and-Livia – were not numerous. Those there would mostly work on their computers all day, or drive off to somewhere bigger if they were teachers or doctors or solicitors. Although, Thea reminded herself, there were several 'business parks' tucked out of sight down tracks that looked as if they must lead to a farm. She had found just such a one in Barnsley, near Bibury, in a converted old mansion house. There was probably one in Northleach as well, if she cared to look for it.

There was a knot of people on the pavement ahead,

staring up at a house. Outside was a police car. As she watched from a respectable distance, an ambulance quietly arrived as well. 'Oh, come on!' she muttered to herself. 'Just somebody fallen downstairs, nothing to get excited about.' But the fact of onlookers was in itself mildly exciting. On the whole, Thea had discovered that people in this area did not easily get worked up enough to go out and gawp at anything.

She would not get involved. It had nothing to do with her; there was no possible way that she could justify showing an interest. Even if somebody had died, having said they wanted a natural burial in Drew's field – highly unlikely in itself – Thea ought not to intrude at this stage. She should turn around and go back to the square and perhaps sit in the little café on the southern side and have a pot of tea.

As she hesitated, another police car arrived and disgorged a familiar figure. DI Jeremy Higgins stood there, four-square, tweaking his collar and flexing his elbows. A uniformed female constable approached him from the house as Thea watched from a distance of fifty yards or so. She tried to recall when she had last encountered Higgins. She remembered him helping her when she put the wrong fuel in her car. And he had been involved in Chedworth when she and Drew had found a body in a barn. Wasn't Northleach a bit out of his usual area, she asked herself, never quite clear about such details. DS Gladwin seemed to roam all over the Cotswolds, wherever violent crime took place. Higgins probably did the same. It was all in the same county, after all.

He had not noticed her standing there with the dog and

she did nothing to draw his attention. Within a few seconds he was entering the house with the young constable, and the little group of onlookers rustled and whispered and one or two of them peeled away to get on with normal life. Thea began to feel uncomfortably conspicuous. 'Come on, then,' she muttered to Hepzie and began to walk along High Street in the same direction as before, taking her right past the house that was attracting so much interest. She crossed over, and gave it a good look from the other side of the street, not expecting to see anything. But as she looked, an upstairs window was thrown open, and Higgins himself leant out. 'Mrs Osborne!' he called. 'Is that you?'

Everybody turned to see who the detective was talking to. Thea grimaced slightly, and stood her ground. 'The name's Slocombe now,' she replied, just loud enough to carry the short distance. 'Remember?'

He rolled his eyes. A passing lorry impeded her view of him, and when it had gone, he was no longer at the window. She supposed he would come down to ground level, so she waited, wondering at the very odd lack of professionalism. Surely he wasn't going to saunter out and ask her how she was getting on, moments into some sort of investigation that carried all the signs of being rather serious? He could not conceivably have connected her to whatever it was, in those few moments. The idea was ludicrous. But she did not have to wait long for enlightenment.

He came over the street to her and smiled. 'Mrs Slocombe,' he said. 'Of course.'

'What's going on here? Whatever it is, it's got nothing to do with me.'

'I'm sure that's true – of course,' he agreed. 'All the same, here you are, and here's a man dead, and I think I might be forgiven for thinking that this has happened before, and it would probably be a mistake to simply let you disappear.'

'A man's dead?' She looked again at the serene old house. 'And it's a matter for CID, is it?'

'Apparently so. I need to get back – but can you stick around for a bit, just in case?'

'Just in case *what*? I've never been near this house before. I have no idea who lives there. I only got here this morning. Honestly, Jeremy, this one is absolutely nothing to do with me.'

'I believe you. All the same . . . aren't you even a little bit curious? Don't you want to know what's happened? If you know people in Northleach, there could well be some sort of connection. It's a small place.'

'Is that house an ordinary residence or holiday lets, or what?'

He twinkled cheerfully at her. 'See? You're hooked already. It's both – neither – that's to say, I'm told it's an Airbnb property, but the owner lives there as well, most of the time, anyway. Somebody foreign, it seems.'

Thea had no experience of Airbnb, and how it worked, but she assumed the fact of a murder in one of its houses would carry a good level of local interest. Already she understood that this was, one way or another, a murder. And 'somebody foreign' would be a good place to start when it came to finding a suspect, however outrageous that might be. 'Okay,' she sighed. 'I'll go and have coffee in the café in the square. You can come and find me there. I'll stay an hour.'

'Thanks,' he said, and went back to his investigations.

It was fifty minutes before he breathlessly joined her in the café. 'They let the dog in, then?' he said, giving Hepzie a quick fondle.

Thea nodded. 'I think they expected us to have gone by now. Or at least ordered some food. But I'd had my lunch already before I saw you. Seems a while ago now.' She glanced at her watch to discover it was quarter past two.

'I can't stop,' he said. 'The wheels are rolling, as they say.'

'So who died?'

'Young bloke. Apparently goes by the name of Sinclair. Not much doubt that it's foul play, judging by the state of his neck.' He gave her a meaningful look. 'And after a wee bit of googling, courtesy of a bright young detective constable, that name popped up in connection with events in Hampnett a year or two ago that involved a certain Mrs Osborne. Slocombe, as she is now.'

'Longer ago than that. It was before I met Drew. But yes – I'm looking after Lucy Sinclair's house here in Northleach, having previously looked after another house of hers in Hampnett. That is clever googling, I grant you. Did you say a young bloke? What's his first name?'

'Oliver. Still not confirmed, no official identification – but there's no real doubt. Is there anything you might be able to contribute at this stage?'

'Lucy is stepmother to a young man named Ollie, who

90

I fear is your murder victim. She's in hospital, so that's one alibi you can put in your notes. I've met Ollie's father, and his current lady friend, this very day.'

Higgins was still standing beside her table, looking down at her with a sudden air of professionalism. Before he said any more, he pulled out a chair and sat down close to her, using his softest voice and keeping his back to the rest of the room. Since speaking to him in the high street quite a lot had changed, it seemed. Having listened carefully to everything she had said, he now placed her firmly at the heart of this latest crime. Thanks to the 'wee bit of googling' she was inextricably embroiled in it. 'Tell me every single thing,' he ordered.

'Oh dear,' she said, before embarking on a somewhat jumbled account of that morning, including the existence of Kevin Sinclair and his lady friend. 'He definitely must be the son,' she concluded.

'Helpful,' said Higgins with a wide smile. 'Very helpful, indeed.'

'So how did he die?' she asked, in a soft, reluctant voice. She was not at all sure she wanted to know.

'Let's just say there was a weapon, for now. According to rumours, it appears he was a drug user.'

'His father said he was degenerate,' Thea remembered. 'That must be what he meant. But you've been amazingly quick to hear rumours.'

'Facebook,' he said, as if it was obvious. Which it was, Thea supposed.

'You mean he's got a blog or something boasting about his favourite illegal substances?'

'Hardly. But there are several local people in a kind of discussion forum. The same clever young DC has highlighted one or two remarks that strongly imply that Mr Sinclair and the proprietor of the house shared a certain lifestyle that did not fit well with the quiet community of Northleach. Something like that, anyway. Nods and whispers. Nothing definite.'

'Is that the same thing as Hunter and his committee?' Thea mused. Higgins waited for enlightenment. 'A man called Hunter runs a committee,' she went on. 'I get the impression that most of the town are involved, and if you resist, you're cast into outer darkness. Or something.'

'You can't just have a committee like that. I mean, it has to represent some sort of organisation. And a whole town can't be on it, can they?'

'I suppose not. It isn't likely to be relevant, anyway.' She shook her head at her own vagueness. Repeating what she had gleaned from Lucy, it sounded faintly ridiculous.

'Early days,' said Higgins.

'But how sad it is,' Thea sighed, thinking of Kevin Sinclair and wondering how badly he had failed as a father. Or whether he had failed at all. It was altogether too simplistic to assume that drug users had been driven to it by their parents. He had seemed relaxed – if somewhat lacking in affection – at the mention of his son. She remembered how he had been unsure of the poor chap's age. 'He was twenty-eight, apparently, if that helps. His father didn't seem very interested in him.'

Higgins nodded. 'I'll make a note, but I think his age is on record already.'

There seemed to be nothing more to say. Thea got up and together they walked down the gently sloping town square to the bus stop at the bottom. 'I go this way,' she said, waving at the street to the left containing Lucy's house and Thea's car. She began to walk away, when she had a thought and stopped. Higgins was still standing there making jottings in a notebook. 'Is Caz Barkley still around?' Thea asked. 'Is she going to be part of this case?'

He rolled his eyes. 'Oh yes, she's around all right. Never makes a wrong move, that one. Must have a very powerful fairy godmother, if you ask me. And yes, she'll be on this case, right enough. The super's gone away for Easter. Took the boys and husband and flown off to Tenerife. Or was it Lanzarote? Somewhere nice and hot, anyhow.'

'Really? So this one's down to you and Caz, then.' Thea remembered that DS Barkley had grown up in the care system, and had been forced to contend with a lot more trouble and damage than the average person.

'She'll jump at it. Another feather in her cap. Promotion before you can say "Whiskers".'

Thea laughed. 'If that's true, I'm glad. She's earned it.'

'That's what the super says.' He sighed. 'It's right, of course. But she can be a bit . . . exasperating.'

'Well, say hello from me next time you see her.'

'I doubt I'll have to – you're sure to see her one day soon, with this lot kicking off.'

'Right,' said Thea with very familiar mixed feelings. 'And you know what? I'm going home this evening, whatever I promised Lucy. Everything's changed now and I want my family round me.'

'As you like. We've got your phone number.'

She was left with a sense of several conversations not properly finished. Bobby had ejected her visitors with no resolution as to what to do about Lucy. Kevin Sinclair still had not been fully informed on that matter, either. Perhaps, Thea thought, the hospital would tell him if he phoned them. But now that his son was dead, he was less likely than ever to care what happened to his ex-wife. The death of Ollie Sinclair, apparently by violence, threw everything into far greater turmoil. And it inevitably meant that Thea Slocombe, renowned house-sitter, would be at the forefront of everyone's attention.

Chapter Eight

Having securely locked up Lucy's house, Thea went home at five o'clock, feeling like a deserter. This time the A429 carried even more echoes from the past. Here was another murder, only a few miles from Notgrove and Lower Slaughter and all the other little villages she had known for a few days. The trees, not yet showing many signs of spring, had a sinister aspect in the fading light. She remembered Phil Hollis in Temple Guiting remarking on them. Both trees and houses had stood unchanged for three or four centuries in some of these settlements, calmly watching the evanescent humans come and go like butterflies. Perhaps, she reflected, it was being married to an undertaker that made her so aware of the brevity of life – and often its futility, in her bleaker moments. *Too strong a word*, she admonished herself. It wasn't futile, exactly. Every life was precious in itself, almost by definition. Murder was and always would be the ultimate horror. To cast another person into oblivion could never be forgivable.

She gave herself a shake as she took her customary shortcut through Sezincote, where evening shadows stretched across the landscape and a flock of starlings celebrated another passing day. She was going to have to present a cheerful face to the family. Beside her, the spaniel was curled up trustfully on the passenger seat, not knowing or caring where they were going, because life for Hepzie was always all right.

She had not told Drew she was coming, so walked in on a scene of domestic competence and self-sufficiency that made her feel excluded – which was entirely her own fault, of course. Stephanie had decided to prepare the evening meal, without any prompting, as Drew announced with pride. 'Sausages and potato wedges with peas,' his daughter announced. Potato wedges had become something of an obsession with both children, sprinkled with oil and herbs and reliably delicious. Also extremely easy to prepare, although Thea often managed to burn them.

Drew was slumped in the living room, having achieved two more of the week's funerals without mishap. He smiled up at her as she came in, and said, 'Hey! It's you! What a surprise!' He waved a glass at her. 'I've earned a G&T today, I don't know about you.'

'I'd be happy to join you,' she said. 'As soon as I've fed the dog.'

Gin on a weekday was unusual, but very welcome. True

to her word, Thea sat next to her husband on the sofa and told him all she could remember of the day's events, having been briefly assured that his day had gone satisfactorily. 'So,' she concluded, 'it looks as if I've landed up with another murder.'

'What if you didn't go back? What if you just stayed quietly here and forgot all about it?'

'Higgins or Barkley would hunt me down,' she sighed. 'Although maybe not. After all, I told Jeremy everything I know, which is hardly anything. I can't just abandon Lucy, though. Apart from anything else, she hasn't paid me yet.'

'Hm. Stephanie's doing supper.'

'So I see. She's a remarkably good girl.'

'She is. But she had some sort of contretemps at school today. I tried to follow it, but lost the thread. Something to do with two other girls and a torn pocket.'

'Is her pocket torn? Am I expected to mend it?'

Drew shrugged. 'You'll have to ask her. I think it wasn't hers, actually.'

'I tore a pocket in my school skirt once,' Thea remembered. 'It was a serious trauma at the time. You could see my pants through the hole. I caught it on a doorknob.' For a moment she experienced again the panic and horror of the incident. She had been about nine, and prone to embarrassment. The boys had made a big production of it, describing her knickers in lurid and inaccurate detail. 'School is so horrible,' she said. 'I don't know how anybody survives it.'

'And yet they all do,' said Drew. 'More or less.'

'I'll ask her about it after supper. I expect I should phone the hospital again and ask about Lucy's progress.'

'Do that in the morning. You haven't asked me about my funerals.'

'Yes I have. You told me they went perfectly well.'

'And nothing more than that. I was hoping you'd ask for details.'

'Were you?' She was torn between a sense of inadequacy as a wife, and impatience with his indirect approach. 'I'm happy to listen if there are things you want to tell me.'

Drew was clearly impatient too. 'That's putting it all wrong. After the way you were so helpful on Monday, I assumed you'd want to hear how they turned out.' He made a muffled sound that seemed to indicate frustration. 'But I can see that today's events have distracted you.'

'They have,' she confirmed. 'Monday seems quite a long time ago now. But you have every right to be disappointed in me – I've put my own business before yours again. I don't seem to manage to get the balance right.'

'No, no – it's me. I'm whining for attention.'

'You are a bit, but that's okay. A modicum of whining is allowed. And I did think about you a lot today, wondering whether you were coping. And see – I came home, because I reckon I do more good here than sitting in a stupid empty house for no reason.'

He pulled her to him in an awkward hug. 'So you did,' he said. 'And from the smells coming from the kitchen, I think Stephanie's just about to call us.'

On Thursday, she drove Stephanie to school, aware that the child was apprehensive about something, and ashamed

98

of her own failure to elicit the story the previous evening. 'Last day of term tomorrow,' she said brightly. 'We'll have to think of things to do next week.'

'Mm,' said Stephanie.

'What's up, kid? Don't tell me you've got Tim's trouble and someone's been bullying you.'

'Not really. Just girls – you know. Sofia Budd's skirt got torn and they blamed me. It was all very silly, but they've been talking about it on WhatsApp and saying nasty things. Like they do. You know?'

'You should have shown me. What have we said about that? Don't keep things like that from us. We might not be able to put it right, but we really want to *know*. We all live in the same world.'

'Except that's not how it seems. It is like Timmy and his school, more or less. But it'll be all right in the end. It's not going to kill me.'

'Let's hope not,' said Thea lightly.

'Where will you be today?' The question sounded more politely dutiful than genuinely interested.

'No idea. You've got a ride home, haven't you? It's Thursday, isn't it?'

'Oh yeah. No problem. I'll make shepherd's pie if you're not here, with that mince in the freezer. I know how to do it.'

'You're amazing. I'll be sure to get it out to defrost, at least. And maybe I'll make it myself if I'm around.'

They were approaching the road outside the school. Stephanie turned to her stepmother. 'It's okay, you know, you being off and out like you are. Everyone else's mother's the same. They've got busy jobs and are always on the phone, even when they're at home. It's *normal*. You don't have to make excuses all the time.'

Tears blurred Thea's vision as she attempted to park. 'Thanks, kid,' she choked. 'Try to have a good day.'

Drew had the biggest funeral of the week that day, and the back room was still overflowing with bodies and coffins; Andrew was still incapacitated. There must be things she could do here at home, to smooth her husband's path. If Andrew was brought in to answer the phone, Thea could sit with him and help – or even go out to the field and . . . what? She was shamefully ignorant of the precise details of the position of graves, their depth, and any other arcane matters. Perhaps, though, if Drew permitted family members to dig a grave, they might need supervision and support. She could in theory even take part in the actual burials, assembling mourners and listening to their stories. And if any new funerals came through, she could talk Drew through the logistics as she had on Monday.

But she had no desire to do any of that. Andrew was better with the families than Thea could ever be. Despite coming to the business late in life he had a natural skill in treading the delicate path between excessive sympathy and chilly indifference. Having been a farmer for most of his life, he was accustomed to the visceral realities of suffering and death. All he had needed from Drew was a brief course of instruction in the mysteries of the 'coffining up' and the crucial necessity of absolute dignity in the moments around the actual burial.

She reproached herself for her resistance to the close-up details of undertaking. She had no problem with the dead bodies while they lay quietly in the back room, but she shied away from following them to their final resting place. She told herself it was her vivid imagination at fault – she could see the slow inevitable corruption of the flesh too starkly for comfort. The heavy earth piled on top of what was once a living, laughing person was too terrible to witness. Even Drew had once said that this was the worst part of the job – the filling-in of the grave after the family had gone. There was a good reason why it was still unusual for mourners to stay for that final disappearance. They sprinkled handfuls of symbolic soil onto the coffin and left it there.

At nine-thirty Andrew presented himself, walking with a stick and looking pained. 'Drew said I could do something useful in the office, today and tomorrow,' he told Thea. 'I left the car up by the church. Took me about five minutes to get out of it. Yesterday set me back somewhat.'

'Oh Lord,' said Thea. 'You'll be suing us for being terrible employers.'

'I don't think so,' he said through gritted teeth.

A few minutes later, Thea did phone the hospital again, feeling foolishly miffed that nobody had contacted her about events in Northleach. She had half expected Caz Barkley to appear on the doorstep, or even the wretched Kevin Sinclair. However hard she tried she could not dispel images of Bobby and her children, the two smart women and purple-haired Tessa all somehow in opposition to poor Lucy. How, Thea wondered, would they all react to the news about Ollie? Had any of them known him, disliked him – or even possibly killed him? The questions would not go away – rather they proliferated. Each one bred two more.

'Not really any change,' said the woman in the hospital. Thea could not be sure whether or not it was the same one she'd spoken to the day before – from the lack of friendly recognition, she assumed not. But perhaps after twenty similar calls, everyone blurred together. She was lucky, she knew, that they told her anything.

'Oh dear,' she said. 'That sounds worrying.'

'She's comfortable,' said the voice. Wasn't that what they said when a person was dying? Thea ended the call with an even stronger sense that she ought to be taking a more active role. But what could she do? If she drove back to Northleach, who would speak to her? The death of Ollie Sinclair would eclipse any interest in Lucy, at least amongst the local people.

Drew was outside, doing whatever he had to do in preparation for the burial of a woman whose name had not stayed with Thea. The weather was dry but cool. The mourners would be assembling at the burial field, having been told there was no space for parking at the house. This was a drawback at any time, and a real problem when it was raining. There were plans to erect a small building for people to gather in, before and possibly after a funeral, but meanwhile it was very much an al fresco event. The usual practice would be to load the coffin into the hearse well in advance, and then send Andrew over to meet and greet, a few minutes before Drew came along in the hearse.

With only two of them, the coffin would of necessity be loaded onto a trolley and taken to the graveside on it. The lowering was feasible with two, but in the majority of instances, family members would participate. Some would baulk at the trolley and offer to carry their loved one across the field on their shoulders. In very wet seasons, the trolley wheels would bog down in waterlogged ground, although the gentle slope of the field meant it was well drained.

It was all a very far cry from the elaborate ceremonies staged by mainstream undertakers. This, as Thea had recently reminded Drew, was what his customers wanted. They were not shy of the realities of death and disposal, but they did need a guaranteed level of dignity and respect. They wanted time, too, instead of the lurking sense of rush associated with a cremation. No conveyor belts or strictly limited slots for the Slocombe funerals. Everything was accorded its rightful pace, which included a lot of hanging about and debriefing afterwards, more often than not.

Thanks to a nifty piece of juggling with the coffin and the trolley, Drew managed to get the deceased into the hearse without appealing to Andrew or Thea for help. The coffin itself was lightweight, the body inside likewise. He came into the house rubbing his hands. 'That trolley was an excellent investment,' he said. 'It means I can do all sorts of things on my own.'

'Why did you need me on Monday, then?'

'Because this trolley already had a coffin on it,' he replied mildly. 'So we had to use the old one, which has none of the same features. It doesn't even raise and lower any more, since the handle came off.'

'Stephanie's being brave about the horrible girls at school. That's both of them being victimised, poor things. Luckily they break up tomorrow. Maybe it'll all be forgotten after two weeks off.'

'I hate it as much as you do,' he said, with a sudden burst of irritation. 'But there doesn't seem to be anything we can do about it.' He took a breath. 'So what are you doing today?'

'Not sure. I phoned the hospital just now and Lucy's still a bit woozy, as far as I can gather. I need to know what she wants me to do. If she's not having the operation, I guess she can go home once she feels all right again.'

'Which might be weeks,' said Drew.

Thea laughed. 'It's a private room – the whole exercise is private. She'll have to sell the house if they keep her there for weeks. Even BUPA might object – and I have a feeling she's not insured. Just paying out of her savings.'

'That's meant to be cheaper in the long run. Someone was telling me last week about it.'

'Well she won't be there for weeks.' Thea was accustomed to the way her husband picked up a wide range of random information from the people who came to arrange funerals. Some would stay for hours, chatting about topics far removed from the matter in hand. Although she supposed private medical insurance would easily arise when one was arranging a funeral.

'You want to go back to Northleach,' he accused her now. 'You want to see the reaction of those people you met yesterday, and keep in with the Higgins chap.'

'Old habits,' she shrugged ruefully. 'Would you mind?

I've walked the dog and tidied the kitchen. I won't take her with me this time. And I expect I'll be back before supper.'

'I won't even notice you've gone,' he said, only half joking. Then he paused, and turned to face her directly. 'Can I just say that I'm taking it for granted that you want to help, that you're going there in a spirit of . . . I don't know . . . call it philanthropy. I need to know you're not just looking for a way of passing the time because it's boring here. Can I say that?'

'You've already said it,' she pointed out. 'Which was brave of you, I'll give you that. I guess the proof of the pudding will be in what happens next. I'm not as clear as you about my own motives, sorry to say. But I'll keep what you said in mind.'

'Well, let's hope you have fun in the process,' he said.

She drove the same route as before, via Stow and Bourton-on-the-Water, taking the shortcut through Sezincote, where the morning sun was throwing shadows at quite different angles from the previous evening. It seemed like a new world, despite the inescapable echoes from the past. This land had seen starvation, violent uprisings, extreme weather, great flocks of sheep coming and going, smaller flocks of tourists and walkers and photographers and writers all intent on making the most of the accidental beauty of the landscape and its stone. And yet there was no sign of human life until she reached the turning down to Stow. She had not passed another car for a mile or more. Drew's careful words were circling around in her head, trying to take root either in hurt feelings or a determination to show him her best side.

The trouble was that she really couldn't justify going back to the scene of the murder. Nobody had asked her to. There might be nothing to do when she got there. Just because she had blunderingly lent a hand in earlier investigations was no guarantee that she would be useful this time. The dreamy inward-looking Cotswolds could get along quite well without her interventions, and the murder of a young man would be solved by professionals, sooner or later.

But she kept going, and the A429 was busy. She sped along between two large lorries and was soon in Northleach, approaching along the former turnpike that had been bypassed for several decades. Driving eastwards, she noted new buildings, showing how the town was growing uncomfortably fast – as were most others across the country. And yet the heart of the place remained much the same. She carried on down High Street, curious to see whether there were any signs of disturbance after the discovery of a murder victim. Cars were parked at crooked angles around the town square, surrounded by a prosperous range of small shops, with public toilets set usefully at the foot of the incline. The majestic church watched over it all, completing the picture, as it had since the fifteenth century. Nothing looked any different from before, and she turned round to go back to Lucy Sinclair's house. There was a slowly dawning sense of panic at the total lack of visible activity. She had been wrong to come. There were countless tasks she could be performing at home, not just as a wife but also as a stepmother.

Schools, after all, expected a great deal by way of clothes, homework, lunch money, meetings, and commitment to whatever ethos featured in the latest newsletter. There had been two parents' evenings the previous week, which she and Drew both went to. Both came away with a sensation of having been subjected to something faintly Stalinist. 'We've been brainwashed,' said Drew. 'Twice.' It all felt dreadfully relentless, the years stretching endlessly ahead, with the whole treadmill going round and round, term after term. The fact that everybody did it with little obvious complaint only made it worse. Thea Slocombe did not naturally conform to what 'everybody' did. 'So do you want to home school them?' Drew had once demanded in exasperation.

'Only if that means setting them loose in the woods all day,' she had sighed.

But now, she had left it all behind for the day. It was easy to understand those mothers who threw aside their smothering blanket of guilt and signed up for demanding full-time jobs, which gave them the best possible justification for forgetting about homework and school dinners and torn skirts. Hadn't Stephanie said that very thing just that morning, without any hint of criticism? They could pay someone else to do all the tedious stuff and go out to sell things, whether it be cornflakes or futures in gold. Some of the time at least, this made sense to Thea.

She let herself into Lucy's house, feeling oddly intrusive. A lot had changed since she'd spoken to the woman on Tuesday, and she was not at all confident that she was still required. For one thing, there was no knowing when Lucy would come home. Perhaps she had suffered brain damage and would no longer be able to live independently. And surely the sudden, violent death of her stepson would have some influence on future decisions. This gave Thea pause for thought. What would have been the relationship between Lucy and Ollie, now she was divorced from Kevin? Had she been in the role of mother throughout the boy's adolescence? Had he sided with his father and cut off all relations with Lucy? Since he apparently lived a few hundred yards away in the same small town, this seemed unlikely. Perhaps he had deliberately sought her out, hoping for support or money or both.

The living room felt chilly, the curtains left open – for which Thea reproached herself. Unlike Bobby Latimer, Lucy liked to keep nosy pedestrians unsatisfied, although this house did not have heavy shutters like some of its neighbours. Without the spaniel, Thea felt exposed and alone. There was something to the notion of a daemon, a companion who was always there, uncritical and loving. Not to mention the convenience of being able to talk out loud without sounding crazy. 'Oh – just talking to my dog,' she would say, if anyone looked askance.

But she did not have long on her own. Barely five minutes after entering the house, she had a visitor, tapping on the window, as had happened the day before at Bobby's. Evidently this was the preferred means of attracting attention amongst the locals.

It was one of the two women from next door. The one with protuberant eyes and small chin. Faith, if Thea remembered rightly. She went to let her in, reminding herself as she did so that this was Lucy's house, and this woman was not Lucy's friend. Lucy had, in fact, specifically warned against her and her housemate.

'Sorry,' said the woman. 'But I saw your car. No dog?' She looked around.

'No,' said Thea.

'Any news?'

'About what?'

'Lucy, of course. How is she? Nobody seems to know what's happening. All that business down the street has driven everything else out of people's heads. Awful thing to happen.' She lowered her voice to a respectful whisper, but her face showed no sign of emotion.

'I think Lucy's a lot better now,' Thea said stiffly.

'They say it's that boy, Oliver, who died. Using that house for all kinds of disgraceful activities, apparently. He was a drug addict, you know. Shocking waste. I can never understand why people . . . oh well, never mind that now. It's very sad for poor Kevin. To think we only saw him yesterday.'

With difficulty, Thea kept her mouth shut, waiting for something that might account for this visitation. Idle curiosity was the most likely explanation. Faith had probably been sent by Livia to find out as much as she could from the renowned amateur detective who had suddenly arrived in their midst. Inwardly, Thea sighed – going by her reputation, it was perfectly possible that the people of Northleach had expected a murder once Thea Slocombe, formerly Osborne, showed up. But no way was she going to disclose any information that might get this person excited. There was something faintly unwholesome about her, in spite of the smart clothes and expensive hair.

Faith went on obliviously. 'What will you do now, I

wonder? Lucy was expecting to be home in a few days, wasn't she? And there really isn't anybody else she can turn to. Fancy having to use the girl across the road as her main contact for the hospital! I mean, isn't that dreadful, not having any real friends or relatives? Even a cousin or something. I suppose it's the small families people have nowadays. As for me, I've got two sisters and at least eight cousins. And Livia's got her boys, and countless nieces and nephews. We're *awash* with relations.' Finally, she heard herself and came to a sudden halt. 'Sorry – too much information,' she said with smile.

'Have you lived here long?' Thea thought to ask. Not only was it a safe question, but she thought it might tell her something helpful.

'Twelve years or so. We came just after Livia's divorce came through.'

'I see.' Several more questions pressed eagerly to be voiced, but she resolved to take it slowly. If she'd got any kind of handle on this woman, there would not need to be much prompting. So long as she stuck to facts – which would not be difficult.

'Well, you probably don't. We're not a *couple*, you know. Everybody assumes we are, and it's very annoying.'

'Does it matter? What difference does it make?'

'Of *course* it matters. There would be all kinds of silly ideas about us, and sniggering and pointed remarks. There are, anyway, but we make every effort to suppress them.'

'Really?' As far as Thea could see, the fact of two women living as a couple – or two men, come to that – had become singularly unremarkable in recent times. She couldn't recall hearing a single snigger from anyone for ages. Not where same-sex couples were concerned, anyway.

Her scepticism did not go unmarked. 'Yes, really,' snapped Faith. 'But I didn't come to talk about myself.'

'No, you came to find out what was going on with Lucy. And the answer is – nothing, as far as anyone's told me. Now I need to get on, if that's all right. I'm not authorised to offer hospitality, so perhaps you could go?' This, she realised, was the second time in two days that Faith had been asked to leave. Perhaps it happened to her all the time. She certainly showed no sign of offence or surprise.

'I can't stay, anyway,' she said carelessly. 'We've got a committee lunch today.'

'I heard about your committee,' said Thea, before she could stop herself. 'It seems to be quite a big thing.'

Faith blinked. 'What does that mean? What have people been saying?'

'Lucy mentioned it, I think. Possibly Bobby did as well. I can't remember now. Is it the town council or something?'

Faith laughed scornfully, but also flushed before answering. 'Nothing like that at all. It's just a social club, basically. It was Hunter's idea to call it The Committee – capital T capital C – as a sort of joke. It was originally just The C-O-M and that sounded odd. We have lunches and go on outings, and hold discussion evenings. It's a bit like the U3A in some ways, but we don't pretend to be educational, and don't have any age limits.' The words emerged in an unconvincingly careless fashion, as if Thea couldn't possibly be seriously interested.

'Sounds like fun,' said Thea dubiously. 'So does it have an

111

actual committee?' She recalled Jeremy Higgins's reaction – that you couldn't just have a committee in isolation. It had to represent a larger organisation. Somehow there was a logical difficulty with the one under discussion.

'Only a very informal one. Hunter's the big chief, and Livia handles the money, when there is any. That's more or less it. It's enormous fun, I assure you. Very liberating. And enlightening at times. Hunter's incredibly *brave*, you know.'

'Is he?' Thea was bemused. 'In what way?'

'I can't explain now. You're sure to meet him if you're going to stay here. He'll tell you about it, if you ask him.'

'Lucy's not part of it, is she?'

Faith pursed her narrow lips. 'We invited her, and she declined. She doesn't appear to be a very sociable person. To be honest, I don't think she liked the sound of us and what we do. She has some very fixed ideas.'

Thea said nothing to this, and Faith let herself out without any further comment. She gave a little wave through the window as she passed.

'Now what shall we do?' Thea muttered, forgetting that she had come without her dog. The answer came three minutes later when her mobile trilled at her.

It was the hospital in Oxford. 'Mrs Slocombe? I'm calling to tell you that your friend Lucy is asking for you. She's very much better today, trying to make arrangements for being discharged. . Are you able to come this morning?'

'So she's not having the operation?' said Thea, trying to process all this. 'Why didn't she call me herself?'

The woman gave a little sniff. 'Oh, well, we like to give

a very comprehensive service here, you see. Mrs Sinclair gave us all a bad shock yesterday, and we're trying to save her any trouble.'

Of course, Thea remembered, it was a private hospital ward, where no effort was spared to keep the patients happy. 'The operation?' she prompted.

'That's still being discussed. I'm sure she'll explain it all to you herself. All I'm authorised to do is ask if you're available to come and talk to her. She seems worried about how things stand between the two of you.'

'Well – yes, I suppose so. I could probably be there in about an hour's time, if that's all right. Maybe less if Oxford isn't too busy.' The roads around that city were familiar to Thea, but not friendly. She strongly disliked driving anywhere near the place.

'Excellent.' The woman gave some directions as to how to find Lucy's ward – which sounded far from straightforward – and then rang off.

It turned out that finding the relevant room in the private section of the hospital was considerably less complicated than parking the car had been. Lucy was sitting up looking ten years older and decidedly battered. There was a bewildered look in her eyes. 'Thea,' she said. 'What a relief!'

Thea sat down at the bedside and waited for enlightenment. It had occurred to her on the drive to Oxford that Lucy had been in control from the outset, and apparently was still. 'You remembered my phone number,' she said. 'I'm impressed.'

Lucy gave an impatient little laugh. 'I didn't, you idiot. It was in my phone.' She gave Thea a considering look. 'Did you think I'd lost my memory, then?'

'I didn't know what to think. Nobody seems to know what happened to you.'

'It was a really bad instance of anaphylactic shock, so they believe. Just one of those things nobody can predict. It came right out of the blue. I must be allergic to something without realising it.'

'Would that have put you in a coma? I thought they could fix allergic shocks quite easily with one of those EpiPen things. I know someone with a peanut allergy and every time he collapses they revive him within minutes.'

'It was less than one day, actually. And it wasn't a proper coma. I could hear people talking. I didn't respond to the usual treatments, which is why they want to run tests. I feel very odd, even now. And it definitely wasn't a peanut allergy,' she finished with a frown.

'Even so . . . it seems a long time to me. And it must have really scared the hospital.' Thea was marvelling at the realisation that it had been barely twenty-four hours since Lucy's collapse. A lot more time than that seemed to have passed. 'You're right – it was only yesterday,' she said. 'They phoned Bobby Latimer, you know. Why not me if my number was in your phone? Bobby was put in an awkward position, thinking she should come right away, but hampered by her kids. If she's such a good friend, why did you need me?' The final words burst out on a wave of confused resentment that took her by surprise.

'For that very reason. She's not available half the time. Not reliable, either. They should never have called her. I stupidly put her number on a form, months ago now.' She shuffled in the bed, as if unable to get comfortable, and put a hand to her back. Thea felt a pang of conscience-struck sympathy. Poor woman – her presenting problem was still there, possibly exacerbated by recent events. 'What's going to happen about your back?' she asked.

'Lord knows,' said Lucy. 'I've lost my place on the list for the next week or two, that's for sure. And they won't dare give me any anaesthetic until they've worked out exactly what happened yesterday.'

'You sound very stoical about it.'

'These things happen,' Lucy shrugged. 'You can't take anything for granted.'

Thea could find nothing to say to that, and Lucy went on, 'Now listen. Have you met anybody in Northleach? Has anything been happening while I'm away? Is the house all right?'

'Um . . .' said Thea, very unsure as to what she should say. It ought not to be her job to inform Lucy of the death of her stepson. Why hadn't the police asked the hospital to let them know as soon as Lucy was well enough to be told? Perhaps they had, and an officer would show up at any moment. Or perhaps the divorced wife of the dead man's father was not very high on the list of people to inform. Thinking about it, Thea realised that this was probably the case. Having told Kevin, they would leave it to him to pass on the essential facts. Come to that, there was sure to be something on the news, whether television or Internet or both. A murder was always top of the agenda. And if Lucy was a website designer, did that not mean she would be constantly keeping up with online information? 'Haven't you checked your inbox or anything?'

'What?' said Lucy. 'I've only just come out of whatever-it-was. Semi-coma. I've been bombarded with needles and monitors and God knows what. When have I had time to check my emails? Why should I, anyway? I was looking forward to getting away from all that.'

'Well, there's been some trouble. I only got to know by chance, yesterday. I've got absolutely no details and I don't want to upset you.' She looked around for a supportive nurse who might have some advice to offer. What if she told Lucy about Ollie and the woman had some sort of hysterical fit – or another collapse? 'It's not really for me to say,' she finished weakly.

'Tell me,' said Lucy in a startlingly powerful voice. 'What's happened? Is it to do with my house?'

'No, no. The house is fine. The thing is, I met your ex – Kevin. And Tessa. We had a bit of a chat.' This was the best she could do as a gentle introduction to the awful truth. For a moment she felt quite pleased with herself, but Lucy was not impressed.

'So what? They only live in Stroud and know half the population of Northleach. Except – I never told them I was having an operation. How did they find out?'

'A person called Hunter told them, apparently.'

'He would,' said Lucy in disgust. 'That man couldn't stop talking if he was facing a firing squad.'

'Didn't he drive you here yesterday, when I couldn't? Wasn't that rather kind of him?'

'He was coming anyway,' snapped Lucy. 'I don't owe

him any special gratitude. The man's no less of a monster for letting me ride in his car for an hour. I paid for it, having to listen to him talking gibberish the whole way, I can tell you.'

A small silence ensued, while Thea looked round again for some kind of backup, at the same time as wondering just how Lucy came to discover that Hunter was going to Oxford at dawn on a Wednesday, and got herself included in the trip.

Lucy was in a single room, well-appointed with a large television, two good-quality easy chairs, a pleasing view and overgenerous heating. There was no sign of any medical staff, although voices could be heard along the short corridor leading to other rooms. Everything was hard surfaces and pastel colours. Sounds of metal objects rattling together competed with the voices. There was a smell that said *hygiene* – like no other smell in the world.

'What are you not telling me?' Lucy persisted. 'I can see there's something.'

Afterwards Thea wondered what clues she had revealed to make Lucy so sure there was something to be reported. Was it usual for a person to awake from a semi-coma in the belief that terrible things had happened in her absence? Perhaps it was. Perhaps you would be struck by a conviction that the world had carried on without you, getting itself into all kinds of trouble. And Lucy Sinclair already knew that Thea Slocombe was more than capable of attracting just such trouble. Last time Lucy employed Thea as a house-sitter, a man had died, after all. Was it reasonable to imagine that this could happen again?

Surely it was far more likely that lightning would not strike twice, and that Thea was the very last person to run into another murder.

'Come *on*,' Lucy almost shouted.

Thea's resistance snapped. Nobody could say she hadn't tried to be circumspect and gentle. 'It's Ollie,' she said. 'Ollie Sinclair, your stepson. He's dead.'

Lucy sank back with something like satisfaction. She closed her eyes, and Thea felt a momentary panic. 'Lucy?' she said. 'Are you all right?'

'The drugs, I suppose,' came the whispered reply. 'We knew it would happen eventually. Kevin's going to be in pieces.' There was no suggestion of distress either in words or tone. Thea felt slightly foolish.

'I guess so,' she said, with a renewed sense of resistance. There was no way she was going to recount her conversation with DI Higgins. All Lucy needed to know was that the man was dead. Somebody else could take it from there. 'Well, I should go. What do you want me to do about the house?'

'What do you mean?'

'Well – I expect you'll be going home again soon. It's all changed now, hasn't it?'

'They haven't said I can go home. There are tests . . .' Lucy frowned and sank into her pillow. 'I still feel quite wobbly.'

'I know you do. But they don't keep people in for longer than they can help, do they? Although seeing that you're private, maybe they will want to milk you for a few more days.' Private medicine was something Thea vaguely disapproved of, on principle. 'Can you walk?' she asked.

'More or less.'

Again Thea wished there was a nurse at hand. Shouldn't there be someone keeping an eye on Lucy in case she relapsed? Then she realised that she was that person – the staff were relying on her to raise the alarm if there was any cause for concern. They were probably more than happy for her to keep watch while the tests were being processed.

'I liked Bobby,' she said, for the sake of keeping conversation going. 'She seems nice. I'm sure she's all you really need to make sure the house is all right. The thing is, my husband's got a lot of work on this week, and he'd appreciate me being there with him, if you can spare me. Everything's changed now,' she said again. 'Don't you see that?'

'I told you – Bobby's hopeless. I think the word is "flaky". I know she means well, but I would never trust her in a crisis. Besides, she's much too taken up with those children of hers.'

'Even so . . . I can't see what good I'm doing there. Nobody's going to burgle the house or set fire to it, are they? The women next door don't seem to be much of a threat—'

'You've met them?' Lucy interrupted. 'Faith and Livia? When? How?'

'They saw me go into Bobby's house yesterday and came to see what was going on. I mean – it wasn't as nosy as that sounds. They were just being neighbourly.'

'Oh, believe me – it was every bit as nosy as it sounds. Worse, if anything.' Lucy spoke bitterly. 'They're like

119

heat-seeking missiles – homing in on the slightest thing, in the hope of finding something to use against me. You can't imagine what it's like. They've completely ruined any chance I ever had of making friends. And all because I said they were bigots.'

Thea was preparing to leave, and now stood up. 'If you said that, then perhaps they're justified in feeling a bit hostile,' she said mildly. 'It's not a very nice thing to call someone, is it?'

'It's true, though. That idiotic club they're all in – it's just a talk shop for fascists and racists and homophobes. I couldn't believe my ears when I went to one of their meetings. Can you believe they tried to make me join them? Me! And now they're doing all they can to intimidate me, so I don't report them for hate speech.'

'Okay,' said Thea, alarmed at the passion behind the words. 'Don't get agitated. If you don't want me to take you home, or sort anything else out for you, I'll go back to Northleach and lock the house up properly, and maybe you could phone me later on and we'll decide what to do next. The people here are sure to tell you something soon, and then we'll have a better idea. It's great that you've made such a quick recovery. Do you want me to tell Bobby she doesn't need to worry any more?'

'She won't be worrying. Thanks, Thea. You're right, of course. It was very good of you to come so quickly. And don't give up on me. I really do think I'm going to need you for a while yet.'

'Bye, then.'

As she drove away, Thea remembered Lucy's pathetic

old dog from her days in Hampnett. The woman had been quite a different person then – compassionate, creative, witty. Newly divorced, she had been giddy with the prospect of freedom. Something had evidently happened to change her in the meantime.

Chapter Nine

She sped back along the A40 to Northleach, making better time than before. She paid a moment's accord to Witney, where she and Carl and Jessica had lived in a previous life, and did the same to Burford, which had always been a big favourite. There was something about the A40 and the places it ran through, all the way from Fishguard to London. Nobody would use it now for the whole of that route, thanks to the M4 and other bigger faster roads, but it survived, earning its own body of fans with its quirky twists and turns.

There was no real sense of urgency, even though it was past midday. She was not required to collect Stephanie from school, because another local mother was doing it. But there was still a nagging feeling that the children would appreciate her being there when they got home. And the dog would certainly be feeling abandoned. Furthermore, she could not think of anything useful she could do in Northleach. She drove into it, with a feeling of redundancy.

Lucy's house was just as she left it, windows and doors all secure. The police were unlikely to need any input from her regarding Ollie's murder. There was sure to be police tape around the building where the poor man had been found, but she had seen no obvious sign of a temporary incident room in the town. It might be in a back room of one of the pubs, she supposed, but if so, nobody had bothered to put a sign up to say so. She was hungry for some lunch, and opted to buy a sausage roll in the baker's in the town square. Not having Hepzie with her made things simpler, she had to admit. She could run in and out of shops without worrying about leaving the dog in a hot car or tying her up outside. But she missed her, even so.

Coming out of the bakery, she ran into the wheels of Buster Latimer's pushchair – or was it a stroller? It was big, anyway, with padded armrests and complicated accessories designed to accommodate shopping and protect against rain. His mother looked small and breathless behind it. 'Ouch!' said Thea, having bumped her ankle as the vehicle competed with her for space in the doorway.

'Sorry,' said Bobby. 'I always try to take this thing into shops and it never works.'

'It's worse than trying to cope with a dog,' said Thea, following her recent train of thought.

'No comparison,' said Bobby, with some indignation.

'Right. Well, hello again. How's things?'

'What things?'

'Um . . .' said Thea helplessly. 'You know . . .'

'There's been a murder, if that's what you mean. I imagine you know all about that already. Everybody's saying you're always getting involved in that sort of thing. Hunter thinks you're a jinx.'

Hunter again – Thea was beginning to feel as if that man was somehow supernatural, popping up in conversation but never actually physically present. 'He doesn't know anything about me,' she said crossly.

'He does, though,' Bobby contradicted. She smiled triumphantly, and added, 'There he is, look. Why don't you go and talk to him? See if you can put him straight.' She was indicating with her chin, since both hands were fully occupied, a point somewhere in the square. 'By that blue car, look.'

Thea looked. There was only one man it could be, and he was so like her groundless mental image of him that she laughed. 'What – him?' She pointed rudely and the man became aware of being discussed.

'Hey, Hunter! This is Mrs Slocombe, the house-sitter,' Bobby called, far too loudly for the situation. The man was only twenty yards away.

'We meet at last,' said Thea, determined to stand her ground. Something about him brought all her defensive instincts to the fore. He was about five feet ten, with a big head and a lot of brown curly hair. He seemed to be in his early sixties. Like everybody else in Northleach, Thea thought wryly. Except for Bobby Latimer, she corrected. He approached quickly, and she held out her hand; he took it in a strong grip.

'No need to shout, dear,' the man said to Bobby. 'You'll have the whole town joining us.' His voice was deep and musical, with the slightest hint of Gloucestershire. The condescension was breathtaking. It took Thea nearly a whole minute to realise who he reminded her of, and then she laughed again. Here was a British version of Donald Trump, if ever there was one.

He seemed pleased to be the object of her mirth, preening as if he'd made a brilliant joke. 'Mrs Slocombe,' he repeated. 'Pleased to meet you. Hunter Lanning at your service.'

'Mr Lanning,' said Thea, matching his tone and demeanour as well as she could. 'I've heard a lot about you,' she went on, suspecting that he was about to say the same thing.

'Have you indeed?' he said, with an ever-widening smile.

'Mostly to do with your committee, actually.'

Bobby Latimer was still there, having given up trying to get Buster's carriage into the shop. She gave a sharp inward breath, warning Thea that she was on dangerous ground. But Thea was past caring. 'Where's Millie?' she asked Bobby, as a way of showing how little she feared Hunter Lanning. 'She told me it was school holidays already.'

'Dance class,' came the brief reply. Bobby was eyeing Hunter as she spoke. 'It must have been Lucy who told her about the committee,' she said. 'Because it surely wasn't me.' She had become more American in her agitation.

'No problem,' said the man easily. 'It's not a secret, darling. The clue's in the name.'

'Oh?' said Thea. For the past minutes her inborn

curiosity had been stirring and then erupting. She found herself wanting to know it all. And one reason for that was that she had quickly identified this Hunter Lanning as a very probable participant in the killing of Oliver Sinclair. If he hadn't done it himself, she strongly suspected that he knew exactly who had.

'C-O-M. That's the official name for it. The Club for the Open-Minded. A place where anybody can say anything they like without fear of persecution. Or even prosecution. Sounds obvious, but it's a rare organisation these days that will allow such a thing.'

'Oh.' Thea frowned, thoroughly deflated by this assertion. The ground seemed to waver beneath her feet. 'Well, I'm all for that, then,' she said boldly, whilst wondering whether it was true. 'What sort of things do your members say?' Only in that moment did she recall Lucy's attack – the committee was 'fascist, racist and homophobic' according to her. Thea's initial impression of Hunter was that this was indeed only too likely. In which case she was not all for it at all, obviously. Although . . . again the ground seemed insecure. 'Do you have members with a wide range of opinions?' she managed to ask.

'Of course,' he said, but he was looking at Bobby. Something unspoken was passing between them, with Thea receiving only the scrap ends of their attention. This merely increased her curiosity. Buster came to her aid with a shout of impatience at being left in a shop doorway. He had probably been promised a bun or something.

'So what about the murder, then?' she said, heedless of whether anyone else could hear her. There was a woman close by and two lads who looked about eighteen. Further away, between two parked cars, a couple were gazing raptly at the church. It was likely that all of them had caught the heavy word *murder*.

'I beg your pardon?' said Hunter, eyebrows raised. 'I grant you there has been a death, the explanation of which is yet to be forthcoming, but nobody has said anything about murder to me.'

'Well, they have to me,' said Thea. Hearing herself, she winced. There was an echo of the way she had spoken to people in Cranham, a few years earlier. She had been insensitive and feelings had been wounded. She tried to soften her approach. 'I mean – well, that's not entirely true. It's just that I know some of the police detectives on the case, that's all.'

'I expect they'll soon figure out that it was one of his peculiar friends who killed him,' said Bobby, with a glance at her child. No mother could be altogether relaxed when discussing violent death just down the road. However strenuously they all clung to the idea that good parenting was a rock-solid antidote to the lurking evils all around them, the sad facts were against them. Bad things could happen to anyone – even innocuous little Buster, in another couple of decades.

'From what I hear, the poor lad was never going to make old bones,' said Hunter. 'I'm sure it'll turn out that he simply took too much of the hard stuff. Usual story, I'm afraid. Nobody's fault. Tragic for poor Kevin.' He heaved a flamboyant sigh.

'Did he live in that house?' asked Thea, waving a hand

towards the high street. 'Ollie, I mean.'

Hunter inclined his great head, and spoke softly. 'Not officially, no. It's been a bit of a scandal for a while now. The owners are from Poland, I believe. Bought the house as a secure investment – and who can blame them? They don't spend a lot of time here . . . well, almost none, to be frank. So they let some young cousin or such use it for a shockingly low rent. The cousin appears to have been acquainted with young Oliver. They all come and go at random – no proper jobs, of course. I think they have one of those Airbnb arrangements that they go in for these days – which can cause all kinds of trouble with the neighbours. All very secretive and mysterious, which gets everyone windy, if you know what I mean.'

'Did they create any actual nuisance?' Thea asked. It was impossible to establish just how this man viewed the arrangement. He seemed to be speaking for the whole village, but nobody in particular.

'They're not really doing anything too awful,' Bobby interrupted. 'But people object to the *influence*, as they call it. Look at those two, for instance.' She ducked her chin at the pair of young men now drifting towards the pub in the square. 'They've been working on the estate the other side of Hampnett – renovating buildings and that sort of thing. Normally they'd go down to Cirencester in the evenings, but once they got to know there were other young people at the Polish people's house, they've taken to coming here instead. I don't recognise them particularly, but there've been several like them drifting around. People find it unsettling.'

'Are they all Polish?' Thea asked. It was true that there was an element of drifting in the way the two were behaving.

'Something like that,' said Bobby.

'Ukrainian, I believe,' said Hunter.

'Shouldn't they be at work?' Thea wondered.

'Lunch break,' said Hunter, and then thought again. 'It looks to me as if they've been asked to come and answer some questions, and they can't find where to go. The police have set up an incident room in the pub. As I'm sure you already know,' he added nastily to Thea.

Instead of defending herself, Thea was snagged by the mention of lunch. Not only was she seriously hungry herself, but it reminded her of something Faith had said. 'Speaking of which, aren't you meant to be having a lunch today? Faith said as much this morning. The committee was doing a lunch, she said.'

He shook his head with exaggerated patience. 'Today's event does not include me. It's ladies only.'

'Good Lord,' said Thea. 'It just gets curiouser and curiouser.' She permitted herself the tiniest hint of a sneer. 'You sound like Freemasons, keeping the women out of the important stuff.'

Hunter Lanning reared back, eyes wide. 'Then you can't have been listening,' he snarled. 'Since when did anybody characterise the Masons as open-minded? And, I might tell you, we play none of those tedious games concerning charitable giving. How many times have you heard them trying to justify themselves by talking of all the good works they support? In our committee we would never agree on which charities we approved of.' He laughed scornfully and again glanced at Bobby. It seemed to Thea that there was a glimmer of unease as he did so. 'For your information, the women requested their own events, on the grounds that there were topics they felt more comfortable discussing without men present. Nothing to do with sexism or segregation or whatever you might be thinking. And I doubt if it turns on matters gynaecological, either. Even the most free-thinking of women might hesitate to reveal her deepest beliefs and ambitions within a man's hearing.'

Thea was lost for words. Again, she felt there was no solid ground from which to argue with this man. She looked to Bobby for rescue. 'Are you a member as well?'

'Me? Oh, well, sort of. I go once in a while. But Artie – he's my husband – is a lot more involved than I am. He thinks it's great. He's a great fan of the whole thing.'

'Oh. Well . . .' Thea looked at Buster. 'I think he's losing patience. I should go. I'm *ravenous*.' She held up the paper bag containing her sausage roll. 'And I ought to be getting back to my husband.' Too late it occurred to her that this had not been very wise. From what she had gleaned from Lucy, it seemed it would be better to keep the not-altogether-good folk of Northleach guessing as to her movements.

They dispersed in three different directions. A flurry of rain hit Thea in the face just as she reached her car, parked outside Lucy Sinclair's house. Dark clouds had gathered over the past few minutes, and she sat in the car eating her meagre lunch and pondering the day's events. Faith, Lucy, Hunter and Bobby had all managed to fill in a number of holes in the story of the past day or two. But there were still legions of questions. The strange house in High Street

130

became prominent in her thinking. A drug den? A hideaway for illegal immigrants? In some ways it seemed ideal for either purpose, until she thought of the unsettled locals and their suspicions. If anything seriously illegal had been going on, it seemed inevitable that some upstanding citizen would quickly report it. Rather, there appeared to be no actual evidence of wrongdoing – simply a sense that all was not well. And then, shockingly, the worst fears and suspicions had been amply confirmed by the fact of a murder in that very house.

She started the car and drove away, feeling the eyes of Northleach on her, and wondering when she would be there again. She had made no promises to Lucy, who had seemed less anxious about her house than previously. But Lucy was no longer of primary relevance. Instead, Thea was compelled to discover more about Hunter Lanning, his committee and those who were a part of it.

When she yet again drove through the Sezincote estate, the view was entirely different from before. The land seemed to shrink under the weight of the sky, the usual distance invisible. Rain was brewing, grey clouds rolling in from the north, along with a chilly wind. Even as she looked, the first serious drops began to fall. In barely two minutes, it was a downpour.

Sitting at the traffic lights in Stow, she briefly considered turning round and going back yet again to Northleach. She wanted to make notes, to check certain names online, to make one or two phone calls, and be close at hand for Higgins or Barkley if the investigation escalated. Drew and the children would not be surprised, whatever she did. She had given them no assurances. In fact, she had not given anyone assurances, knowing better than to do so. She was essentially free from spoken obligations.

But she was not free of unspoken ones. She was a wife and a stepmother. She had a dog, and a house to think about. Affairs in Northleach were tenuous and far outside her sphere of influence. For the time being at least, she knew she had to go home.

The last stretch of road to Broad Campden was slick with rain, already forming puddles here and there. The Easter holidays were about to start. Drew had a lot of funerals – which would be badly affected by heavy rain. Everybody had their place, knowing where they should be and what they should be doing. Everybody except Thea, in fact.

The spaniel greeted her with easy adoration, before she was through the door, and Drew gave a hurried sigh of relief as he came around the side of the house. 'You're back,' he said.

'I am. All present and correct. Is everything all right here?'

'More or less. We just dodged the rain, and nobody got wet. There were forty-three people. It was lovely, actually.' He smiled at the memories of his success. 'Everybody admired the way it was done.' Then his expression changed. 'But tomorrow's going to be a nightmare, though, with three to get through. None of the families like the idea of lowering the coffin, for a start. The twelve o'clock has got horribly whiffy. It's all the drugs they give them.'

'Right.' Thea cut him off quickly. 'He's not in the corridor, is he?'

'He was, but I've switched them round. I wish I hadn't said I'd do them all in one day. What on earth was I thinking?'

'We've been through all that,' she told him sternly. 'It would be very bad for business if you turned people away.'

'Yes, but I could have done one of them on Saturday. Why didn't I think of that? When will I learn to check my assumptions before I speak? There's nothing sacred about weekends any more. Even people like Daphne Plant are loosening up about that now.' He was referring to the mainstream undertaker, where he had once worked, and where he learnt the business. Unable to tolerate some of the less admirable features of the work, he had chosen to go it alone, setting up his own business in Somerset and charging very much less for a simpler service.

'You see plenty of Saturday funerals these days,' he went on. He wasn't really speaking to her, Thea realised, with her thoughts still stubbornly fixed on the whiffy gent to be buried next day. In her mind's nose she could detect the cloying smell of decomposition, even before she got into the house.

'Oh well, too late to do much about that now,' she said. 'Is Stephanie home yet? What are you doing for the rest of the day? Not a lot, I imagine, given that it's raining.'

'The usual,' he shrugged. 'Only more so. And yes, Stephanie got in five minutes ago.'

'Well, if you ask me it's good that we've got the weekend free. You're going to need to unwind, the state you're in.'

'Are you going to be here to help me do that?' He gave her a small-boy look that both irritated and amused her.

'Probably,' she said cautiously.

Stephanie seemed subdued when Thea found her in her bedroom. 'Awful weather,' said Thea. 'Let's hope it improves for the weekend.'

'Did you go back to Northleach?'

'Yes, I did. I've been out all day. Are your clothes all right for one more day? You can wear the same skirt tomorrow, can't you?'

'It's a bit dusty. I dropped my pen and had to crawl under the table to get it. The floor was filthy.'

'You could wear trousers just for one day, then? It baffles me the way you prefer skirts. I thought they'd have been given up long ago. I remember all sorts of battles when Jessica was your age, with the girls all wanting trousers.'

'Yes, you said. Trousers are too hot. And skirts look nicer.'

It was a conversation they'd had several times. In a world where hardly any adult women wore skirts or dresses, it seemed perverse to Thea that schoolgirls insisted on them. At first she had blamed the headteacher, but it seemed that was mistaken. 'I agree with you,' she had said when Thea broached the subject. 'But apparently we're out of date on the subject. They all want to look feminine, I'm told.'

'Not all,' Thea had observed. 'I'd say about a third of them have opted for slacks.'

Mrs Metherington had sighed. 'You would not believe how fraught the whole subject is these days. All I can do is

134

leave everybody to make their own decisions. Any minute now there'll be boys showing up in skirts, and we'll just have to go with it. My worst fear is making an issue of it and ending up in the headlines.'

Thea had sympathised and said no more – except to Stephanie. The child was growing fast, which meant regular purchases of expensive new garments. 'I'm sure there's more leeway in trousers,' she grumbled.

'Dad said you'd had a bit of a barney with someone in your class,' she said now. 'Is that right?'

'I don't know what a barney is.'

'Yes you do. It's an argument. Disagreement.'

'I thought it was a fight. I haven't been fighting, if that's what you're worried about. Didn't we say all this already? You don't have to keep on about it.'

'I do, because you haven't told me anything about what's actually been going on.'

'You wouldn't understand.' Stephanie looked at her. 'I don't mean that nastily. You just wouldn't. There's a sort of gang – it's mostly an online thing, but they talk about it as well. The whole thing's stupid – that's what you'd say, and you'd be right. But – it's always *there*. They don't like people who don't want to be part of it.'

'Like you.'

'Yeah. Anyway, it's the end of term tomorrow. I can forget all about it for a bit.'

'Okay. Well, you have to keep us informed, you know. Talk about this sort of stuff and it often loses its power over you – if you see what I mean. But you're right, I'll never properly understand what it's like. So I'm not going to interfere unless you ask me to, okay?'

'Thanks,' said Stephanie. 'I expect it's all very character-forming.'

'Sure to be,' said Thea, only too aware that she was being quoted back at herself.

Thursday was generally Thea's favourite day, harking back decades to when the school timetable had nearly always suited her very nicely on that day. History, Art and English seemed to predominate, and never any games. This evening, with her family in Broad Campden, something of these echoes still lingered. 'What do you want to do at the weekend?' she asked the children. 'We should go and buy Easter eggs, I suppose.'

'Isn't that meant to be kept secret, like Christmas?' Drew wondered. 'My mother always pretended there wouldn't be anything special, and then there it was – a great big egg in a box on the breakfast table.'

'That would only work once, surely?' said Thea.

'Nope. Somehow it always came as a splendid surprise.'

'Your mother's a good actor, then.' Drew's mother had been widowed recently, and after years of estrangement, had decided to bury the hatchet and pay regular visits to her son and grandchildren. She had last shown up in February, with her big, unreliable dog that followed Timmy everywhere. The next visit was scheduled for late April. 'Making up for lost time,' said Drew. 'Brace yourself for her appearing every couple of months.'

'I rather like her,' said Stephanie.

'You like everybody,' the other three chorused.

It was past five o'clock when Caz Barkley came to the door. Hepzie greeted her like an old friend, but Drew and Timmy both withheld any enthusiasm. 'For heaven's sake, we're just about to eat,' muttered Drew. 'Why is she here now?'

'Hush, Dad,' Stephanie admonished him. 'She'll hear you. We're not eating for ages yet, anyway.'

Thea took the young detective sergeant into the living room. 'If I'm not done by six, start without me,' she called into the kitchen. 'I don't expect we'll be that long. Supper time,' she told the visitor.

'Right. Sorry. I'll be in the doghouse with your husband, then.'

'You and Gladwin both. Can't be helped. I haven't seen you for ages.'

'Last summer,' Barkley nodded. 'And now here we are again.'

'Northleach I suppose.'

'Right. Oliver Sinclair, twenty-eight, died of injuries to head and neck. Bled to death, essentially.'

'Horrible! And I was looking after his stepmother's house and had just spoken to his father and his . . . whatever she is, when they found the body. She calls herself his partner, I expect.' She waved Barkley to a seat. 'Which really doesn't make me very useful – does it? I'd never heard of Ollie until yesterday.' Numerous thoughts were popping into her head, making speech less coherent than it might be. 'What was the time of death? Who found him? If he'd only been dead an hour or so, I can provide a whole string of alibis. That would make me useful, at least.'

'DI Higgins says you might have some insights and the

SIO agrees. You've met the parents and probably half the people in the village by now. We've been running round in circles for two days trying to figure out the story. No two people tell it the same. And the time of death's a nightmare. There was heating on full blast in the house, which plays havoc with the pathology. Nobody had seen him since Sunday, as far as we can discover. The closest we can get is that he was in the house all day Monday and Tuesday, alive or dead. There's stuff in the fridge, the Smart Meter shows quite high usage of power for most of that time. There was a laptop showing activity. And a phone, obviously. The forensic bods have been having a field day, going through it all and fitting it all together. There are countless factors to be considered. Was he killed in his sleep? Did he know his killer? There's no sign of any sort of fight or resistance. I could go on.'

'What about the drugs? Everybody says he was an addict.'

Caz shook her head in despair. 'That's another thing. The woman who found the body told the first responders that he was known to be on drugs, so it was the first thing in the notes. It's on the G5. But bizarrely there's no actual evidence that he was taking any sort of addictive substance. The tox screen is completely clear. He was in work, we can't find a doctor who'll admit to having him on the books, and the PM couldn't find a thing. No score marks, no nasal inflammation, and nothing recent in his system. But at least four people have categorically told us he was a druggie.'

'Blimey!' said Thea. 'That's weird.'

'It is,' Barkley agreed.

'Who was the woman who found him?'

'A friend of a friend, who says she'd been trying to get him on the phone since Tuesday morning, to talk about something he really cared about. It's still a bit confusing, but there's a girlfriend in the picture, and she's the one who asked this other woman to go and have a look. We found all the messages she left, so the story checks out. Anyway, the girlfriend knows a woman who lives locally, by the name of Ms Shapley, and sent her round to see what was what. The door was unlocked, so the poor thing just walked in and found him. Most people would throw a fit if that happened, but not this lady. You should hear the tape of her call. Dead calm, giving his name and the address clear as a bell. Then she says, "He must have got into trouble with his drug supplier." Just like that. She was still there when the paramedics showed up, but she didn't talk to them. Just explained that she was only a messenger and had never even met Ollie before.'

'Weird again,' said Thea.

'We've interviewed her, of course, and Ollie's girlfriend. When pressed, neither of them could give any real evidence for drugs. The girlfriend was especially blank about it. Ms Shapley said it went with the territory, as far as she was aware. Mr Sinclair was a film editor, apparently working mostly from that house. She said she had always assumed people in that sort of work took drugs as a matter of course.'

'The girlfriend ought to know best, presumably.'

'You'd think so. Did you know that Ollie was a very successful athlete some years ago?'

Thea blinked. 'I did not,' she said. 'Would that fit with

drugs? Some sort of agonising injury leading to stronger and stronger painkillers? Would you be able to spot evidence of prescription drugs, rather than heroin or cocaine or something?'

'The pathologist says there was nothing chemical in his system at all. He had eaten bread, apples and cheese for his last meal, and drunk nothing but water.'

'Sounds too pure to be true,' said Thea.

Caz nodded. 'Could be. Even if he was on something, that might have nothing to do with why he was killed. The oddest thing is the way everyone was so sure about it.'

'Including his father,' said Thea. 'Who I'm sure you've spoken to.'

'We have, obviously. The wretched man's in pieces.'

'Is he? So you're not suspecting him, then?'

'Go back to how he was when you saw him. Was that yesterday?'

'In the morning. Before anybody knew about the murder.'

'So what did he tell you about his son?'

Thea racked her brains. 'Nothing much,' she reported. 'Just that Ollie was not Lucy's son, and that he couldn't remember exactly how old he was. It was Tessa who knew.'

'No mention of drugs?'

'Ah, yes. He said Ollie was degenerate, and he seemed to actively dislike him. Sorry I forgot that part. A lot's happened since then.'

'Degenerate. That's a strong word.'

'I know. I was shocked.'

'Is there any way you could have been speaking to his

killer, do you think? You've had plenty of time to think back and ask yourself the same thing.'

'It's an unfair question. Far too subjective. But I would say no, with a fair degree of certainty. He was more concerned with Lucy, wanting to know what had happened to her. It sounds daft, but he was too *relaxed* to be a murderer. None of the *wildness* you'd expect. If you see what I mean. And now you say he's fallen apart. Grief-stricken, in fact.'

'That's the impression Higgins got when he spoke to him. Have you ever seen anyone just after they've committed a murder?'

Thea said nothing, trying to sort through the many occasions when she had been close to a violent death. 'I probably have,' she said slowly, 'but nobody specific comes to mind. I would venture to say that women hide it better than men. I've been very thoroughly taken in by women a few times.'

'So everybody believed Ollie was on drugs, but nobody appears to have seen any evidence of it with their own eyes.'

'More or less. You'll have asked more people about it than I have. With me it was just a kind of background fact they all took for granted. Like that woman, Faith, who mentioned it this morning.' A new thought struck her. 'Oh – I should confess that I told Lucy that Ollie was dead. I went to see her in hospital and she hadn't heard. *She* said something about drugs, as well.'

'You went to see Lucy Sinclair?'

'She was asking for me. She got over the coma or whatever it was, and seemed pretty well back to normal this morning. From what I could gather, there's not much wrong with her, and she'll be home again before long. She didn't have the operation on her back as planned.'

Caz was visibly floundering. 'This is what the super means about you,' she groaned. 'You get right in there, sorting out the relationships and passing on the latest news, before we've even got a list of relatives. I really don't know how you do it.'

'It's not deliberate,' said Thea humbly. 'It just sort of *happens*.'

'Well, it's lucky for us. Who's the Faith person?'

Thea repeated everything she could remember about Faith and Livia, finishing with, 'They live next door to Lucy, and she doesn't like them much. In fact, she more or less said she wanted me to guard the house against them.'

'Really?' Caz gave this some thought. Thea watched her as she sat in an armchair, leaning forward. Her hair was roughly tied back. Both feet were firmly planted on the floor. She had gained some weight since the previous summer, Thea noticed. *Big-boned*, as Thea's mother would say. But no fool, as had been evident from their first encounter. 'Why would that be, then?'

'I don't know, really. They seem perfectly civilised to me. But I could tell they don't really like Lucy or approve of her. And she really doesn't like them. Says they spy on her and make life impossible, and she doesn't trust them not to snoop round her garden – even the house, if it's left empty. She said that's why she wanted a house-sitter. It might have all started when she wouldn't join their committee, although that doesn't seem any reason to worry about the house. She was annoyingly vague about it, but she did seem worried. I had a feeling she was trying to explain something without actually giving any details. If so, I was too thick to get the message.'

'How well do you know her?'

Thea explained about the earlier house-sit in Hampnett. 'She'd just got divorced and was celebrating with a month in the sunshine. I assumed she got quite a generous settlement. She seemed quite light-hearted and perfectly sane. I wouldn't swear to either of those now.'

'Which would imply that the husband was in the wrong and had a guilty conscience, if she got a good settlement,' said Caz.

'Or maybe she just had a better lawyer. The fact is, I hardly know her at all. It's the same story with all my house-sitting jobs – I never get to spend time with the owners of the houses. They show me round, hand me the keys and leave. Sometimes there's been a bit more time when they come home again – but not always. And quite often things have gone horribly wrong in the meantime,' she said regretfully.

Caz laughed. 'The way I hear it, that's nearly always.'

'No, no. I've had quite a few where nothing happened at all. But they don't make the news, of course.'

'But Lucy came back again, so you can't have made too much of a mess of it in her case.'

'Well, the house didn't burn down. But I wasn't entirely successful with her animals. And I kicked her dog.' She sighed. 'I wish I hadn't done that.'

'I expect you had good reason.'

'I thought so at the time. He's dead now, anyway.

Nothing to do with me kicking him, I should add.'

Caz rightly shrugged the dog's story away as irrelevant. 'Faith and Livia – interesting names. Are they a couple, or what?'

Thea brightened. 'Ah – that I *can* tell you. It annoys them terribly that everybody jumps to that conclusion just because they live together, and they go out of their way to insist that they're just friends. Nothing more. No way. Absolutely not.'

'As in, they protest too much?'

'Sort of. Except I assume it's true – that they're not, I mean. After all, who cares?'

'So what *are* they? How often do female friends live together like that?'

'I suppose it's possible. It probably makes perfect sense in a lot of ways. Faith said something about a divorce. And Livia's got some sons. I can't remember how many. They've obviously got a lot in common.'

'What age are they?'

'Sixties. Most people in Northleach appear to be in their sixties.'

'You'll have seen *This Country* I suppose?'

'What?'

'It's a sitcom set there. I think the blurb calls the place "picturesque but depressingly dull" if I remember rightly.'

'What – Northleach? Surely not!'

'Thea Slocombe, you have to be the only person in the Cotswolds who doesn't know about it. It's very funny.'

'But – Northleach! Aren't the residents hopping mad about it?'

'I'll leave you to find that out for yourself,' said Caz with a smile. 'My guess is that they do their level best to ignore it.'

Thea nodded. 'Nobody's mentioned it to me. I've got to watch it. Does it point fun at anybody in particular?'

'I think not. And it can't possibly have anything to do with the murder. That's what I'm here about, remember?'

'Yes, and we'd better get on with it. My supper's going to be cold at this rate.'

'We've said most of it.'

'Pity about the time of death being so vague,' Thea said. 'That must make everything a lot more complicated.'

'We'll get pretty close with a bit more work. The house is full of clues – we just have to sift through them all. There's something suspiciously *neat* going on. The others renting the house, for a start, so conveniently hopping back to Poland and leaving him there all by himself. The friend who was worried enough to get someone else to investigate, but not to do it herself. It has a weird feeling of a kind of chess game, with every piece set up well in advance, clearing the way for the final blow. It's premeditated murder times ten.'

'They were making films, did you say? Not pornographic ones, I take it?'

'We're still looking into that. YouTube seems to carry most of them. And so far, they're entirely innocent – aimed at quite young kids, encouraging them to take more exercise. More or less what you'd expect from a former athlete, I suppose.'

'Right, but – kids? Doesn't that ring a bit of an alarm bell?'

'A bit,' admitted Caz Barkley.

'Anything's possible. I realised years ago that the bland façade of these pretty villages hides an awful lot of bad behaviour. It's actually easier to get away with it – whatever "it" is – here than it would be in central Birmingham.'

'So Gladwin keeps telling us. It still feels wrong. I mean – *Northleach*!'

Thea laughed. 'I thought that was my line,' she said.

Voices from the kitchen were growing louder, and Thea understood that her absence was increasingly intolerable to the family. The door was open and she could see Stephanie laying the table and Drew peering into the oven. Even Hepzie had transferred her allegiance and was sitting reproachfully beside her empty dinner bowl. 'You'll have to go,' Thea told Caz.

'Okay. Thanks for talking to me. You've been helpful. I think we're more up to date now.'

'Ollie wasn't into drugs,' Thea recited as if ramming this idea firmly into her brain. 'Is that for public consumption? It can't be right for his reputation to be sullied like this.'

They were on the doorstep. Caz was thinking. 'Actually, it might be good to keep that bit quiet for a few days – see if we can figure out who knew the truth and who didn't. Somebody must have spread the story on purpose, don't you think?'

'Could have just been jumping to conclusions. A group of men living in someone else's house, coming and going at odd times – it wouldn't be much of a leap.'

'Well, don't say anything yet. Are you going back to Northleach any time soon? It would suit us rather nicely if you did. You could come in handy. Probably.'

'I don't know,' said Thea, glancing back towards the kitchen. 'I'll have to see.'

Caz gave her a knowing look, and grinned. 'You're not convincing me. All you wanted was to be asked.' She started towards the lane, before pausing. 'By the way, your house is a bit whiffy – did you know? Smells like dead bodies. Just saying.'

'And good night to you too,' muttered Thea before closing the door.

Chapter Ten

'No new funerals for next week, then?' Thea asked Drew, once the children had gone to bed. 'From feast to famine, as they say.'

'There's sure to be something over the weekend. Or if there's not, I won't complain. It'll give Andrew time to get right. He's insisting on helping out tomorrow, which will probably set him back.'

'Can I do anything?' She knew she had to ask, just as she knew what the reply would be.

'Well, if you're here you could answer the phone. But it doesn't matter – we'll switch the calls through to the mobile if you're going out.'

'I feel horribly useless,' she confessed. The next day loomed ahead like a brick wall, with poor Drew left to scale it as best he could, all by himself. Even if she stayed at home, she would not be of any real help.

'Just useful in different ways,' he said gallantly. 'Don't worry about me. What's the worst that can happen?'

'Don't say that!' She shivered at the possibilities. 'People get murdered, you know.'

'As if I could forget. So, you'd better bring me up to date on the Northleach business, hadn't you? It's obvious that your detective chums aren't going to let you stay out of it – even if you wanted to.'

'I'm not at all keen to be involved,' she assured him. 'I don't even feel I owe Lucy anything. I think she's being ridiculously paranoid about the neighbours, and never needed a house-sitter in the first place.'

'Unless there's things she's not telling you.'

'Well, yes. That's possible, I suppose.'

'Quite likely, it seems to me. And the police presumably think there's a connection between you being in her house, and her stepson being killed just down the street. How could there not be?'

'You don't mean because it's me, and murder always follows me around, do you?'

'Sort of. The thing is, you've got a big reputation in the area now, more so since you married me. Neither of us can escape the associations with death of every hue. Violent, natural, accidental – the whole range, between us.'

'Yes, but – where's the logic in suggesting that somebody killed Ollie knowing I was going to be there? Surely that would be a deterrent, since I'm pretty good at fingering the killer. Any murderer with any sense would steer clear of a village I was scheduled to be staying in.'

'Maybe he saw it as a challenge. An extra twist, or some sort of double bluff.'

She frowned doubtfully. 'I'm not sure real people think like that,' she objected. 'Besides – hardly anybody knew I was going to be in Northleach.'

'How do you know that?'

She faltered. 'Okay. Bobby Latimer obviously knew, and probably her husband. Possibly the women next door, and they might have said something to the silly committee outfit. Oh dear.'

'"Silly committee outfit"?' he repeated. 'What's that, then?'

'Some sort of debating society – Club for the Open-Minded, apparently. C-O-M. Lucy says they're all bigots who want somewhere to air their racist views. Something like that.'

'Gives open minds a bad name, then,' smiled Drew.

'That's it.' She smiled back. 'In a nutshell.'

'The victim's name was Ollie, was it?' Drew was evidently taking a genuine interest, which Thea was quick to prolong. It had been quite a while since he had initiated any conversations to do with her house-sitting adventures. Even when local friends had been closely involved in a killing, Drew had tried to remain detached. At some point over recent months he must have concluded that this was unwise.

'Oliver Sinclair. Lucy's stepson, as you've already noted – which is impressive, may I say? And appreciated. It's nice to be able to talk it all through with you.'

'You make it sound as if this is the first time. What

about when you were in Cranham? I took enormous interest that time. There were those puppies . . .' His eyes went misty with nostalgia.

'You were trying to ingratiate yourself,' she accused him.

'Not at all. I enjoyed your company and wanted to be your friend.'

'Pooh!' she said.

'So tell me more about the murdered man.'

'Okay, then. He was said by everyone in town to be a drug addict, but actually appears not to have been. The pathologist couldn't find any sign of anything you could call a drug. Which is strange.'

'Rumours spread very easily in a place like Northleach. For better or for worse.'

Thea chewed her lip for a moment. 'I never really thought that was true around here, though. So many people spend half their time, or more, somewhere else. They don't know their neighbours, or care what they get up to.' She remembered something Caz had told her. 'Did you know there was a sitcom set in Northleach? Called "Our Country" or something. We should see if we can get it on Netflix.'

'It's *This Country* and yes, I've heard of it, as of this week. Penelope Allen's people mentioned it when we were arranging her funeral.'

She blinked at him and laughed. 'Is that where I went wrong, then, when I made such a mess of arranging that funeral last year? I didn't get onto chat about television programmes.'

'You didn't make a mess of it. They didn't like the field – that wasn't your fault.'

'They didn't like me, either. I was too buttoned-up. Too scared of saying the wrong thing. You're always so *natural* with them, as if the whole thing was just another predictable event in their lives, to be taken in their stride.'

'Which it is,' he said. 'Very nicely put, if I may say so. I should make a note – it would go well in one of my Women's Institute talks.'

'Glad to help,' she quipped, happily. Moments like this with Drew had become scarcer than either of them liked, especially during the previous spring and summer. Despite efforts to get closer, it had taken a long time for the situation to improve. When it became clear that Stephanie and Timmy were alarmed by the way things were going, the efforts had been increased, with modifications, so that now Thea felt there were definite results. She loved Drew, and felt obligated to him. He had taken a bigger risk than she had in setting up this new home together. The baggage they had both brought with them was heavier for him and he found the work of processing it harder than she did. Thea had a flippant streak in her character that her second husband lacked. 'I mean it,' she said for emphasis.

'I know you do. That was obvious on Monday. You were a huge help. And look – here I am on Thursday, still standing. Just.'

'You'll be fine,' she said. 'Three funerals in one day sounds a lot, but think how fantastic you're going to feel at the end of the day, when it's all over and everybody loves you.'

'Let's hope so,' he said.

Thea spent the next hour on her laptop exploring websites about Northleach. How she had ever managed to overlook the existence of *This Country* she could not imagine. She read the summaries of every episode and some of the reviews. It would appear that the sitcom had really put the little town on the map in a way it had not been since the turnpike had been abandoned and the bypass constructed. But far more interesting than that were the heady descriptions of the town's past. There had been a dozen inns serving the constant stream of traffic passing through on the main route from Wales to London. In the Middle Ages it had been all about wool, but then experienced a lengthy slump. It had been revived with the advent of the turnpike and the increased use of stagecoaches. More familiar to Thea were the accounts of drovers taking great herds of cattle and flocks of sheep to London – much of the Cotswolds had been traversed by them for centuries – the huge capital city sending demands for fresh meat all across the land.

What a fitting symbol of this current century then, that the place should become famous for a third time as a 'picturesque but depressingly dull' little place. A whole new kind of tourist would be putting Northleach on their itinerary now. No longer the 'cathedral of the Cotswolds' built by rich wool merchants, but the silent stone cottages and sheep-filled fields would attract people who only came

153

to mock. They would find the allotments and the bus shelter and be somehow gratified. And now that there had been a murder, perhaps this would find itself woven into the imagined world of Kerry and Kurtan. Thea smiled to herself at the thought. Ollie Sinclair might find himself a lot more famous after death than he had ever been in life.

She knew she had to go back there, first thing next morning. Or at least after she'd taken Stephanie to school. Drew had stated flatly that he was not going to be available for any domestic tasks, which included ferrying his daughter. 'If you're going out, can you please make sure you're back in time for the afternoon school run,' he said.

'Shouldn't be a problem,' Thea assured him, knowing that the coming day was impossible to predict, and therefore any promises were risky. 'But if I get caught up somehow, I'll phone Mandy and get her to do it.'

Mandy and her son Giles were part of a family that lived on the road to Blockley, one of very few in their immediate area with school-age children. Inevitably there were shared car journeys back and forth to school. Giles was fifteen, spotty and resentful. The school was barely two miles away and he knew he could easily walk there and back. And if he did that, Stephanie could sometimes walk with him. But they hated and despised each other, and the suggestion was forcefully and repeatedly rejected by both parties. *Two miles!*' one or both would exclaim, as if the walk were ten times as long. Giles would stand at the roadside thumbing a lift rather than use his own two legs. Which made him almost worse than useless where Stephanie was concerned.

Mandy's husband was a hard-working horticulturist, raising fuchsias or forsythias or something of the sort, and claiming to be utterly unable to take twenty minutes off occasionally to collect a son from school.

Drew demolished her easy assumption of backup. 'She can't. Don't you remember she said she's going to Cambridge today for a long weekend? She's got her aunt's funeral there tomorrow afternoon. That's why she was happy to fetch Stephanie today. We're supposed to get Giles from school tomorrow.' He exhaled, exasperation unmistakable. 'You *can't* have forgotten.'

'I did,' she admitted meekly. 'I'd better not be late, then. But you know how things happen. I might get a flat tyre.' She knew better than to voice her true concern – that she would find herself immersed in murder business and forget all about her obligations at home. 'What about Fiona? Can I ask her to do it?'

Fiona Emerson, wife of Andrew with the lumbago, was generally free on a Friday. Her work schedule was impenetrable to Thea, but she had been known to come over for tea and a chat on a Friday afternoon. Asking favours of her was, however, a breach of protocol in Drew's eyes. He grimaced. 'She won't be able to say no, even if it's a nuisance. She's a bit feudal in that way. I'm the boss and you're the boss's wife.'

'I'll make it very clear that she can refuse. She's not like that with me, anyway.'

'I can't stop you,' he sighed. 'But go carefully.'

'You could stop me, but I hope you're not going to.'

* * *

155

Fiona gave very convincing assurances that it was really no problem, and she felt bad about Andrew being so useless, and it would be a pleasure to help, and it was only five minutes' drive and she liked Stephanie, and where should she park.

Thea texted her stepdaughter to tell her who was driving her home. The risk of security issues and objections from an overprotective school regime ought to be thereby allayed. She exhaled with relief and thought no more about domestic matters.

Despite having to deal with these complicated responsibilities, Thea – this time accompanied by her dog – was heading down the A44 yet again at twenty past nine on Friday morning. The absence of any word from Lucy implied that the woman was still in hospital, and her house standing empty. Rather to her surprise, Thea was glad about this. She joined the A429 with a sense of an adventure yet to reach its climax. 'Here we go again,' she sang to Hepzibah. 'All good friends and jolly good company.' It was childish and silly and feckless, but she felt ridiculously happy for no reason at all.

The road itself was much of the reason. All those places she had got to know, scattered across the landscape over to the west – Slaughters and Swells and Guitings – with their secrets and their burdensome histories, called to her. To the south was Chedworth, which had a character even more powerfully unique than the others. Chedworth was both Roman and thoroughly sylvan. There were gods and goblins in equal measure in Chedworth.

Even Lucy's house had acquired a rosy aura in the past twenty-four hours. It was a haven that Thea could legitimately use while she tried her best to gain further insights into local networks. Sanctioned by Caz Barkley and armed with a wealth of fresh information, she was developing a glimmer of a Plan. Admittedly, the story as she currently understood it had several gaping holes – which only made the project more enticing. Kevin Sinclair intrigued her, giving an impression of rootlessness, living on the road, never in the same place for five minutes. Almost a goblin himself, in his way, she thought whimsically. And then to collapse into pieces at the news of his son's death . . . a son he had not appeared to be remotely fond of. Feeling wise and insightful, Thea evolved a comprehensive theory about unfinished business and long-standing guilt. The relationship was sick, but the man no doubt believed it was salvageable. One day, he would have told himself, he would gather his courage and approach the son for a reconciliation. Perhaps a third party would come to their assistance. Perhaps Ollie would make the first move. However it was to be accomplished, the father must have cherished a belief that one day all would come right. Perhaps it was all about the putative drugs. If they could be transcended, then there would be ground for hope. And now, all hope was gone forever. All chance was lost. No wonder the poor man was in such a state.

Then there was Livia, the non-partner of Faith, who needed to be observed as an individual and not half of a non-couple. Had Faith made a special effort to present herself without Livia, the previous morning, to make the point that they were two separate people? Could one of them commit a murder without the other one knowing about it? It seemed highly unlikely.

And why would they? That nagging, insistent question of motive was sure to raise its annoying head before long. In order to get close to answering it, the people had to be understood, their stories checked for mendacity. That was what the police strove to achieve, against fearsome odds. That was where Thea Slocombe could contribute something – her own special brand of inquisitive ferreting away at the backgrounds and the connections so very often producing vital leads. To her great credit, Detective Superintendent Sonia Gladwin had grasped this from the first moments of meeting Thea, and had used her extensively ever since.

Hunter Lanning was another individual worthy of scrutiny. He gave the impression of arousing strong feeling in those who knew him. If he made a point of voicing his opinions regardless of the sensitivities of his listeners, this was sure to lead to aggravation of all kinds. Thea could imagine threats flying in all directions, but not to the point of murder. And if it did get that far, wouldn't Hunter more probably be the victim than the perpetrator?

The police were almost certainly concentrating on discovering all they could about Ollie, and must have learnt considerably more than Thea had, as a result. His prowess as an athlete was an element of his life that might reward investigation. Even more productive would be a quest to trace the origins of the story about him being an addict. Although it could have been unintentional, the likelihood was that it had been a deliberate slander, for a specific reason. If his murder had been carefully planned, then it made sense to blacken his character in advance. That would reduce the level of outrage at his death, as well as weakening the efforts of the police to find his killer. However earnestly they might believe themselves to be impartial and non-judgemental, they would be under less pressure to bring the killer of a druggie to justice than that of an upright and useful member of society. The media would reinforce this innate prejudice, too. And the wretched Ollie would go unmourned by all but his immediate family.

There was a definite pressure to achieve something useful while back in Northleach, as justification for abandoning Drew. She could hear the voices of her mother and sisters reproaching her for the lack of wifely support, despite the very reasonable argument that just because her husband worked from home did not mean that Thea ought to be actively at his side when things got busy. Drew himself would not expect it. Even Stephanie would agree that Thea had every right to do as she liked – within reason. Solving a murder, albeit it unofficially and without any payment, was a public good, after all.

So she wasted no time lingering in Lucy Sinclair's house. Instead she took the dog and walked along to the town square. It looked very much the same as it had the previous day and the day before that. As she stood there, wondering where to go next, a minibus found a space at one side of the parking area and disgorged a group of five or six people clearly intent on exploring the church. One woman with long grey hair stopped and stared first at Hepzie then at Thea as she and her companions passed. 'Good Lord – is it you?' she asked foolishly. 'You've still got the same dog.'

Thea looked closer, failing to recognise the face. There were so many candidates from so many villages, as well as further afield. Would someone from the local area be riding in a minibus to see a church she presumably already knew? Could it be a former schoolteacher, or somebody she had briefly worked with decades ago? This had happened a few times before, and it always turned out to be somebody quite peripheral to one of the house-sitting commissions, who had paid more attention to Thea than had been reciprocated.

'You *are* Thea Osborne, aren't you?' the woman went on impatiently. 'Surely you know me? It's only a few years ago. Winchcombe – remember? Where there were those horrible murders.'

Thea did remember Winchcombe and the murders, mainly in association with Drew, because Karen had just died and neither Thea nor Drew knew what to do next. 'I'm Thea Slocombe now,' she said, still unable to put a name to the face in front of her. 'And I live in Broad Campden.'

'Really? Well, I'm still Priscilla Heap, older and not a bit wiser. I gather there's been some trouble over here in Northleach? Don't tell me you've got yourself involved yet again?'

Priscilla Heap . . . horsey, lonely, nervous of dogs . . .

the memories slowly came into focus for Thea. 'Gosh, yes,' she said belatedly. 'Now I remember.'

'Such an awful time. Such misery – I'll never forget it.' She threw a look of mild reproach at Thea, who so obviously had forgotten much of it. 'And now there's news of another killing,' she repeated, as if unsure that Thea had heard the first time.

'Yes,' said Thea. 'And yes, I do know the people concerned, slightly. Er – I think you're wanted,' she finished, seeing the group of sightseers all standing close by, clearly waiting for Priscilla.

'Oh! I'm supposed to be showing them round the church. It's a little freelance job I picked up. They're from Belarus,' she added in a whisper.

'Gosh!' said Thea. 'Do they speak English?'

'Surprisingly well. You know how it is – pretty much everybody speaks, or at least understands, English, while we can barely cope with a few words of French. And I still haven't worked out exactly what their native language is. Anyway – it was good to see you.' The expression on her face did little to confirm these words. Thea sympathised. She had not wanted to be reminded of events in Winchcombe either. It was one of the murkier and more distressing of all her brushes with violent killing. And the echo of past horrors was unsettling. It brought to mind another buried memory – of events in Snowshill, which had been even worse than Winchcombe in some ways.

In the interests of exercise as much as anything, she carried on along High Street, and past the house where the body had been found. There was police tape across the front door, but nothing else to see. More recently-created smaller roads branched off on both sides, and Thea was aware that there was a hinterland that she had never seen. High Street mutated into East End and eventually met up with the A40 on a straight stretch that made a mockery of the old turnpike as it rambled through the town. That turnpike, Thea knew, had been thronged with traffic three centuries ago, the road rutted and deep with the dung of horses, cattle and sheep. No potager would ever lack for fertiliser in those far-off days.

The weather was turning milder with each passing day, spring bulbs filling the gardens in the few houses with space between the front door and the pavement. But there was little sign of any horticultural activity. Cars passed sporadically, but the pavement was almost deserted. Priscilla Heap's group of Belarussian tourists was the morning's main excitement, it seemed. The atmosphere was soporific, lulling Thea into a state of mental idleness that she could not easily climb out of. 'This won't do at all,' she muttered to the spaniel. 'We've got to find someone to talk to.'

The choice lay between Bobby Latimer and Faith-and-Livia, as far as she could see. Bobby might have news of Lucy, although Thea had assumed that she herself would now be the first point of contact, having been the one to actually visit the patient. There surely had to be high emotion and considerable activity caused by the killing of Ollie Sinclair, going on invisibly somewhere.

Idly walking along the street now seemed futile, and unlikely to make anything happen. One of Thea's habitual

162

methods of delving into the background lives of those associated with a murder was simply to go and knock on doors. Failing that, there had sometimes been good results from sauntering through villages, but it was much less reliable, especially in inclement weather. 'So let's knock on a door,' she said to Hepzie, and turned to go back into the centre of town.

But then all her conclusions were abruptly turned on their heads. A large car pulled up beside her and a purple head poked out of the passenger window. 'Hey!' said Tessa, friend of Kevin Sinclair.

'Oh – hello,' said Thea, uncertainly. Should she offer condolences? She bent down to look at the driver, who was indeed the bereaved father. 'Mr Sinclair,' she said.

'You heard about our Ollie.' It was a flat statement from a man who had been transformed into a grey-faced wreck, in two short days. All three of them focused on the house, a few yards along the street.

'I'm so sorry,' said Thea, trying to make the words sound sincere. 'It must have been a terrible shock.'

'You can't imagine,' said Tessa. 'It's like the world just stopped.' She turned to Kevin almost warily. 'We can't settle to anything.'

'You're in with the police, right?' Kevin stared hard at Thea. 'That business in Hampnett, when you were watching over the barn – chap was killed in the snow? Lucy said you'd been helpful – that you know the high-up detectives. So – what's going on here? Who've they got their eye on for my Ollie?'

It was worse than awkward. The physical discomfort

163

of talking to people in a car, while holding the dog and watching for approaching traffic, made it almost impossible. 'I honestly don't know anything,' she assured him. 'I only came back today because . . .' She hesitated, aware of several difficulties in finishing that sentence. Because she wanted to do a bit of ferreting on behalf of the police? Because she couldn't abide unfinished business? 'Well, because Lucy wanted me to,' she concluded. 'I went to see her in hospital yesterday.'

Kevin Sinclair shook his head, as if to say there was so much wrong that he didn't know where to begin to set her right. 'Get in,' he said, to Thea's great surprise. 'Bring the dog and get in the back.'

In the absence of any convincing excuse, she did as she was told. No warning voices screamed inside her head; they never did. She trusted people and that was not going to change, despite her repeated first-hand experience of the awful things they could do. It was probably a character defect. But she did have a phone and a dog with her, and they were in a street in broad daylight. All the same, when Kevin put the car into gear and began to drive off, she did feel her heartbeat quicken. 'Where are we going?' she asked, her voice a trifle shrill.

Kevin replied wearily, 'Only to the square. We can't stay here – we're impeding the traffic.'

Tessa gave a little laugh, in recognition of the flicker of panic. 'Did you think we were kidnapping you?'

'It happens,' said Thea tightly.

There were a few free spaces in the car park and Kevin deftly manoeuvred his big vehicle into one of them.

Ignorant about cars, Thea had been slow to observe that this was something flashy and expensive. There was a smell of leather and an impression of solidity. She glanced at Hepzie's feet to see if she'd left mud on the seats.

'So,' said Kevin, turning round easily to face her. He put one arm over the back of his seat and rested his chin on it. It would have appeared relaxed and friendly if it had not been for his grey skin, red eyes and slow delivery. Everything was a visible effort. All that was keeping him going was a very obvious wish for information. 'What do you know about the murder of my son?' he asked heavily. 'If I can't find out who did it, I doubt I'll ever sleep again.'

It was a raw, uncompromising question to which an answer was expected and needed. It left Thea in no doubt about how deep the man's need went. Her earlier theories about the father–son relationship were being confirmed. Everything between Kevin and Ollie had been dysfunctional, and to have it cut short now, before it could be put right, was intolerable. He was resting his chin because his neck was too tired to support his head. His eyes were sunk far into their sockets, and there was stubble all over his lower face. How he had managed to drive so capably was a mystery. At his side, Tessa remained quiet and still, facing forward.

'I know he was violently attacked in the house just down there. That's all.'

Kevin stared at her. 'All right. So what do you know about his life? Who he was, who he lived with, why he was ever in that house?'

'You think I'm part of the police investigation,' she realised.

'Aren't you?'

'No.' She was going to add *Not at all*, but hesitated. The truth was that after speaking to Higgins and Barkley she sort of *was*. They had told her far more than they would tell an ordinary member of the public. And they had effectively asked her to lend a hand in ferreting out all available background information.

'But you know things,' Kevin persisted. 'You and the police are hand in glove. Why else are you here again today, hanging around that house?'

'I know that lots of people thought your son was a drug addict,' she said. 'And that they can't be sure of the exact time of death.'

'He was a drug addict,' said Kevin heavily. 'Who says anything different?'

'Well – apparently there might be some doubt about that.' *Keep it vague*, she told herself, belatedly recalling that Caz had asked her to keep that detail quiet. But she was so sure that Kevin had not killed his son, that discretion seemed unimportant. 'I suppose it's not always easy to tell,' she added.

'Easy enough, I'd have thought. They only have to look at those useless friends of his. So-called friends. One of them must have killed him in a drug-crazed frenzy.'

The words were in implied quotation marks, but none the less sincere for that. It did conjure a vivid picture, which was all too likely to be running in a ghastly loop inside Kevin Sinclair's head. 'I don't think it was quite like that,' said Thea, treading as carefully as she could.

'So what was it like, then?' The words were softly

166

ominous. Thea's heart rate was not slowing down.

'I don't know. I just happened to be walking along the high street on Wednesday when Jeremy Higgins showed up. They'd only just found the . . . Ollie, I mean, at that point. Higgins and I had a short conversation a bit later, when everything was still completely confused. He only really had impressions to go on – and he thought then it was some kind of squat, used by people on drugs. Later on, they got a very different idea of how it had been. Haven't they told you all this? You're the next of kin, after all. Didn't you know about it already?'

'Jeremy Higgins?' Kevin repeated. 'That'd be the senior investigating officer, would it? Your pal Jeremy?'

'There's a chief superintendent above Higgins, who'll be the SIO. I can't remember his name.'

The man shook his head as if to dispel irrelevancies. 'He was a druggie,' he repeated. 'He lived with druggies. Everybody knew that.'

'Which drugs exactly?' Thea asked. 'Did he tell you?'

'We didn't talk about it.'

'There'll be plenty of evidence in the house, I expect. And the friends will have to answer a lot of questions. Don't worry – they'll find who did it. They've got so much technology and so forth to help these days. Nobody gets away with murder any more.' A statement she knew quite well was far from true. During this exchange, Thea had become more acutely aware of Tessa's immobility. It began to seem unnatural, as if she was suppressing tears or words so violently that the effort paralysed her.

Kevin seemed to be thinking along the same lines.

'Tess?' he said. 'You tell her.'

'We don't know for certain, do we?' the woman said, without turning her head. 'We don't know *anything* for certain.'

'We know he's dead,' came the gravelly reply. 'The rest of it doesn't much matter now, does it?'

'Oh, Kev.' The tone was that of a helplessly fond mother trying vainly to console a small boy. 'Yes, he's dead. Poor Ollie. Such a waste.'

It was exactly the right thing to say, in Thea's view. The death of a young person was always a waste. Parents put in all that love and attention and worry, finally getting their offspring to adulthood, only for it all to wither away if the son or daughter then died. It cast a terrible pall of futility over everything. 'Was he your only one?' she asked, thinking of her own Jessica and how dangerous it could be to have all your eggs in a single basket.

Kevin nodded absently. 'He did take drugs,' he repeated, as if trying to convince himself. 'They all did. That house was a drug den. The whole town knew it was. Isn't that what Lucy said? For God's sake – if that wasn't true, then what was stopping me from fixing things between him and me?' That felt to Thea like something close to the crux of the matter.

'She did,' Tessa confirmed, referring to Lucy's words. 'So did those two women next door to her.'

'They wouldn't say it if it wasn't true.' He looked hard at Thea. 'So the police are idiots,' he said accusingly.

'That's possible,' said Thea, her head full of images from *Breaking Bad*, with Barkley and Higgins following all the wrong leads, ignoring the facts. 'But they do seem to be having trouble proving it. The drug part, I mean.'

'Some drugs don't leave much of a trace,' said Tessa, finally altering her position to look at Thea. 'It's not always injected, is it? You can smoke most of them or snort them up your nose. There won't have been time for the post-mortem people to test for everything.'

'No,' said Thea doubtfully, aware of the depths of her own ignorance on the subject. 'Well, if that's all . . . ?' She reached for the door handle, alerting her dog in the process. 'I hope we haven't made mud on your car seats.'

Kevin shook his head again, as if appalled at the shallowness of this remark. 'Go on, then,' he said sourly. 'Can't say you've been much help.'

'Kev!' Tessa reproached him. 'Don't be nasty.'

'That's okay,' said Thea. 'I really am very sorry about your son. It's a terrible thing to happen.'

'Right,' said Kevin with a heavy nod. 'I dare say we'll be seeing you.'

Thea and her dog left the car, and began walking away before it moved. She was displeased with herself for the way she had reacted, but unable to pinpoint any precise misstep. The confusion about Ollie and drugs was the biggest mystery, which overshadowed any other questions, such as the crucial one: who killed him? The two were obviously connected – if he had been living in a 'drug den' then an early death was not entirely surprising. If, on the other hand, the house had been used for thoroughly harmless and legal purposes, with Ollie an innocent victim of a savage attack, there was a much bigger mystery to be solved. But it seemed to Thea that the police were in little doubt as to which scenario was the true one. Caz had told her enough to persuade her that the latter was almost certainly the case – and yet Kevin Sinclair was not convinced.

The absence of any message from or about Lucy was beginning to seem peculiar. Whether she had had a relapse or was shortly to be discharged, Thea would expect to be informed. She had been careful to keep her phone on, and close by so she would hear a call if it came. She was also braced for a panic summons from Drew, if something went horribly wrong with his schedule for the day.

There was no sign of life back at the house in the West End street, nor next door. The Latimer family opposite were unlikely to be visible, given that they spent most of their time at the back of the house. Nor had she noticed any police activity anywhere in the town. It was as if everything had quickly returned to the usual Cotswold invisibility on every front, only two days after a murder victim had been discovered in the heart of Northleach.

The house felt cool, as before, but she made no attempt to warm it up, thinking she would not be in it long enough to warrant doing so. There were one or two envelopes in the metal cage attached to the inside of the letter box on the front door, which she left untouched. Everything seemed horribly uncertain. Should she assume that Lucy would be home for the weekend, needing milk and bread, but quite likely to be able to get them for herself? Whatever had happened to her in the hospital had not affected her back. It would be no more of a handicap than it was before she went in for her now-cancelled operation. Thea realised that she was watching the street window in the expectation that the woman would turn up in a taxi at any moment. Or one of those hospital cars, driven by volunteers.

And then a woman did come to the door and ring the bell. Hepzic yapped uncertainly, not sure whether she was supposed to defend this house as she did the one in Broad Campden.

Chapter Eleven

'I was told you might know something about my boyfriend and how he died,' came the stark assertion, with no preamble. 'I've just had a word with his father, and that's what he told me.' She bent down to pat the spaniel as if they were old friends.

'He told you wrong,' said Thea angrily. 'And he knows that perfectly well.' She made no pretence of not knowing who the boyfriend was.

'Well, can I talk to you anyway? My name's Vicky, by the way. I've got nothing else to do, and nobody wants me around.'

Thea gave her a searching look. Early twenties, thin, bad skin, straggly hair – the epitome of a drug addict, in Thea's limited experience. 'This isn't my house, you know. I can't just invite any strange person in.' The thought had occurred to her that this Vicky was highly likely to pocket a valuable ornament, and insist on eating something from Lucy's store cupboard. She did look hungry. And she upended all Thea's latest notions about Ollie and drugs.

'I'm not strange. Lucy knows me well enough. She wouldn't mind me being here.'

'I don't know that I can just take your word for it, though, can I? I'm always getting into trouble through letting people into houses.' She thought back to her days in Barnsley, near Bibury, and the awful consequences of letting a woman into a house that was not hers.

'I've heard stories about you,' said the girl. 'You're always in the news.'

'Not lately,' Thea defended herself. *Not this time*, she promised herself. Which led to a realisation that by now there would be quite a lot of coverage of the Northleach murder, with quite possibly a mention of Ms Thea Osborne, also known as Slocombe, who so often found herself involved in such episodes. To her knowledge, no journalistic person had observed her presence, but that was no guarantee. When this Vicky person had gone, she would have to check.

'Look – I've been standing here long enough for the neighbours to notice me. That's my car, which someone will probably recognise. I'm fairly well known around here, as it happens. If I meant to do anything illegal, I'd never get away with it, would I?'

'Okay,' said Thea, regretting that many of her thoughts must have been clear on her face. 'Come on, then.' After all, she had brought Faith from next door in already. Why not make it open house and stop fretting?

'I suppose this is all very familiar to you,' said the visitor when they were settled in the living room. 'People trying to get to grips with a death, I mean. Your husband's an undertaker, isn't he?'

'That's right. Although—'

'I know,' Vicky interrupted. 'I don't seem very distraught. I can still string sentences together and drive a car.'

'Except you haven't brushed your hair,' said Thea. 'And those clothes look a bit grubby. And nearly every bereaved person can still drive – including Kevin Sinclair.'

Vicky emitted a great peal of laughter, close to hysteria. 'Well said! I'm a lot more of a mess than I think, obviously. Can I talk about Ollie? Will you just listen for a bit?'

Thea wordlessly spread her hands and nodded. This was something she could do; a simple human response that ought not to be nearly as rare as it was. Drew had observed countless times that a very major part of his work was to just sit and listen to the story. Only by telling it repeatedly could the newly bereaved come to terms with the huge change in their lives.

'So – we'd only been together a few months. Not even living together properly. He had a very complicated arrangement, being at the house here some days, but also in his own place in Minchinhampton.'

'On his own?' asked Thea, assuming there was no way the young man could be the owner of property in affluent Gloucestershire.

Vicky nodded. 'Yes, actually. He had his own house

there. He bought it when he was about twenty-two. With the money he was making then.' She frowned at Thea. 'You really don't know much about him, do you?'

'Hardly anything,' Thea agreed. 'Just bits and pieces.'

'He's an athlete. Was, I mean. Professional. He earned half a million in the four years from when he was nineteen to twenty-three. It's been tailing off since then, though. More than tailing off, to be honest. More like falling off a cliff. He was going to concentrate on teaching from here on.'

'What sort of an athlete?' Thea's thoughts were frantically reorganising themselves. 'How is it possible to earn so much?'

'It's not in this country. He was in the Middle East with his mother for most of that time. Qatar, mainly. I didn't know him then, so I'm hazy about the details, but he was a champion high jumper, in the top five ranking at one point. Lots of competitions with big prizes, all sorts of fabulous contracts. Anyway, he put all the money away and bought the house with it.'

'Very sensible of him.'

Vicky shot her a suspicious look. 'That sounds snarky,' she said.

'Sorry – it wasn't meant to. Only none of this sounds like the same person I've been hearing about. I mean – what about the business with drugs? Maybe I can finally get to the truth about that, at least.'

She heard herself sounding like someone who had a right to know – which she was not. But it had to be asked. It was the single most burning aspect of the whole case.

Now that this girlfriend had presented herself, apparently confirming all the accusations, the matter could not – nor should not – be avoided.

'Drugs?' Something like exasperation clouded Vicky's face. 'What do you mean?'

'Ollie's father, for one, insists that he was an addict. And you – this sounds rude, I know, but you look like one, as well. Why are you so thin?'

The same peal of laughter came again, followed by a collapse into sudden tears. 'Is that what people are really saying about us?' she managed to ask.

Thea handed her a crumpled tissue from her pocket, and Hepzie nudged at her knee. 'So it would seem. The house in High Street was believed to be used by a group of men on drugs, according to a number of people I've been talking to.' She stopped to think. 'Although the police think it was all a misunderstanding. Local people jumping to the wrong conclusion on scarcely any evidence.'

'You don't know what you're talking about. It's absolute nonsense. The house is an Airbnb property, if you must know. Ollie's got two friends, and they all use it during the week for *work*. Somewhere they can get together in peace and quiet and do their thing. No girlfriends or anything are allowed. It's very intense. Was,' she finished miserably.

'Their thing?' Thea queried, dredging up something she'd heard about film-making but not getting very far.

'Making films for YouTube. Sport-related. Exercises, fitness regimes. So people can work out on their own. Kids. It's all very clever – they make a game of it, with incentives and rankings. It's a bit difficult to explain.' She blew her nose. 'But it's nothing to do with drugs.'

'I see,' said Thea, not entirely honestly. 'So it was all a wicked slander. Or just narrow-minded neighbours getting suspicious over nothing. And these two friends – did one of them kill Ollie, by any chance?'

Vicky gave her an angry look. 'Of course they didn't. They couldn't have done, even if they'd wanted to. They're both in Poland. They're Polish, see. Ollie's been there in the house on his own since the weekend, designing the next series of films, and doing background stuff. Now do you get it?'

'Sort of. More than before.' She smiled. 'If you came here to get information from me, it looks as if we've swopped places, doesn't it? I told you I barely know anything at all. But I was told that there are quite a lot of Eastern Europeans working in the area and some of them were in the habit of dropping in at the house here. Is that right?'

'Might be. They needed people to be in the films – to demonstrate the exercises. Fit. Young. They'd have been paid to do it. All totally straight. I mean – the films are there, on YouTube for anybody to see. There's nothing secret or sinister about them. The people at the pub can tell you. I met them there sometimes. Why would people get hold of such awful ideas about them?'

Thea thought she could understand, to some extent. 'There's a man called Hunter Lanning, who seems to be a big cheese locally. When I spoke to him yesterday, he said very plainly that the place where Ollie died was a "druggie house". I think those were his very words, or something like.'

Vicky put out a hand, waving it blindly to make Thea stop talking. 'Wait,' she begged. 'This is making no sense. The police must know all about Jan and Nikola by now. They've probably sent Interpol to talk to them, if that's what it's called now. They can't have found any drug paraphernalia in the house, just ordinary stuff for the films – laptops and cameras and a few lights.'

'Okay. Don't get in a state about it. I don't know what's true and what isn't, do I? But Hunter Lanning seemed very sure.'

'Who is he exactly?'

'Oh – a local man who runs some weird sort of club where they talk about politics. Or at least things that are controversial. I got the impression nearly everyone in town belongs to it.'

'He said Ollie and Jan and Nikola were druggies, did he?'

'He certainly gave that impression. I couldn't have got it wrong.'

'And does he know who killed Ollie as well?' She was crying tears of anger now, her words pouring out as if making an accusation. Thea was very unsure as to what to make of this surge of explanations.

'I don't expect so,' she said calmly. Then she changed tack. 'I presume the police have interviewed you, and you told them everything you've just told me?'

'Yes, and now I understand some of the things they asked me. It was all quite gentle, which was a bit surprising. And they can't have taken the drug story very seriously, because they didn't go on about it. I never dreamed they'd already been told the whole house was full of drugs. Somebody here in Northleach must have started the story on purpose, for some reason. And that's not fair.' She wept fresh tears. 'And you think I'm an addict as well!'

'And you're not?'

'Of *course* I'm not! I look like this because my boyfriend just died. And because I had leukaemia up to last Christmas. I might still have it. I've been having all sorts of ghastly treatments for it, and this is what's left of me after all that. Now do you understand?'

'Oh dear,' said Thea weakly. 'That's awful.'

Vicky shrugged her words off and launched into further indignant explanations. 'This story about drugs makes no sense, if you really think about it. Who would rent us the house, if they thought it would be full of drug addicts? How would we *afford* it? Ollie and the others were struggling to survive on the money they managed to make from the films. Nikola worked a few hours a week in a call centre to boost the income.'

Thea took her lead, and tried to focus. 'So who does rent you – them – the house? Where do you fit in?'

'Well, there it starts to get a bit more complicated,' Vicky admitted. 'The plan was for me to be in the videos, demonstrating the exercises – but I haven't been well enough. And then there are Ollie's parents . . .' She heaved a profound sigh. 'Not to mention Lucy.'

Lucy! Thea looked at the kitchen clock, which indicated an incredible twelve-thirty, and felt a sudden panic. The day was half over, and nothing had been settled. The opposite, in fact. The notion that this was to be Crunch

Day, with answers to every question and justice prevailing now seemed insanely optimistic. 'Where on earth is she?' she said aloud.

'Who? Lucy? Isn't she in hospital?'

'She must be, I suppose, but when I went to see her yesterday, she thought she'd be sent home by now. You heard what happened, I assume?'

The girl cocked her head and frowned. 'No – did something happen? Wasn't she expected to be in for a week or more? Was it a more minor operation than they thought?' She snorted. 'But when did *that* ever happen?'

'She collapsed just before the operation was due, so they didn't do it. They can't work out what caused it – some sort of allergic reaction, they think. She was unconscious for a while, but by the time I saw her she seemed fairly normal. A bit confused, maybe. They were doing tests. Could be they've found something that means they need her to stay in for a while.'

'But nobody's told you? That must be awkward.' Vicky regarded the dog, as if there might be enlightenment to be found in the soft spaniel head. 'She's gorgeous, isn't she?' she said. 'What's her name?'

'Hezpibah,' said Thea distractedly. The dog could not conceivably hold any relevance to the matter in hand.

'Lucy told me about her old dog – Jimmy. Did you know him? He died before I ever met any of the Sinclairs. She cried whenever she talked about him.'

'Did she?' Thea felt a familiar pang of guilt at this reminder. Of all the careless and irresponsible things she had done with other people's animals, her treatment of Jimmy was the worst. She could hardly bear to think about it, even now, years later.

'That's very weird about her collapsing. I had no idea. All anyone's talked about is Ollie.'

'That's not surprising. Tell me about his mother,' Thea invited. It seemed to her an encouraging sign that the girl was so willing to keep talking. The hope was that it was proving therapeutic. But it could not go on much longer. There was a dawning sense of urgency that meant she would soon have to take some sort of action. If she only knew what that action should be.

'She's very sweet. She comes from Qatar originally, with a rich father. She met Kevin when she was about sixteen and ran off with him. Luckily, it's not a particularly devout family, but they are Muslims and it was still a scandal. More so when they separated, apparently. She's been absolutely dedicated to Ollie and his career, since then. And it paid off. They're both minor celebrities in the Middle East.'

'How old was he when his parents split up?'

'Four or five. There's a sister as well. I've never met her. Kevin ignored them both for years. Nothing for birthdays or Christmas. Then when Ollie got so famous, he tried to come back.'

Thea was wondering why a well-to-do young Muslim girl should take up with Kevin Sinclair. From what she had seen of him, it seemed highly unlikely. 'Wasn't he much older than her?'

'Who? Kevin? No, I don't think so. It was years before they had the children. Everyone fought to stop them getting married, but they managed it eventually.'

'But it didn't last. That seems very sad. A waste of all

that determination and effort. Wouldn't you think they'd stay together because of all that, if nothing else?'

'I guess the strain got to be too much. And Ollie wasn't easy, by all accounts. There are some horrendous stories about him as a toddler. Hyperactive doesn't come close.' Her eyes filled as she remembered her boyfriend's fate. 'Poor Sayida! She's utterly destroyed now, of course.'

'So is Kevin.'

'Serves him right,' said Vicky darkly.

'Well . . .' Thea began. 'I think we've put the picture straight between us, haven't we? I need to get back home before much longer. I shouldn't really have come at all, but they thought I might be useful.'

Vicky looked confused. 'But surely you'll be staying here until Lucy gets back? What if she needs help?'

For the first time, Thea gave some thought to the apparent existence of a relationship between this girl and Lucy Sinclair. Was it not slightly odd? 'How well do you know her?' she asked.

'You mean Lucy? Very, as it happens. That's how I met Ollie in the first place – through Lucy.'

'But now you're close to his mother, Sayida? Isn't that a bit complicated?'

Vicky looked even more confused. 'Why would it be? It's not particularly unusual these days, is it? They're all on amicable terms, even Tessa, who's an idiot, obviously. But a nice idiot. Harmless.'

Thea remembered that a murder had been committed. Was it safe to think of anybody as 'harmless' in the light of that fact?

'Well . . .' she said again, in a firmer tone, 'that's enough for now. We can talk again if you like, but I don't know when I'll be here. It's possible I won't be coming down to Northleach again at all.'

'Let me give you my phone number, then. And I'll take yours. You've been brilliant to talk to.' She took a deep breath as if testing her own condition. 'I feel much better,' she reported with a look of surprise. 'All thanks to you.'

'And I've been set straight about the drugs,' said Thea. 'That's a relief. It was bothering me, to tell you the truth.'

'Maybe you can straighten a few more people out about that, then.'

'I doubt it.' She thought about Hunter Lanning, and Kevin Sinclair and Faith-and-Livia. 'They all seem totally convinced, even his father. That's very peculiar, isn't it?'

'It suits their prejudices,' said Vicky tightly. 'You see, the fact is, nobody really likes Ollie. Nobody except Sayida and me, that is.'

When Vicky had gone, Thea found herself coming up with a long string of questions she wished she'd asked. The story that had felt so frank and convincing with the girl in front of her now began to develop holes and leak much of its credibility. Something about Lucy nagged at her. If she and Vicky were such good friends, how come Lucy hadn't heard about Ollie's death by Thursday? Even if Kevin had not thought to tell her, it seemed odd that Vicky hadn't. And precisely what was their original connection? Where was Vicky's home, and who did she know, if anyone, in Northleach? And – she realised with a shock – Vicky had made no attempt to follow up on her initial question of what exactly had happened to Ollie. She had accepted Thea's denial of any special knowledge, and willingly diverted into background information, which Thea had assumed to be what she most wanted to splurge. Thinking about it now, she wondered just how cathartic it could have been to explain such facts. Had there not been something strangely *cool* about it?

She had not made the wretched girl a drink, or offered her a biscuit, she reproached herself. They had launched into conversation with such intensity that there hadn't been a moment in which to get up and put a kettle on. Lucy's kettle was very slow, Thea had discovered, and her teabags very wishy-washy. There was no sign of any instant coffee and Thea disliked messing around with coffee machines. So far, she had managed to obtain more palatable beverages elsewhere.

It seemed wrong to just lock the house up again and head for home with Hepzie. She should at the very least call the hospital to see what the situation was regarding Lucy. Anything could have happened, after all. If the tests could not diagnose the reason for her collapse, there would be no way of preventing it happening again – which might mean keeping her in for further monitoring and supervision. The absence of so much as a text from her did suggest that she must be incapacitated again.

Instead of phoning the hospital, she called Lucy's mobile number, feeling foolish not to have thought of doing so earlier in the day. Hospital patients were no different from everybody else in being glued to their phones, day and night.

Charging points were automatically provided and nobody made the slightest objection to constant use, since it served to keep the patient quietly occupied. The days were long gone when hospital authorities had believed that mobiles interfered with vital equipment and should therefore be banned.

Lucy's phone was off, so Thea left a brief message saying she was unsure as to what she was expected to do. Then she sat down with a cup of weak tea and slightly limp ginger biscuits and tried to think.

Chapter Twelve

She thought first about Ollie Sinclair and the new information she had been given about him. *Nobody really likes Ollie*, his girlfriend had said. Did that mean nobody would grieve for him, attend his funeral, care who killed him? She tried to rerun everything Kevin had said, looking for evidence that he did in fact love his son. On the face of it, there was plenty. He had looked ravaged, and had wanted to know all he could about the police investigation. And surely any father would be distraught at the death of his son. But the Sinclair family was beyond complicated. There were alliances and schisms that confounded expectations and logic, according to Vicky. And there were the people Thea had met here in Northleach who all seemed to be connected in one way or another. Even Hunter Lanning, who had effectively dismissed Ollie as a lost cause, thanks to drug addiction. Where, Thea wondered, had that slanderous belief come from? Had somebody done it deliberately, as part of a complex plan to murder the man? If nobody much cared whether he lived or died, it would be a lot easier to get away with killing him.

All this was successfully keeping her in Northleach, when she really ought to be at home, ready with tea and a listening ear for her exhausted husband. At least Stephanie was catered for, her lift home assured. The child could provide an intelligent and sympathetic ear for Drew, probably better than Thea could. Stephanie had watched funerals being arranged from infancy. She understood precisely how to pitch her remarks, not just to her father, but to families of the deceased. She had been allowed to answer the phone to them, take messages and even discuss the relative merits of cardboard coffins and willow baskets. She did all that with greater confidence than Thea did.

Having Hepzie with her was a mixed blessing. It was risky to leave her alone in Lucy's house, with the owner potentially turning up and letting her out by mistake. Or objecting to her unsupervised presence. So Thea would have to take her everywhere with her – and since that was likely to be neighbouring houses, her reception was uncertain. Except for Bobby Latimer, who had made no complaint at all about a strange dog turning up. And Bobby Latimer seemed as good a place to start as any. She appeared to be familiar with all the main players, and yet to be sufficiently detached to be free from emotional outbursts. It was almost impossible to imagine her as a murderer, too.

So Thea took the dog and crossed the road and knocked

on Bobby's front door. 'They should call me She Who Knocks on Doors,' she murmured to herself and the spaniel, thinking of all the occasions when she had done something very similar in other Cotswold villages. Hepzie wagged her tail in agreement.

Bobby had her mouth full as she answered the door. 'Lunchtime,' she mumbled, rolling her eyes.

Thea took her to be thinking *Haven't we seen enough of each other for one week?* 'Oh – sorry!' she said. She noticed that she was more than ready for a midday meal herself.

Bobby made no move to invite her in, but simply stood there, slowly chewing. There were sounds of children from a room close by. 'I'll come back later, then,' said Thea.

'Uh-uh.' Bobby shook her head. 'Won't be here.' At last she swallowed. 'Was it important?'

'Not exactly. No – not at all, really.'

'Go and talk to Livia, then. I think she's there on her own at the moment.'

Such levels of neighbourly surveillance made Thea shudder. 'Why? Where's Faith gone?' she asked, mainly to test the extent of Bobby's knowledge.

'How would I know?' came the swift response.

Thea just tilted her head slightly and raised her eyebrows. Sometimes a look could speak volumes. 'You think I'm a nosy neighbour,' Bobby concluded. 'I expect I am by some people's standards. But I can't see any harm in it.'

Still Thea said nothing. Silently she ran through a few options. *Whatever turns you on* was one of them. She smiled at her own thoughts.

'Right, then,' said Bobby decidedly. 'If you'll excuse me.' She was trying to be British, Thea realised – formal, pronouncing all the consonants and standing tall. It was actually quite endearing.

'Of course. Sorry,' she said again. And crossed the road for a second time.

It was galling to be seen to do exactly as Bobby had suggested, but there seemed to be little else available. She knocked on the door of the house next to Lucy's and was rewarded by its opening instantly. She had been watched, she thought resignedly. 'Hello! Good to see you. Come in. Have you had any lunch? How about a nice dry sherry first? I was furious when Faith told me she'd seen you yesterday morning without me. Now's my chance to catch up.'

This too was appealing in its way. The people of Northleach were beginning to seem more likeable than they had at first. 'Is it okay if the dog comes as well?' she asked.

'Of course. You wouldn't get far around here if you couldn't cope with a dog now and then. She's not even muddy, as far as I can see.'

'She's not,' Thea confirmed. 'We haven't been anywhere yet today.'

The sherry materialised with no further consultation, followed by a magical plate of food. 'Sit down,' Livia ordered in her husky tones. 'Faith's made one of her risotto things. It's got mushrooms and lumps of haddock in it – hope that's to your taste?'

'Isn't she here?'

'She's upstairs, I think. Wanted to get a cardy. It has turned a bit chilly, hasn't it?'

'Oh,' said Thea, thinking that Bobby had been quite wrong in her belief that Faith was out somewhere, leaving Livia on her own. Perhaps the village surveillance system had its limitations, after all. She sat down as instructed, but was unsure about accepting food.

'Have you eaten?' she asked. 'I can't sit here and take your food if you're not having it as well.' She hesitated to explain that it made her feel at a serious disadvantage, like a waif who had to be rescued from starvation. Somewhere there was a suspicion that the woman was perfectly well aware of that already. Livia was standing beside a large pan on the hob. Thea couldn't see whether there was one plate or three about to be filled – or any plates at all.

'Oh, don't worry about that. We don't normally have lunch until nearly two, for some reason. But it's ready now, just keeping warm. We can eat with you.' She turned and beamed in a parody of hospitality. 'The thing is, it doesn't always work to wait for a person to decide whether or not to accept an offer of food. Had you noticed? They try to calculate all the implications, and waste a lot of time in the process. Much simpler just to ladle out a plate of whatever's cooking and take it from there.'

'I suppose so,' Thea said, thinking that while this might be true, there were subtler ways of handling it. You didn't plonk it down in front of your guest without sitting down yourself – or waiting for the third person to put in an appearance.

But people were strange. They developed strange routines and forgot what normality looked like. In any case, the sherry was welcome and she sipped it thoughtfully. Hepzie

190

was at her feet, having a gentle scratch to pass the time.

Then Faith was clattering down the stairs, coming into the kitchen, expressing a welcome at least as enthusiastic as Livia's. 'Well, this is nice,' she gushed. 'Lucky I made a good lot of risotto.'

Thea smiled uneasily and looked around the room. It was twice as big as Lucy's kitchen, with a solid pine table at one end, at which she had been told to sit. A big window looked over the garden, and a tall dresser housed a quantity of china. As she watched, Livia took down three plates from the middle shelf.

'We saw your visitor a little while ago,' said Faith shamelessly. 'Friend of yours?' The wide-eyed gaze was far too guileless to be believed. Even Stephanie or Timmy would grasp the not-very-well-hidden agenda: *We'll have to tell Lucy Sinclair that you had a strange girl in her house.* Except that, according to Lucy, there was very little amicable communication between the neighbours. Wasn't that a large part of the reason for wanting Thea there in the first place?

Thea still said nothing, bending down to make sure the dog was behaving, and then ostentatiously looking out at the garden, which had a big flowering cherry in a prominent position. Livia placed a generous lunch in front of her, and Thea smiled her thanks.

Neither woman had missed her failure to answer Faith's question. They exchanged a very obvious glance, and Thea remembered the insistence that they were not a couple. She found herself trying to define the term in any way that would not include these two. They lived and ate together.

191

They had specific routines. They read each other's thoughts. Many a husband and wife lived in the same house for decades without being as intimate as Faith and Livia clearly were.

'I haven't heard from Lucy,' she said. 'Not a word. I'm not sure what I ought to do.'

'One assumes she remains in hospital,' said Livia, apparently intending to be funny with her pompous syntax. She smiled, as if to make the point more clearly. Then she took a mouthful of the risotto, which Thea had already judged to have been cooked by an expert. Something herby, something else slightly tangy, all combined to create highly enjoyable food.

Having taken a matching mouthful, Thea replied, 'I suppose that's it. I can't think of anywhere else she would go.' But then, Thea thought, she did not know very much about Lucy's life. There could be friends who would whisk her away for recuperation – but everything she did know strongly suggested otherwise. The death of her stepson could have changed all Lucy's plans, or simply rendered her too upset to remember to speak to her house-sitter. Then Thea tried to remember everything that had been said between herself and Faith the day before. It seemed a long time ago. She'd had a lot more conversations since then. In fact, the whole of the past two days had been filled with dense conversations that she could not hope to recall verbatim. She just trusted that the salient points remained in her head.

'I went to see Lucy in hospital, actually,' she said. 'She didn't seem too poorly. She said she might be home by now.

But I haven't heard anything since.'

'Have you tried her phone?' asked Livia.

'Yes, but it's switched off.'

'Does she know about Kevin's boy – being dead, I mean?'

Thea nodded, with a strong sense of a minefield right in front of her. The central issue had finally been brought into the limelight, giving her a theoretical opportunity to discover more about it. But somehow it felt impossibly difficult. Who knew what; who had said what to whom and when; and who was telling outright lies – it all sat there in a great tangle, and she could see little prospect of sorting it out. Far more likely that she could make it worse with a few careless words. So she ate some more, wishing the plate had been even more generously filled.

'We all knew him by sight, of course. Such a handsome young man was bound to turn heads. Not that we ever saw him visit Lucy, even though she was only just down the street.'

Thea smiled and gave a wide-eyed look that said *That's interesting.*

'She's quite an unreasonable person, you know,' Livia went on mildly. 'Takes great exception to the most innocent remarks. Hunter's in despair of her.'

'I saw him yesterday,' said Thea, thinking she'd done impressively well in collecting local characters, most of whom had links with the murder victim. Hunter Lanning was of growing appeal as a likely killer, if only because he seemed to be so prominent. By some kind of logic, that gave him more to lose and therefore a more powerful motive than any other that had occurred to her.

193

'Oh? What did you think of him?' This was Faith, whose prominent eyes were fixed on Thea's face with great interest.

'I imagine he must be a very good orator. Persuasive. Even a bit charismatic on a good day.' Thea had good reason to know charisma when she saw it, having come dangerously close to falling under its spell not so long ago.

Faith and Livia both glowed; Faith even put down her fork and clapped her hands. 'That's right!' she applauded. 'Exactly right. He's a wonderful man.'

'What are his politics, I wonder?' She held her breath, expecting defensive reactions, or a lot of flummery about individualism or freedom of speech.

Instead there were two matching smiles, with the merest whiff of condescension. Livia spoke first. 'It would be impossible to put a label on him in that regard. He deals with every topic on its own merit, as he sees it. He agrees with aspects of every political theory, and votes for the candidate he thinks will do the most good.'

'Or least harm,' supplied Faith.

Livia nodded, and went on, 'Although sometimes he might opt for abstention. You should hear him talking about democracy. It's a revelation.'

Thea thought she spotted a flaw. 'And you all agree with him, right?'

It backfired. 'Of course not. That would go against everything COM stands for. We're not there to agree with each other. The whole point is that there is no single truth on any subject. There's always another side to the coin.' It was Livia again, looking down her nose like a Victorian schoolmarm.

194

'Oh. Is there, though? I mean surely there have to be some absolutes?'

'We haven't found any yet – but it's always enormous fun trying.' Faith gently tapped her fork against her plate to indicate enthusiasm. 'It's so marvellously *stimulating*. Like sunshine on a frosty morning. Just so *liberating*, as well.'

'Sounds great,' said Thea, struggling to find any grounds for thinking otherwise. Scraping the last grains of rice from her plate, she let a few moments elapse, during which she remembered that she was supposed to be asking about Ollie Sinclair, not the local debating society. Because probably that's all it was, when it came down to it. Nothing remotely linked to violence in any form. 'Hunter told me that Ollie was a drug addict,' she ventured, once again forgetting that Caz had asked for discretion on the subject. 'The same as you did,' she addressed Faith. 'But other people insist that wasn't true at all. It's not a very nice thing to say about a person without any proper evidence.'

All three plates were empty, and the diners sat back to enjoy the residual flavours loitering in their mouths. Thea took some water from the tumbler beside her plate.

Faith was the first to speak. 'There never seemed to be much doubt about it. The drugs, I mean. Not that the people in the house were causing any actual nuisance. It was always very quiet – not even very much coming and going. We thought it was all a bit of a joke, actually. I mean – lots of socially acceptable substances are really drugs, aren't they? People get addicted to all sorts of things.'

There it was again, Thea noted. Open-mindedness taken to the level of a rigorous doctrine. It sounded good, but somewhere there was a strange lack of substance to it, as if words were the only thing that mattered.

'So you never bothered to find out whether or not it was true?'

Both women blinked at this. Clearly the idea had never crossed either of their minds. 'Why would we?' asked Livia. 'It has nothing to do with us.'

The concept of community flashed through Thea's mind, bringing echoes of other Cotswold settlements where nobody interfered with anybody else, but simply left everyone to battle or flounder or exploit or kill in whatever way they saw fit. Community existed only as a negative. Even Hunter Lanning's club obviously failed to qualify. At least, she thought wryly, he had used a different word for it, based on the first three letters. 'Committee' might not be an accurate description, but it was closer than 'Community'. 'You might have helped to save his life if you'd shown a bit of interest,' she said sharply. 'Don't you think?'

A curtain of silent hostility descended. 'No,' said Livia. 'We really don't think anything at all like that.'

No further lunch courses were in evidence, and Thea knew well enough that her welcome had expired. It was apparently one thing to express an outlandish opinion about Israel or race or people changing their gender – but personal criticisms were clearly unacceptable. The openness or otherwise of a person's mind did not extend to tolerating insinuations about their actual behaviour. 'It's all theory with you, then,' Thea accused. 'That's the long and short of it.'

'We'd rather you didn't pass judgement,' said Livia,

stiffly. 'If it's all the same to you.'

Thea got up and jerked her head at the spaniel under the table who moved an inch or two with an enquiring expression. 'I should go,' she said, wary of finding herself in the wrong. 'That was the best risotto I have ever had. It was truly delicious. Thank you very much. Come on, Heps.'

'We had heard about you, of course,' said Livia thoughtfully. 'But we reserved judgement until we'd met you. I have to say your reputation is entirely justified.'

'Oh?' Thea's blood felt chilly in her veins.

'"Impertinence" is the word, I think. Overstepping normal bounds of acceptability. Intruding where you have no business to go.'

The automatic instinct was to defend, either by making counter-attacks, or by disarming through humour or apology. Over the years, she had taught herself to do none of these things. 'It gets results, though,' she said. 'That's the trouble. I've learnt something from you today, and if it takes a bit of plain speaking to get there, then so be it. But I didn't want to upset you in the process.'

'Is that an apology?' asked Faith, obviously hoping it was.

'Not really. You see, there are other people far more upset than you, not far from here. And they have a lot more reason to be. The truth is, you two are just mildly offended, and I don't feel a bit sorry about that.'

Ten minutes later, once again in Lucy's house, she reran her little speech. It had been masterly, she concluded. She would repeat it to Drew, and Barkley and anyone else who might be interested. Then by some association, she thought of a boy – young man – called Ben whom she had met the year before in Barnsley. He had shown her the importance of learning as much as possible about the victim in a murder investigation, and would not be at all impressed by her almost total ignorance concerning Ollie Sinclair. Intent on putting this right, she sat down with her phone and did some googling.

Vicky had been right that Ollie had formerly been a very high-profile high jumper in Qatar. But he had not been included in the Olympic team, due to a very badly timed injury. The implication was that he had been slightly too young for the previous one, and too old for the next one, rendering his career ultimately disappointing. She found a picture of him, looking decidedly handsome, with black hair and big brown eyes. Beside him was his mother, older and stouter than Thea had imagined. The woman with a romantic story behind her, and now perhaps nothing to live for. Unless she and Vicky were so bonded that they continued to support each other.

She could find nothing about the YouTube activity that Vicky had described, which seemed very strange. Ollie would surely retain his original name, since it must carry some clout in the sporting world, and yet nothing came up when she searched. It was of course possible that she was missing something, looking in the wrong places. Or perhaps the venture was a lot more embryonic than Vicky had implied. Various explanations came to mind – the Polish colleagues had taken it all to themselves and kept it under their names; the business was unlicensed and therefore only accessible by people in the know. Something underhand like that anyway, Thea thought vaguely. From there her thoughts strayed to the two Polish men who worked with Ollie and had conveniently left the country before he was killed. It added to the growing impression of a well-planned attack – Ollie alone in the house, nobody in the area especially fond of him, and some of them actively hostile. The way had been clear for the killer, who had been further assisted by the uncertainty over the time of death. The complicated account of how the body was found further strengthened the idea that all the ducks had been in a very neat row.

She should have asked Vicky why she hadn't missed her boyfriend sooner, she realised. Whoever it was who last saw him, it was not Vicky, nor was it his mother. Not unusual for a man in his late twenties, of course, but worthy of note, just the same. Thanks to the online information, Ollie was beginning to become more of a real person to her, which inevitably meant that she was ever more intent on discovering who had killed him. Even if he had lacked friends, nobody had said anything damning about him. The Poles evidently found him congenial, and there was something benevolent in his choice of career, once the high jumping had to stop.

But it was mostly guesswork, she had to admit. There were stark anomalies and contradictions, largely centred on the assertion that he was addicted to drugs. His mother sounded fond of him, his father not so much. Would the loss bring the two together somehow? And what about the sister who nobody but Vicky had mentioned?

It was now almost two o'clock, and she wondered idly whether Faith and Livia were annoyed at having their schedule spoilt by a visiting amateur detective. Having lunch so much earlier than usual would leave them with a long afternoon to fill. *Serves them right,* she thought. Even though they had welcomed her in and been entirely pleasant for the most part, she found herself disliking them. They had been difficult to assess on the first encounter, at Bobby's, but the few conclusions she had reached on further acquaintance were consistent with early impressions. They were too pleased with themselves, for one thing. They seemed to float above common little human troubles like murder, or cancelled operations, putting all their attention into sterile discussions with people like Hunter Lanning. Did they continue the discussions between themselves every evening at home, Thea wondered. It was only too easy to imagine that they did. It would come as no surprise to hear that one of them was writing a book about the importance of an open mind – although she fancied that if such were the case, they would not have desisted from telling her about it. There was something genderless and passionless about them – the word *sterile* recurred. They were both shaped more like young men than ageing women. Their active lives, if they'd ever had them, were over and now all they could do was talk.

Ollie, she told herself sternly. Somebody killed him, and it could quite well be a person she had met here in Northleach. The list of suspects was sadly thin. Even if Vicky was right that nobody really liked him, that was nowhere near motive enough for killing him.

The missing Poles had to be on the top of any list, surely, despite their apparent cast-iron alibi of being out of the country? Remembering the young Ben Harkness again, she found herself writing names on a sheet of paper, in the hope that a pattern might emerge. *Jan and Nikola* looked like female names; only when pronounced Yan and Nik-OH-la did they become male. Amusing glints of *Twelfth Night* went through her mind, with half the cast being a different gender from that believed to be the case. Did they have a bizarre system in Northleach where men were women and vice versa? 'Of course not,' she said aloud to herself. It would not help things at all to get as silly as that.

Twiddling her pencil, she tried again. Where did Kevin Sinclair fit into the picture? Something was evidently very awry between him and his son – but if he was the killer, he would need to be a brilliant actor to have come over as he had that morning, persuading Thea that he might be feeling guilty and desperate, but not because he was a murderer. She had seen men with very much the same look coming in to talk to Drew about a funeral.

She had no doubt that the police knew everything she had managed to discover, and probably a whole lot more. Her strengths lay elsewhere, despite what she had learnt from clever Ben and his logical processes. Thea was never going to match his skills and knowledge. Instead, she had always focused on networking, burrowing beneath local veneers of calm respectability. Had she not just found herself questioning Kevin's state of mind – something that would never turn up on an Internet site? He would show up as a serial monogamist, on at least his third woman, an inattentive father but a consistent and reliable earner – probably. He did have that expensive car, which suggested a certain level of success. Driving a lorry could well be quite lucrative if he put in long hours or accepted unpopular routes that involved long waits for Channel crossings and took him down to Turkey or across Europe to Lithuania. All she could conclude was that Kevin was rather a stereotype of a man of his time, poor at commitment and not very emotionally mature. Even that much would require some guesses and dodgy interpretations. Having actually met him, Thea suspected that he was a frightened man, out of his depth and ready to blame himself for his son's death. She also suspected that he knew almost nothing about Ollie's life – his friends, work, opinions or skills. Someone had told him that Ollie was on drugs and he had abandoned him from that point on.

All of which raised the issue of timing. For how long had the house been used by the three young men? How long ago had the drug story taken root? It all felt fairly recent. Wouldn't the inaccuracy of the rumour quickly become apparent, in the absence of any evidence whatsoever? Assuming, of course, that it *was* inaccurate. So far there were the police findings – or lack of them – and Vicky's assurances to outweigh the assertions of Hunter, Kevin, Faith-and-Livia and Lucy. It was not safe to give total credence to either camp, especially as 'drugs' covered such a multitude of sins.

The light outside was fading, thanks to a mist that was gathering. There were hours to go before sunset, but visibility was not good. Northleach was on comparatively high ground, with no river close by, which Thea thought should ensure good light – but mist could descend anywhere, as she had learnt. This particular mist came from above, a cloud that had carelessly flopped itself down onto the little town and made everything blurry and damp. The morning had been fine, which was no guarantee at all that the afternoon would not be unseasonably chilly. Had Drew not reported dour predictions for Friday's weather, way back at the start of the week? Perhaps this mist was the vanguard of something particularly nasty.

'Just the weather for a funeral. Melancholy without being too much of a nuisance,' she muttered aloud, before recognising that this was her subconscious reminding her that she had a hard-working husband twenty miles away who would appreciate her presence. But, 'He'll have to wait,' she went on, pretending to herself that she was talking to the dog. Hepzie knew better and took no notice of her.

And yet – what was she meant to do here in Northleach? The total silence from Lucy was puzzling and annoying, to the extent that she felt justified in phoning the hospital to ask for the latest news. Which she did, to receive an even more puzzling and annoying response.

'Mrs Sinclair was discharged this morning,' she was told.

'Really? What time?' Perhaps, she thought, Lucy had taken a bus, which would meander across Middle England for hours before arriving at Northleach.

'About eleven, I think. A hospital car took her home.' The woman giggled. 'And I should know, because my uncle was driving it.'

The nurse's uncle was of no interest to Thea. 'Well, she's not here,' she said crossly. Then she revised her opinion of the uncle. 'Do you know where he was taking her? Did you hear her give an address?'

'No, I didn't – not exactly. But he knew he'd have to go to Northleach, which is a lot further than he would have liked, to be honest. He's seventy-six and prefers to stick to places he knows.'

'I'm in Northleach and she's not here,' Thea repeated.

'Oh God! What if there's been an accident! Poor Uncle Roy. What's the weather like over there?' A very unprofessional panic filled the woman's voice. Thea felt a pang of remorse at being the cause of it.

'Don't worry. It's a little bit misty, that's all. There's sure to be a perfectly good explanation. I'll try phoning her again – and you could call your uncle as well. Don't worry about it. I'm sorry to have bothered you. Honestly, there's really no reason to get in a state.' *I hope*, she added silently.

The nurse gave an inarticulate reply and the call was ended.

Despite knowing full well that it was unworthy of her, and that Drew would not approve, Thea felt slighted. It was as if Lucy had forgotten all about her. How hard would it have been to send a quick text or even make a proper call? It made her think of Hunter Lanning and the implication that he thought it was fine to offend people. It was, sort of, but it did not help to oil the social wheels or maintain good relations. She did not think she would ever feel really warm towards Lucy Sinclair again. Even if she was upside down in a ditch beside an elderly volunteer who wasn't safe to drive, she could still have made her intentions clear at the outset.

All of which left her with no clearer idea of what to do next. Everyone seemed to have deserted her, which was quite a Fridayish feeling, she noticed. After the positive emotions around Thursdays, the next day was all too often a let-down, with grey realities intruding. The weekend was going to be wet, or too busy, or not busy enough. There would be annoying commitments, meetings with people one did not really like. Businesses were closed – though far less than they used to be – making it difficult to fix appointments or catch up with bureaucratic matters.

'Oh, stop it!' she told herself. 'Just go home and forget Northleach completely.'

That wasn't going to happen, but it was a tempting idea. While she was savouring the temptation, the Gloucestershire police arrived to settle the matter. Caz Barkley was at the door, bright-eyed and excited. 'Developments!' she gasped. 'You might want to come.'

Chapter Thirteen

'What about the dog?' Thea asked, putting first things first.

'Leave it. We won't be long – probably.'

Telling Hepzie to be good, Thea locked the street door and hoped for the best.

Caz set off towards the town square with Thea a step or two behind. There was no chance of any sort of explanation, which Thea felt was putting her at a very real disadvantage. 'This is very unusual,' she protested. 'What if somebody's got a gun?'

Caz slowed and turned round with a broad grin. 'Don't be daft,' she said.

'Okay. So – what?'

'You'll see. Don't worry – it won't be dangerous.' She set off again and barely a minute later they were at the top end of the town square, where a child was squalling and two dogs were barking. It was still misty, but not enough to obscure the goings-on in the middle of quiet little Northleach.

'That's Millie,' said Thea. 'Where's her mother?'

'Good question. I believe the man with her is Dad, though.'

'Artie? Albie?' Thea wasn't sure of his name. He was standing over the howling child, arms folded, head bent, making no attempt to console his daughter. 'I don't know him at all,' Thea told Caz. 'Why did you bring me here?'

'I couldn't think what else to do. It's not exactly a police matter, but something's obviously not right. I was supposed to be going over to Cirencester, when I saw all this carry-on. That's my car.' She pointed at an inconspicuous grey vehicle left crookedly across two parking bays in the square.

'Nobody seems to want to interfere.'

Several things struck Thea as being wrong. Millie had seemed a particularly sensible little girl, only two days earlier. The man was behaving strangely. The barking dogs were attached to an old man sitting at a table outside the café, with his back firmly turned. 'Why did you say "developments"?' she asked Caz. 'What's this got to do with anything? Isn't it just a bigger-than-usual tantrum?'

'It might be,' said the young detective. 'But that's not what it looks like to me. All I know is that the man strongly objects to any interference from me – or probably from anyone. He says the kid isn't hurt.'

Thea had no patience with such hesitancy. 'I still think it's for you to sort out, not me, but we can't just stand here wittering, can we?' So saying, she walked up to the distraught Millie and bent over her. 'Hey Millie – remember me? What's all this about? Is this your dad? Did something happen?'

'Ollie!' she wailed. 'I want Ollie!' Tears and mucus flowed down her face. 'Where is he?' The words were screamed out in a helpless despair that went through Thea like a bayonet.

'Oh, darling. Is that it? Ollie isn't here, sweetheart. Hasn't your daddy told you that?' She gave the man a belligerent stare, to show him just what she felt about his performance as a parent.

He met her gaze slowly. 'I told her,' he said. 'Why do you think we've got all this ballyhoo?'

'So take her home and tell her properly. You can't just *stand* there. What's the matter with you?'

'We've been home and there's nobody there. So we came to look for my wife and son. Millie wanted to go and see Ollie, so I had to tell her she wasn't going to be seeing him any more, ever again. She's been playing up like this for a good twenty minutes and I've had enough of it.' He glared from Thea to Caz and back again. 'Who are you, anyway?' he demanded.

Millie was clinging to Thea to the point of discomfort. The old man's dogs were quieter, and Caz was regaining some much-needed authority. 'You knew Ollie Sinclair, then?' she said, clutching at the single pertinent fact to emerge.

'Obviously,' said Mr Latimer – Albie? Artie? – with no sign of deference to the representative of the law. Unless, of course, he had not been advised that here was a detective sergeant in plain clothes.

208

Thea was preoccupied by the small Latimer's devotion to Ollie. Here, then, was an exception to Vicky's claim that 'nobody liked Ollie'. 'How?' she asked. 'How did you know Ollie?'

'He does a bit of sport at her school, one day a week or so,' said Albie/Artie carelessly. 'Mill's besotted with him. He's used her in his little films a few times, as well. All perfectly kosher, of course.' His accent was much more American than his wife's. Thea wondered idly whether the children would grow up sounding transatlantic.

'Perfectly kosher,' Caz repeated thoughtfully. 'Right.'

Millie had grown quieter once her misery had been properly acknowledged and even discussed by no fewer than three adults. Thea disengaged herself and stood up. 'Go to your father,' she said, with a little wave. 'He didn't mean to make you so upset, I'm sure.' She was asking herself a string of questions about this family, members of which kept popping up in the town square. Perhaps if you lived so close to shops and pubs and cafés, you treated it all as a kind of extended garden. Add in a private infant school and a murder scene, and there could well be plenty of reason for frequent sallies forth, with a child or two.

'Artie,' she said suddenly. 'That's it, isn't it? Bobby mentioned you yesterday, when we were standing almost exactly here. She said you were a keen member of Hunter Lanning's club. It's all coming back to me now.' She gave him the first proper look since joining in the whole episode. He was fairly short, wore a neat-looking suit and was only marginally younger than almost everybody else she'd met in Northleach. That was, he seemed to be at least in his mid fifties. Too old to be coping with a heartbroken child in a public place. Embarrassment came off him in waves.

'Come on, Millie, we're going home,' he said, making it sound like the very last option available to him. 'Mum and your brother will be back before long.' He had ignored Thea's words and barely even glanced at Caz. The child heaved a great sigh and nodded.

'Will she be all right?' Thea asked. 'I mean—'

'I'm her father, so yes, she will be quite all right, thank you. Won't you?' he demanded of the child. Again she nodded.

Thea noted the effort to avoid sounding so American, to adopt a more dignified diction. The British spoke so formally, with their clipped t's and proper sentences, that any American living amongst them must hear himself as sloppy, if not downright slurred, by comparison. Artie Latimer might have a very British surname, and he must have some money to afford that nice house, but he was still an alien abroad.

The group dispersed and the quiet life of Northleach resumed without a ripple. The old man patted his dogs and drained his cup of tea. There was a faint misting on his shoulders, from sitting so long outside. Were his dogs not allowed into the café? It was the same one that had admitted Hepzie on Wednesday.

Caz went back to Lucy's house with Thea. They had not discussed it first, but it was clearly inevitable. Thea accepted effusions from the briefly-abandoned dog and then made tea, prepared for a lengthy update on the murder investigation. It was close to three o'clock; Stephanie and

210

Timmy would soon be home, and Drew would be finishing his third burial of the day. Thea calculated that she could justifiably give herself another hour in Northleach.

'Well,' she said. 'That was exciting. Although I still don't understand why you called it a *development*.' She ran through the incident again. 'Did you already know that Millie was crying about Ollie, when you came to get me?'

Caz shook her head. 'Nope. The man had already told me to back off, that it was a private family matter, and he had it all under control. I had no grounds for interfering, so I came to get you. At least, I hoped you'd be here. I thought you might know them,' she added with a grin.

'But why give it any attention at all? A child bawling in the street is hardly unusual. None of the locals were taking any notice. There was no blood.'

'I know. Just a gut reaction, I guess. I mean, she was so upset, I couldn't just ignore it. But I had no authority to intervene, either. So—'

'Yes, I see,' said Thea, feeling rather smug at the obvious implication that she was regarded as a kind of all-purpose saviour when it came to distressed locals near the scene of a murder. 'Well, we learnt something, which means you did the right thing. The Latimers knew Ollie, which for me anyway is fresh information. Although . . .' She thought back to the encounter with Bobby and Buster the day before, 'I suppose it was assumed that Bobby knew him when I was talking to her yesterday. She didn't actually say so. She certainly didn't seem very upset.'

'The Latimers,' said Caz heavily. 'You know practically everything about them, don't you? What they all do for a living and where they were born.'

'Mostly, yes,' Thea confirmed. 'Don't you? I talked about them yesterday, remember?'

'Remind me,' Caz invited. 'Now we've got a firm link between Ollie and the child.'

Thea did her best to encapsulate everything she had learnt from her two meetings with Bobby, whilst trying to fill in some gaps. 'She never said anything about Ollie working at the school. She must have known yesterday that he wouldn't be coming back and that Millie would be upset about it. She sounded as if she disapproved of him and his friends – wouldn't she object to letting him work with small children? What about the drugs? She must have known what everybody was saying about him and the others. It doesn't fit.'

'Maybe she knew better. Who runs this school? It hasn't come up in any of our interviews as somewhere Ollie worked. They've got to have been satisfied that he was no risk to the kiddies. There are all those hoops to jump through.'

'I know,' said Thea. 'Unless he just popped in on an informal basis. Artie seemed to be saying he did outdoor stuff with them once a week. Maybe he taught the older ones how to work a camera.'

'Pardon?'

'He made films. You obviously knew that. That's what they were doing at that house. YouTube and all that sort of thing. About athletics. Oh – there it is!' She held up a finger. 'He'd have been getting the kids to exercise, to improve coordination or stretch their muscles. That sort of thing.

He'd be ideally qualified for that.'

Caz had her phone in her hand, tapping and swiping and peering at the text that came up. 'Okay,' she said sheepishly. 'I hadn't caught up with that bit. It wasn't in the briefing,' she added defensively.

'Oh?' Thea was vague about police briefings, but had an idea that a senior officer would assemble the team each morning and bring them up to date with all information and avenues of investigation that had occurred the previous day. The day job of a murder victim surely had to be of considerable interest. 'But you are on the team, aren't you?'

Caz nodded. 'They've got me looking into the father – Kevin Sinclair. That's more than enough to keep me busy. That man's life has been seriously messy, I can tell you.'

'But he didn't kill Ollie,' said Thea, without pausing to think. She had already reached that conclusion, and now it was simply axiomatic. Whoever the killer might have been, it was not Kevin Sinclair.

'He might have done,' Caz argued. 'They certainly didn't get along very well.'

Again, Thea remembered what Vicky had said. *Nobody really liked Ollie.* 'Lots of people disliked him,' she said aloud. 'According to his girlfriend.'

'Vicky Upfield,' Caz nodded with a look of relief. 'She's been interviewed.'

'I know she has. And she didn't say anything about Jan and Nikola, which was bad of her. But I expect you've located them by now, anyway. She came here this morning, by the way. You told me about the filming and the Polish friends and all that, didn't you?'

'Of course I did,' said Detective Sergeant Caz Barkley wearily.

They talked for an hour, sharing ideas and making connections, with Caz repeatedly grimacing at Thea's appeals for detail that were strictly meant to be kept confidential. How exactly had Ollie died? And when? Who were the main suspects? What exactly was so messy about Kevin's life? They went around the same questions and guesses and contradictions three or four times, getting nowhere. As always happened when Thea was talking to a police detective, the professionalism fell away and they were just two people trying to solve a puzzle. It had been the same with Phil Hollis and Sonia Gladwin – both senior ranks and both putty in Thea Slocombe's hands.

'Where's your friend?' Caz asked at one point, quite out of the blue. 'The owner of this house, I mean.'

'Lucy? Good question. She left hospital this morning without telling me, and I've no idea where she's gone. It's quite weird, actually.'

'Especially as she's stepmother to the murder victim,' said Caz meaningfully. 'Could be she's got reason to go into hiding.'

'You think she knows who did it and is scared of them?'

'It's got to be possible.'

'She'll show up eventually,' said Thea, feeling the same uncomfortable sense of offence as she had earlier. 'It is quite rude of her, though,' she added.

'Yes.' Caz was clearly pursuing the subject, thinking through some of the implications. 'She might well be scared the killer's after her as well. So she's waiting until we've caught him before coming home.'

'Have you heard anything that might even remotely suggest that?'

Caz worked her shoulders. 'Not really – have you?'

'Absolutely not. And after all this talk we've just had, it's pretty obvious that neither of us has got close to the crucial facts. There's a story hidden away that we're a million miles from grasping.'

'Where should we be looking?' Caz asked, with a wild expression. 'Nobody in this place will tell us anything. They all belong to that committee thing, which isn't really a committee at all, but that doesn't seem to have anything to do with anything.'

'None of them seem to like each other much,' Thea observed. 'Vicky said Ollie was unpopular. Lucy couldn't find anybody she trusted enough to watch out for her house. The Latimers are interlopers and Faith and Livia are just odd.'

They had already gone over much of this ground. The police had seen no reason to interview Lucy's neighbours, and Thea couldn't supply one. Now she considered them again. 'Could be they're the reason Lucy hasn't come home,' she speculated. 'She said something about them watching her all the time. I wouldn't be surprised if they've made her jittery.'

'So, are they a couple or not?' Caz had asked at the start, with utter predictability. Thea had tried to explain, with scant success. 'Sounds to me that there's not much of a question about it,' said the detective. 'As if anybody cares.'

'Exactly,' said Thea. 'Nobody cares except them – they apparently think it's something awful. And the irony is the more they insist it's not true, the more people assume it is.'

'As you say – odd. But not really suspicious.'

Before they could go round it all again, Thea stood up. 'I've got to go,' she said. 'And you're probably meant to be somewhere, aren't you?'

'Duty calls for both of us,' said Caz. 'Are you coming back here at the weekend?'

Thea spread her hands in a gesture of ignorance. 'Who knows? I did tell Stephanie I might bring her here so she can explore a bit. She might like to see the church. But I'm not staying overnight, whatever happens.'

'Your dog looks hungry.' Hepzie was pushing an empty water bowl across the floor and Thea realised she had not filled it even at the start when she and the dog had first arrived. Lucy must have put it out for her.

'Thirsty more likely, poor thing. I can't imagine when she last had a drink. Sorry, Heps.' She filled the bowl at the sink and gave it to the spaniel. 'Did I tell you about Lucy's old dog, Jimmy?' she began. 'The one I had to look after in Hampnett when she lived in a converted barn?'

'Another time,' said Caz decisively. 'Unless you think it's evidence of something.'

'It's not,' sighed Thea. 'Only my own bad character, anyway. It amazes me that Lucy's asked me to be a house-sitter for her again, after that.'

Caz cocked her head. 'So why did she? Either you're

much more responsible than you think you are, or she really couldn't find anybody else.' She looked round the room, and out into the back garden. 'And why have a sitter anyway? What's so precious that it needs guarding?'

'That's exactly what I want to know,' said Thea.

Chapter Fourteen

There was a strong sense of failure swirling through Thea as she drove home through the persistent mist. The day had cut itself short, any potential sunlight giving up all pretence that it might yet break through, and the still-bare trees glistening with damp. It would be close to five when she got back, walking into the family home and dealing with tired, hungry people all wanting to debrief at the end of their week.

Her own debriefing had already been provided by Barkley, rather to her relief. She was all talked out, dumping her observations without the slightest idea as to what they suggested about the people she'd met. Nobody seemed particularly likeable, but nor did they give any clue that they might be capable of murder. If she had been forced to lay a bet on any of them, she supposed it would be Hunter

Lanning. He at least had said or done nothing to make her want to defend him, unlike poor Kevin Sinclair. The two Polish men had to be kept in mind too, she presumed. A fight over a piece of film editing could have ended tragically – the two foreigners dashing back to their motherland for fear of retribution. Hadn't Caz admitted that the exact time of Ollie's death was very uncertain? But Vicky had implied, if not said directly, that the two had been out of the UK for a while. She could have been lying, of course. There were plenty of wild scenarios that would make that perfectly likely.

And now she had met Artie Latimer, she cautiously put him on the list, as well. He wasn't big, but he looked as if he might have lurking anger issues.

Plus, of course, there were all those women, any one of whom might have wielded a sharp instrument quite effectively, too.

Broad Campden was murky under its generous provision of trees, the track down to the Slocombe house close to night-time darkness. Thea let Hepzie out of the car before she reversed it into the opening at the side of the house, as she often did. The dog would run up to the front door and yap, to announce her presence. She noted that the hearse and van were both neatly in place behind the house. If her calculations were correct, there would be no bodies in the back room for the whole weekend. Unless, of course, something had happened during the day to change that. If so, she couldn't think who would do the removal, or when.

Drew was waiting for her on the doorstep, unsmiling. 'We've got a visitor,' he said, without lowering his voice.

'She's been here for quite some time.'

Thea's first thought was it must be Gladwin, the detective superintendent who had not so far put in an appearance in connection with the Northleach murder, but had perhaps zoomed back from her holiday in order to take over the investigation. Drew had never been entirely reconciled to the relationship between her and Thea. His glum expression strongly suggested Gladwin. 'Who – Sonia?' she asked him.

'No. Lucy Sinclair,' he said, still speaking loudly enough to be heard throughout the ground floor. 'I've been trying to phone you.'

'Have you? I should have heard it, then. It's been switched on all day.' But mostly out of earshot in her jacket pocket, she remembered. Not since about two o'clock had she given any thought to its existence. 'Why is she here?' she asked, in belated bewilderment. 'I've been waiting for her all day in Northleach.'

All day echoed inside her head. What a very long day it had been, with so many conversations and ideas and questions that she knew she would never get it all straight, piled as it all was on top of similar encounters on Wednesday and Thursday.

'Well, come on then and talk to her,' Drew ordered impatiently. 'It's Friday evening and everybody's exhausted. Stephanie's in a state about something again, and I haven't had a minute to find out what the matter is.'

'How did the funerals go?' Thea asked dutifully. If she didn't say it now, she might not get another chance until it was too late. Better not to ask at all than to leave it to the next day, or even bedtime on this day.

'Fine,' he said as if that was the very least item to be considered.

Lucy was in the sitting room looking small but dogged, in one of the armchairs. Timmy and Stephanie were both on the sofa, looking very uncomfortable. The television was off and there was no sign that they'd been doing anything at all – just sitting there with this unknown woman. Had Drew ordered them to entertain her while he got on with something important? There was not the slightest hint of any preparations for an evening meal. *Takeaway Chinese*, Thea decided on the instant. That was one major item off the list, which came as a great relief.

'Lucy,' she said, trying not to sound too friendly. 'What's going on?'

'I'm sorry.' The voice was wobbly, but the expression behind it did not waver at all. 'Your husband did try to phone you . . . and your children have been very hospitable.'

The only way any of this could make sense was if Thea had somehow missed a large and crucial part of the day's story. Her thoughts were filled with questions about logistics as she tried to comprehend the mental map that included Oxford, Northleach and Broad Campden. 'Where's your car?' she asked, idiotically, forgetting what the nurse had told her.

'What? My *car*? It's in Northleach, of course.'

'Oh – yes, that's right. Nursey's uncle drove you, didn't he? But surely you haven't been here since then? That was *hours* ago. Five hours, at least,' she calculated. 'Drew's been doing funerals all day.'

'I was in Chipping Campden for most of the time. I had

221

lunch there and looked round the shops. Then I came here.'

'But *why*?' Thea almost wailed. Protocol had been breached, lines crossed, rules ignored. It had been wrong when Lucy showed up on Tuesday – now it was unforgivable. The woman was turning into a stalker. And Drew was cross about it.

'You're the only person I can trust,' came the manipulative reply. 'I can't go back to Northleach with things the way they are.'

'Of course you can,' said Thea, feeling ruthless. 'I'll drive you there myself, if I have to.' And then she could go and collect a lavish Chinese dinner from Chipping Campden on the way home, she thought – which might go some way towards consoling her disgruntled family. If she went now, the meal would not be too drastically much later than usual. Stephanie could phone in the order . . . and Lucy Sinclair could just sort her own problems out as best she might.

'I was hoping you'd let me stay the night,' said Lucy, with another unwavering stare. Just how this battle of wits – or, more accurately, *wills* – had developed, Thea wasn't sure. It was as if it had all been prepared in advance, ready for her to walk into.

'Well, you hoped in vain,' she said. 'I'm not obligated to you, Lucy, not the least little bit. You've messed me about all week, one way or another, and wasted a lot of my time. Now the hospital have said you can go home, that's where you should go.'

She had forgotten Drew's children, sitting there so quietly. For a moment she saw herself through their eyes – unkind, unsympathetic, refusing to listen. It was not

222

an image to be proud of. 'Look,' she started again. 'I can see you're nervous about something, but I can't imagine what it might be. Your house is right there in the main street, with people on all sides. There's even a police presence at the moment, after what happened. You can't possibly be in any real danger. If I'm prepared to do another hour's driving to take you back, I think that's about as much as you can expect from me. Any reasonable person would think the same.'

'She's *scared*,' Stephanie interrupted. 'She thinks she might be murdered next.'

Thea hesitated, mainly in the hope that she could redeem herself. Then she took a deep breath. 'Okay,' she said. 'I know the whole situation's quite unsettling. Probably everyone in Northleach is feeling a bit paranoid at the moment. But life has to go on. I don't suppose the person who killed Ollie is still in town, anyway. Most likely he's in Poland or somewhere.'

Lucy gave a half-choked laugh at this. 'I don't think so,' she said.

'If I let you stay tonight, how will that help anything?' Thea asked, aiming for a calm and reasonable tone. 'Will you want to stay another night after that, and then a week or a month?' Reasonableness was rapidly evaporating, despite her best efforts. 'You'll be leaving your house vulnerable to whatever it was that worried you in the first place, won't you?'

'Things will settle down,' said Lucy vaguely.

'What about your operation? Have you got another date for that? Do they know what caused your collapse on Wednesday? And how can you expect to just stay here stranded without your car? I've got a *family* to run,' she finished breathlessly.

'I can help.'

Now it was Thea who laughed, expressing the same kind of scorn and exasperation as Lucy had done. 'No. Sorry,' she said. 'It's not going to happen. Get your things and I'll take you home. Just let me go and tell Drew what's happening.'

Lucy seemed to sink more deeply into the chair as if trying to root herself in it. Again, Thea noted how many social rules were being transgressed. You didn't insist on staying where you weren't wanted. To do so was both mad and bad. Police could be called to eject you. They called it 'home invasion' in America. Which made her think of the Latimers, who were at least neutral on the matter of Lucy Sinclair, as far as she could tell. 'What if I call Bobby Latimer and ask her to keep an eye on you?' she said, trying not to sound as if she was pleading.

'Don't you dare!' Lucy flashed. 'I told you – I can't trust *anybody* in Northleach.'

'Which is quite obviously ridiculous,' Thea flashed back.

'She's scared, Thea,' said Stephanie again, as if this trumped everything. 'Can't you see?'

'But what's she scared *of*?' Thea demanded. 'If her fear is baseless, then it's neurotic and needs to be addressed by professionals. Maybe I should just take you back to the hospital,' she said nastily to Lucy.

The woman had begun to look deranged. Her eyes sparkled and she barely blinked. It occurred to Thea that she really knew next to nothing about the undercurrents running through Northleach society. And it was true that there had been a murder. That much was impossible to deny. 'Let's see what Drew says, then,' she said, with a horrible sense of cowardly compromise. Thea Slocombe had never liked the notion of compromise, even when she had been Thea Osborne or Thea Johnstone before that.

'He'll say it's up to you.' It was Timmy who piped up, with total certainty.

'I expect he will,' sighed Thea. 'And I say this is all completely unreasonable and unnecessary and the best thing for Lucy as well as everyone else is for her to go home. The sensible thing is surely to get to the bottom of whatever's wrong with doing that. Specifically. Actual threats. Not just all this vague nonsense about not trusting people.' Lucy was seriously rubbish at answering questions, she noticed. There were still quite a few from twenty minutes ago floating around the room.

And before there could be any attempt at giving answers, Drew had come into the room. 'Well?' he said. 'What happens now? I'm hungry.'

Thea knew that time was running out. If she left it any longer, Lucy would have to stay, because it was late and dark and damp and nobody would want to drive through the Cotswold lanes on such an evening. 'I'm trying to persuade Lucy to go home. I'll take her now, and collect Chinese in Chipping Campden on the way home. But she doesn't want to go, and won't explain why.'

It was annoying to observe the effect Drew's presence had. Lucy sat up straight and felt for the handbag on the floor beside her. 'Well, I do see your point,' she said, far more meekly than she had spoken so far. 'I expect I am just being foolish. Although the people at the hospital *did* say it would be best if I had somebody with me for a day or two. Just in case . . . Anyway, I feel perfectly well now, so probably it would be best . . .' She looked forlornly up at Drew, who, to his credit, was clearly not being swayed. If the woman was willing to go, he certainly wasn't going to stop her – as everyone in the room could see. 'All right, then,' she conceded. 'If you don't mind all that driving.'

Thea did mind, and for a moment wondered why she thought it preferable to just making up a bed for the night and starting again next morning. But she had gradually come to the conclusion that she did not really like Lucy Sinclair in her new persona. In Hampnett she had seemed breezy and full of good humour. She'd rejoiced in her divorce from Kevin and shown extreme kindness to abandoned animals. But they had only spent an hour together, in total, and Thea supposed almost everyone could manage to be likeable for that long. Now there was so much unexplained, so many inconsistencies and phobias, that Thea could no longer be patient with her. The prospect of having her hanging around throughout the weekend was intolerable. 'Come on, then,' she said.

The car journey was deeply uncomfortable, which Thea had somehow failed to foresee. It was not so much that Lucy was patently sulking, but that her thoughts were so intense that they made the air crackle. There was a constant impression that a great tirade was about to burst forth, but it never did. Thea had no problem with silence, as a general rule, but a brooding passenger on a dark evening drive was a whole different challenge. She went as fast as she dared, half hoping that Lucy would protest at the speed, which would at least be relatively normal.

The final sweep along the A429 was achieved at almost eighty miles an hour. 'I always like to go fast along here,' Thea said, breaking the prolonged silence. 'I know I shouldn't. When I was house-sitting here one time, I realised how dangerous it is for wildlife and pedestrians. But I still can't resist it when there's hardly any traffic.'

'Not great visibility, though,' said Lucy tightly.

'I'm pretty sure I could see headlights well enough.'

'I would think it's tail-lights you need to see, not headlights.'

'True,' Thea agreed with a small laugh. But she slowed down. It was less than half a mile to the roundabout where the road crossed the A40, and anything in front of her would be braking in another few seconds.

They reached West End and Lucy's house without incident, and Thea debated with herself whether or not she ought to get out and spend a few minutes ensuring that all was well. Common courtesy dictated that of course she should, but Lucy had forfeited quite a lot of that sort of thing by her behaviour that day. 'I think I've left everything as I found it,' Thea said, trying to remember whether she did in fact tidy the kitchen adequately. 'I wasn't sure whether I'd be coming back or not.'

'Believe it or not, I have spent the past fifteen minutes trying to put myself in your shoes, and I can see I've messed you about. I took too much for granted. I thought we had a stronger friendship than it's turned out to be. It's a bit of a pattern with me, actually. I never seem to get it right. But you don't have to look after me. Of course you don't. Why would you?'

'Well . . .' said Thea weakly.

'Just one question,' Lucy cut through. 'What does "nurse's uncle" mean?'

'Oh Lord!' Thea groaned. 'That was awful of me.' She explained about her phone call to the hospital that morning. 'And I called him "*Nursey's* uncle", with a "y" – which makes it even worse.'

'Nursey,' Lucy repeated. 'That is rather awful. He was a really nice man, as it happens.'

'Look – you will be all right, okay? The house is perfectly secure. Nobody's going to be breaking in or harassing you. Keep the curtains shut and they'll barely notice you're here. Honestly, I wouldn't be doing this if I thought you were in any real danger.'

'That's what people always say,' Lucy muttered. 'But you're probably right. It's easy to get worked up over nothing.'

Except they both knew that it was not nothing, because – after all – a man had been murdered in the high street.

Chapter Fifteen

Thea drove home more slowly, tempted again and again to turn back and rescue Lucy Sinclair. Had not fate been sorely provoked, with so many groundless assurances? Had Thea not behaved disgracefully in ejecting the frightened woman from the sanctuary of her own home? A home where there was no threat, nothing to fear, warm and cheerful – except for Drew's glowering. There were endless questions she still wanted to ask Lucy. Why did she feel so uneasy in that quiet little town? Was there one person in particular she was afraid of? There was an implication from people Thea had met that Lucy had been critical, perhaps even antisocial. She had rejected Hunter Lanning's wonderful committee, for a start. That alone might be enough to make her an outcast – although Bobby Latimer appeared to have a lurking sympathy for Lucy's opinion of it. After all, Hunter had driven her to Oxford on Wednesday, which suggested a pretty low level of animosity. And what about Kevin? Were things still hostile between him and his former wife? Had Tessa taken against Lucy? All three of Kevin's women still lived in the area, which would inevitably produce tensions. What about Ollie's mother, who had to be at the heart of everything, at least in terms of the grief quotient being suffered? Driving back along the same increasingly familiar route, Thea let speculation run riot, along with regret that she might never find answers to the multiplicity of questions. Despite that frustration, it was better than worrying about what Drew was going to say.

The arrangements for the Chinese meal ran smoothly, and it was ready for collection at the estimated time. She was dreadfully hungry, she realised, as the wonderful smells filled her car. It was barely five minutes before she got it home, to find the table laid and a bottle of wine in the fridge. 'Wine!' she said, when they were all seated around with their plates well filled. 'Gosh!'

'We're celebrating having managed seven funerals in four days,' said Drew. 'At least, I am.'

'Well, congratulations!' she smiled, raising her glass. 'I'm afraid I can't pretend to have anything to celebrate from my week. All I've done is fill my head with a hopeless muddle and been mean to poor Lucy Sinclair.'

'You *were* mean,' said Stephanie.

'But it's better here without her. She wasn't any fun,' said Timmy.

'No fun at all,' said Drew. 'It would be like having one of my funeral people to supper. Somebody whose husband had just died – imagine it!'

The subtext, as Thea very well knew, was that work and family should be kept separate. If he could do it, with everything happening in the same house and tiny village, then why could she not manage? He could tolerate a little light house-sitting, if that was what she wanted, but he did not relish having it brought home and thrust under his nose. And she really couldn't blame him. On the other hand, she would very much have liked to talk it all through with him. She would enjoy describing Faith-and-Livia, and the poor parenting skills of Artie Latimer. He had, she remembered, shown a certain amount of interest in Hunter Lanning and his open-mindedness. The problem was, she had gleaned nothing more about the man since that conversation and so had nothing new to convey.

'What if she gets murdered, though?' said Stephanie, with a frown. 'What if she knew there was some terrible danger, and that's why she wanted to stay here?'

'If she really knew that, she should go to the police. They'd protect her.'

'They wouldn't, though, would they? I mean – *how* would they? Probably they wouldn't even believe her,' Stephanie persisted.

'Stop it,' begged Thea. 'Why are you guilt-tripping me like this? Don't forget I was there all day, trying to understand what was going on. I couldn't see the slightest reason for Lucy to worry. She's obviously not ill. Even her back seemed a lot less stiff – maybe the hospital gave her something for it before she was discharged. It's her own fault if she couldn't make friends. You can't expect me to take responsibility for that.'

'Thea's right,' said Drew. 'Just drop it, okay?' He gave his daughter one of his looks, from under his floppy fringe. Drew's hair was doing the opposite of most men his age. Where their hairline receded, leaving more and more brow, his seemed to be trying to cover his whole face. If he had it cut short, he looked all wrong and it grew back in unruly tufts. So he only went to a barber when it passed his eyebrows, leaving a perpetual look of a fair-headed Paul McCartney in about 1969.

'Tell me about the funerals,' said Thea, hours later than she had intended.

That night she dreamt about Kevin Sinclair, who was spying on his son through a small window, watching him smoking some lethal and illegal substance while Hunter Lanning and Artie Latimer stood behind Kevin muttering that they'd known it all along. Clouds of blue and purple smoke billowed around Ollie's head, and as Thea watched him, in the dream, he slowly sank to the floor and turned into a corpse.

'It's all about the drugs,' she was saying to herself when she woke up. 'It's got to be.'

The weekend was empty of any real plans. Drew wanted to go and talk to Andrew, and catch up with some paperwork. Stephanie was writing up a lengthy report about an experiment she and others were conducting at school, to do with photosynthesis. It had been going on all term and the family had long ago lost interest. Timmy was reluctantly learning a poem – something that Thea and Drew thought had been abandoned by schools long ago. The only way it was going to succeed was if the entire family learnt it with him. When Thea had mentioned this to her mother the previous weekend, Maureen Johnstone had been ecstatic. 'We had to do that!' she cried. 'I've never forgotten all those poems.' But it turned out that she had, with only a scattering of first lines still lodged in her brain. 'He's got a very old-fashioned teacher,' sighed Thea. But she did in fact like the idea, and had even gone through a short phase of learning poems by heart herself, only a year or so ago. 'Margaret, are you grieving over Goldengrove unleaving?' she would mumble to herself, now and then. But she could only get as far as the sixth line before her memory failed her.

Tim's poem was every bit as obscure as the Hopkins, it seemed to Thea. A sonnet by John Updike of all people, entitled 'Iowa'. It didn't rhyme and the scansion sounded wrong. But it had more than enough images to conjure the American West – which neatly dovetailed with another school project concerning history. Every line carried an idea that the old-fashioned teacher managed to pursue and elaborate to a remarkable extent. She had spent a week on fireflies, for one thing. And the transgressive reference to cigars made Thea happy. 'I love the smell of cigars,' she said.

All of which meant that the family were quite nicely occupied on Saturday morning, and Thea had very little to do. Wash the school clothes, sew a button on one of Timmy's school shirts, get some shopping in and maybe run the vacuum around. Hepzie's hairs required regular removal from furniture and rugs if all four of the Slocombes were not to appear in public lightly coated with them. But those tasks, however conscientiously performed, could not possibly take more than a couple of hours. Even the supermarket, close by in Chipping Campden, was a quick job accomplished shortly before lunchtime.

The sun came out in the afternoon and the dog made it clear that a walk would be in order. Stephanie was the default person to attend to this need, escorting Hepzie down the track to the big field at the end. Various crops came and went in this field, sometimes requiring walkers to stick to the path that ran through the middle, but mostly it was permissible to run all over it. After nearly two years, the Slocombes still had not met the farmer who owned it. There were never any animals on it, which made it a very restful recreation ground.

'The thing about the Cotswolds,' Drew once said, 'is that there's so much *space*. Even if you had a thousand walkers roaming about, one summer Sunday, they'd hardly even see each other.'

'Even more so in the Lake District,' said Thea. 'Or the Yorkshire Dales.'

'It's because there are so many footpaths,' said Timmy, preparing to share yet again his knowledge of the exact length of all the major pathways.

'I should go with you,' Thea said now to her stepdaughter and dog. 'But I'm feeling lazy.' In truth, she was hankering for enough undisturbed solitude to make a few phone calls. Drew had taken Timmy with him to see Andrew, because it was generally believed that Drew needed to spend more time with his son. 'You said you'd take me to Northleach,' Stephanie reminded Thea. 'Isn't that happening now?'

'I don't know. It might. I'll keep you posted.'

So Thea began with Caz Barkley. The young detective answered quickly, with undiluted friendliness. 'I was just thinking about you,' she said.

'Have there been any more developments?' asked Thea, putting great emphasis on the word as a tease. She still thought it had been a great exaggeration to use it for a crying child the day before.

'Nothing concrete. Interviews. Background searches. The DI is seeing the father again. I think they called the girlfriend back. I've been on the Internet all day up to now.'

'Did they find Jan and Nikola?'

'Who?'

'The Polish men who worked with Ollie – duh! Aren't they the main suspects?'

'They're not Polish, Thea. They're from the Ukraine and we interviewed them days ago. Didn't I tell you that? And they work on the fruit farm down near Chedworth with a whole lot of others. Mostly it's seasonal, but there are some who stay all the year round. They just hung out with Ollie in the evenings now and then.'

'No, not them,' said Thea impatiently. 'There's another pair who made films with Ollie. Ask Vicky. She told me about them.' A sudden sense of frustration and urgency gripped her. Had the police really been stupid enough to amalgamate the two lots of East Europeans?

'But they went back to Poland last week. Why would we want to talk to them?'

'I don't know – doesn't it seem suspicious to you? Why don't you think they could have killed him and then rushed off to Warsaw or wherever, where you'd never find them? At the very least, they'll know more than anyone else about the set-up in that house – how much time Ollie spent there and who else dropped in.' She paused. 'Why am I saying this to you when you must know it already?'

'Good question. I don't think either of us actually knows the whole story about that side of things. The Polish chaps are not on any lists of interesting persons, which is really all we need to know.'

'But – what if they arranged for someone else to kill Ollie, on their behalf? What if everything was planned down to the last detail, with their tracks cleverly covered?'

'As I understand it, there's no suggestion at all of anything like that.'

'Okay. So you *have* eliminated them, then.'

'Yes, in a way. You don't understand how it works. We're really not stupid, you know. And neither are Jan and Nikola, by all accounts – so you got that bit right. One of them is head of a film department at a big university and the other one's making a name as a director.'

'And Ollie did film editing and had a Muslim mother and only just missed being an Olympic high jumper,' Thea finished for her. 'I know that much, at least. Plus, he was or was not on any sort of drugs.'

'No, he was not. He might have smoked a bit of pot, and he wasn't teetotal, but not a hint of anything stronger. Any suggestion otherwise is definitely false.'

'It's all about the drugs,' said Thea, remembering her dream. 'It's got to be. That's the only part that makes absolutely no sense.'

'That doesn't make sense in itself.'

'Well I hope it isn't a secret any longer, because I think I might have mentioned it to Kevin Sinclair when I probably shouldn't have.'

Caz clicked her tongue, but did not sound too perturbed.

'I doubt if that did any harm. We think it's just a lot of hidebound villagers jumping to conclusions. When we ask them directly for evidence, they go all vague and say somebody told them that's what was going on, but personally they'd never been too sure about it.'

'Still peculiar, though. What about Hunter Lanning? He was so convinced when I saw him on Thursday. Not to mention Kevin Sinclair, of course.'

'Remind me. Who's Hunter Lanning?' Thea could almost hear the worried cogs turning in Caz's brain.

Thea made the same tongue-clicking sound as Caz had just done. 'He's a big man in town. I think I mentioned him to you yesterday, and you can't possibly have missed the fact of his existence. He's in charge of the committee. Wake up, Sergeant Barkley.'

The detective laughed, but Thea was aware that she might have gone too far. 'Right. Yes. Nobody seems to think he's important. I think DI Higgins might have interviewed him. We're not stupid, you know. Why do I have to keep saying that?'

'I never said you were. But I do think the Lanning man

237

could be significant. He knows everybody. Everybody knows him. He runs the *committee*. Didn't I tell you about him yesterday?' She was almost shouting.

'Thea – we don't interview the entire town, you know. We set up the incident room as close as we can get to the scene of crime, and mostly wait for people to come to us if they think they can be useful. Just for a few days. It'll be packing up tomorrow, I think. Other than that, we've spoken to the entire family, even the sister, who lives in Liverpool and is so disaffected she might not even come to Ollie's funeral.'

Thea savoured that fresh snippet for a moment, still feeling there'd been some oversight. 'I can't believe Hunter wouldn't present himself,' she insisted. 'He's that sort of person.'

'It's possible he did, but I don't recognise the name. Or I didn't – now, I think Higgins did speak to him, so you can stop nagging about him. I don't think you did mention him yesterday, actually.'

'Okay. So the sister – is she older or younger?'

'Oh Lord. You never stop, do you? I think she's younger. I think she was only a baby when the parents split up, and growing up with a single mother and a chaotic big brother was really no fun. She got out early and has hardly been back. These are just impressions from the briefing, remember. She gave a credible account of where she was last week, so she's also not interesting.'

'So – where has the investigation got to, then? It sounds to me as if you've crossed just about everybody off the list of suspects.' The question had been slow in coming, and she felt a bit silly leaving it so late. 'If I may ask.'

'Let's just say it's a bit sluggish. There's a mass of stuff to go through from the house – computers, phone and so forth, but nothing that really stands out as evidence. I was rather hoping you'd phoned to tell me you'd unearthed something new. I've learnt to assume you have, even when you don't bother to tell us about it.'

'Lucy Sinclair came here yesterday. She wanted to stay, but I made her go home.'

'Was that as unkind as it sounds?'

'Probably,' Thea admitted. 'I don't think I'm very good at hospitality.'

'But now she's in Northleach?'

'Right. And she could be hoping for a bit of police protection, because she's scared, although I got the impression she wasn't going to ask for it. She wouldn't say what she was frightened of. I told her everybody in town would be jittery and it was quite normal and she should face her fears. I mean, she lived down a farm track in a converted barn for years, all by herself. Even I found that scary, when I was there in the snow. She can't be a complete wimp if she coped with doing that.'

'I'll pass it on,' said Caz. 'Send someone to go and talk to her, maybe.'

'Yes,' said Thea, feeling a flicker of satisfaction that was not altogether benign. Lucy had not seemed too enthusiastic at the prospect of talking to the police. 'She can probably tell you quite a lot about Ollie, while you're at it.'

'Stepmother,' said the detective, after a tiny hesitation. 'What a family! I haven't met the father, but he sounds quite a case.'

'I've met him. And his current woman. They're very shocked – all over the place. I felt quite sorry for them.'

'But not for Lucy?'

'Not very. I can't see that she's lost anything – but Kevin's lost his child. Though I don't think he knew what he'd lost till it had gone – to quote the song.'

'What song?' said young Caz Barkley.

The conversation had done nothing to suggest what Thea should do next. The afternoon still lay before her, with all the nagging stereotypes of family life falling away. Timmy was not in the mood for a board game. Drew was still tinkering with his paperwork, which included bank statements, and eyeing the phone as if willing it to ring. 'What if there are no more funerals all week?' he said. 'It might well go like that.'

'Take the chance to catch up with other stuff,' said Thea. 'You could even go and see your mother. You'll have to do that soon, or she'll be wanting to come here again.' The family was still shuddering from a visit several weeks ago. Drew's mother had almost forgotten about him for years, especially after he married Thea – but then resurfaced eager to make up for lost time, when her husband died. It had been Drew's father, apparently, who maintained the distance from his son, in some mangled psychological problem he had with the fact of funerals and undertaking. As it turned out, he was buried in a North Country field very much like Drew's burial ground. 'He wanted it all kept very simple,' said his widow.

'She'll insist on coming at Easter, anyway,' Drew argued.

'I thought that was all fixed.'

'It probably is,' said Thea. 'But I live in hope. Caz and I just decided that I'm a very poor hostess. Inhospitable.'

'I've known worse,' said Drew comfortably.

Now she hung around in his office, liking to be with him, whatever he was doing. She enjoyed watching him being methodical, which he generally was, while conducting a dilatory conversation. She had no reason to be anywhere else, after all. Drew was easy company, easily pleased and slow to complain. 'Any thoughts about tomorrow?' she asked him idly.

He shook his head. 'I wasn't sure we were in any position to make plans, with things so unpredictable down in Northleach. I did wonder if you'd like us all to go there for lunch in one of the pubs. That would make a change.'

'Oh! Really? Gosh!' She savoured the suggestion, once she'd recovered from the surprise. 'That would be great. Not The Wheatsheaf, though. I get the feeling it's not really us.' She pushed aside thoughts of the chicken she had just bought at the supermarket, and the inevitability of roast Sunday lunch and hardly anything else on most pub menus the following day. 'I wonder if there's anyone doing a carvery,' she mused. That would be a compromise she could cheerfully live with. 'I'll check the websites and see.'

Five minutes later she reported that The Sherborne Arms would most likely be their best bet. 'Nothing at all pretentious about it,' she concluded. 'And they're fine with dogs.'

'That's most likely the one in the sitcom I was telling you about. Maybe we should try and find it later on, and watch one or two episodes.'

241

'Good idea.' She was still wondering how she had failed to notice him watching a Cotswolds-based comedy series, and assumed she must have been lost in a book, ignoring the TV, which would not be unusual. 'You mean doing the iPlayer thingy?'

'Don't pretend you can't manage that. It's pathetically simple.'

'I wasn't,' she said. Her technophobia had long ago ceased to amuse Drew or his children, so she was making a bigger effort to move with the times. To date, she was only about ten years behind everybody else.

The prospect of going back to Northleach accompanied by husband, children and dog made her uneasy. Would they just wander up and down the main street? Would she show them where the murder had taken place? No way did she want to bump into Lucy Sinclair, which would mean parking at the further end of town, and not walking along West End at all. The church would have a service on, most likely – though not in the afternoon. Drew was trying to take an interest and involve himself in her main preoccupation of the moment, but it was sadly misplaced – and she could not tell him so. Stephanie had already said she wanted to go there, after all. She might even have put the idea into her father's head. There was, however, the Coln Valley nearby, with a string of enchanting little villages that nobody had heard of. Winson, Ablington, Yanworth, and then the very famous Bibury. The whole area was strewn with big beautiful houses, lovingly built and carefully preserved. Gardens, rivers, sudden vistas – the whole works in one small stretch of English countryside.

'We can go for a long walk after having lunch,' she said. 'But only if Timmy can say that poem right through, and Stephanie finishes her botany project.'

'That's all sorted, then,' said Drew with an expression not far off complacency.

She made a conscious effort to dispel all thoughts of murder from her mind for the rest of Saturday. She had done it at Christmas, with moderate success, and that had been a killing within walking distance of the house. Northleach was twenty miles away – surely it could be out of mind? But it seemed not. Questions would not be repressed. What was Ollie really like? That was the main one. You should always start with a close analysis of the victim, but that was far from easy when you'd never met him. Not for the first time, she appreciated the magnitude and complexity of the task facing the police when trying to make sense of such a crime. However diligently you questioned those who knew the dead man, some of them would lie, some would forget and some would simply get it all wrong, with the best of intentions. For example, this bizarre insistence that Ollie Sinclair was addicted to drugs, when Thea was now fully persuaded that he never was. So who could have told such a powerful lie to the man's father that he clung to the belief so tenaciously? It had to be more than an idle rumour.

Kevin Sinclair was the person who kept recurring to her, as the one she should talk to again. She was uneasy with the way she had behaved with him on Friday, when he so badly wanted her input. He had seemed so genuinely bewildered, with his woman not helping very much, that Thea had not known what to say. In her experience, a great deal took place in the heart and mind of a newly bereaved person over the early days of the loss. Disbelief, denial, rage, guilt, despair, detachment, blame and bewilderment were just a few of the stages a person went through. Kevin might well be a different man on Saturday from the figure he had cut on Friday.

She had forgotten where he lived, but she knew it wasn't Northleach. She tried to recall any hints, but all she could remember was that he drove a lorry. His first wife, Sayida, was also in the area somewhere, but Thea couldn't remember whether Vicky had named the place. Cotswolds villages and small towns numbered in the hundreds – or over one hundred, anyway. There were many names Thea still had never heard, and Drew was even less well-versed than she was. And neither of them could say for certain whether Winchcombe was north or south of Stow, or Moreton-in-Marsh east or west of the Slaughters. They were constantly consulting maps, until Thea suggested they pin one up on the wall somewhere and try to learn it by heart. The only one in the family who seemed to have a natural grasp of the layout was Timmy, because he was keen on the ancient pathways and canals.

But She Who Knocks on Doors knew her limitations. She could not capriciously approach Kevin or Sayida or, really, anyone else, the way things stood. The police were deeply into their investigation, with their background searches and lengthy interviews. Caz had told her almost nothing when she phoned, but focused on learning what Thea might have discovered. Only if specifically requested to act as an informal investigator – and given an address – could she knock on any more doors. It felt like a dead end, with not so much as a hint of a suspicion as to by whom, or why, or even *when* the killing of Ollie had been perpetrated.

It was Stephanie who broke the blockage down, without meaning to. Tired of her homework she had begun checking out some YouTube offerings, sitting with her tablet in the living room. Thea and Drew had both insisted she do all her online activities in plain view, to avoid the more obvious hazards associated with it. 'We still can't know everything she's doing,' said Drew. 'She could be being bullied right under our noses. Or groomed.'

'Unlikely,' said Thea. 'Though it might be easier if *she* was doing the bullying.'

'What? My perfect daughter? What are you saying?'

'We have to be prepared for anything,' she had teased.

'This Oliver Sinclair,' Stephanie said now, out of the blue. 'He was very handsome, wasn't he?'

'Pardon? How do you know that?'

'He's trending. Gone viral, pretty much. There's a film of him doing his high jumping. And a whole lot about his life.'

'Of course there is,' said Thea, feeling old and foolish. 'I saw some of it.'

So Stephanie showed her a vast gallery of images, and a Wikipedia entry she had somehow managed to miss, and pages of condolences from athletes she had never heard of. Being dead, especially by mysterious and violent means, evidently brought you to extreme Internet prominence, however obscure you might have been in life. And Ollie had not exactly been obscure, Thea was beginning to realise.

'Fancy you being right there, in the middle of it all!' Stephanie marvelled. 'And we had his mother here in the house. That's awesome.'

'Stepmother, actually. Not even that, probably, now she's divorced from his father. I don't know if it still counts then.'

Stephanie gave Thea a worried look. 'Does that mean you'd just forget about me and Tim if you left Dad? Wouldn't you be our stepmother any more?'

'I'm not leaving Dad. You've got me for life,' said Thea lightly.

'I want to go there,' said the child earnestly. 'I want to *see* it all.'

'We are going tomorrow. All of us.'

'Are we?' Stephanie frowned. 'Why?'

'Well . . .' It was a good question, on consideration. 'I think Dad wants to take an interest in where I've been most of the week. He wants to see for himself.'

'No,' said Drew's devoted daughter. 'He doesn't really. He just thinks *you* want to go, so he says he'll go with you – to be nice. You should tell him he doesn't have to. We can go now, just you and me. There's time, isn't there?'

'Not really. Not if I'm going to produce a decent supper for everybody. It's three o'clock already.' Stephanie rolled her eyes, which made Thea think she ought to take the idea more seriously. 'And anyway, what would we do there? There's not really anything to see. I've wasted enough petrol driving there and back so many times.'

'But you were going to go again tomorrow.' The logic was unarguable. 'Which would be sillier than us going now.

Dad and Tim would just be in the way. Hepzie as well. You can't be a proper detective with a dog to consider.'

'It'll be dark before we know it.'

'It won't. We're on British Summer Time now, remember. It'll be light until after six.'

'That still doesn't give us much time. An hour or so, that's all.'

'More than that,' Stephanie asserted confidently. 'If we go right away.'

'But Steph, it's bonkers. What do you think will happen when we get there? For a start, I definitely don't want to bump into Lucy again. I was already working out how we could avoid her tomorrow. *Nobody's* going to be pleased to see me, come to think of it.'

Stephanie was again attending to her tablet, looking for more information. 'It says he was an instructor, making films about high jumping for schools and clubs and stuff. It doesn't say he lived in Northleach, though. There's a person here says he was a neighbour, but he's put Minchinhampton for where he's from.'

'I know. I mean – I know he just rented the Northleach house, to work in. So what?' Stephanie's dawning detective skills were beginning to seem alarming. Drew was never going to approve. There were ominous echoes of that boy Ben Harkness who had worked such magic in Barnsley the previous year.

'So where *did* he live? Why does everybody seem so sure the murderer is in Northleach, when he knew people all over the world?'

'Probably because he was killed in Northleach. Who else

247

knew he would be there? A local person could just come and go without attracting any attention. And because the entire town thought he and his friends were drug addicts and they wanted to get rid of them.'

'They thought wrong, didn't they?'

'Apparently. That's the weirdest thing about the whole case. Especially as his own father seems to have believed it.'

Stephanie's eyes widened, not so much at the information itself but because her stepmother was so freely disclosing it. Almost without knowing it, Thea was treating her as a fellow detective and she was thrilled. 'His own father!' she repeated.

Thea's eyes were half closed, as she tried to keep pace with her thoughts. 'It was as if he *needed* to believe it,' she said slowly. 'For his own peace of mind.'

'That's *very* weird,' Stephanie agreed.

'Well, what about this . . . What if Kevin had been a really bad father, never seeing his son, never trying to find out if he was okay, off with his other women and driving his lorry and generally pleasing himself . . .'

'Like Grandma,' said Stephanie, thinking of the way Drew's mother had been absent from their lives for years.

'A bit, yes. But Kevin would say he had good reason, because there's nothing you can do with a drug addict. They won't let you help them, and they tell lies and steal your money and give the family a bad name.'

Stephanie laughed. 'Are you trying to put me off ever taking drugs?'

'Only incidentally. I expect I'm exaggerating, but that is more or less what people think – isn't it? I bet they tell you all the same stuff at school. Just Say No, and all that.'

'More or less,' Stephanie agreed. 'Go on about the Sinclair family.'

'Okay. So, what if Kevin absolutely can't cope with any suggestion that Ollie was actually a perfectly respectable person, well thought-of and making his way in life – everything a father could wish for? If he had to believe that instead of the drug thing, when it was too late to make amends, he'd be in an awful state. He'd refuse to believe it, because it would make him such an awful father. Even *more* awful, I mean.'

'I see. But what does this have to do with the murder?'

'I don't know. Except it does seem to mean that Kevin isn't the killer. Don't you think? Even if he wanted his son right out of his life, he wouldn't *kill* him. He'd have no reason to go that far.'

'Mm,' said Stephanie doubtfully. 'That's a bit too complicated for me. Some of it seems a bit back to front.'

'Real life can be like that,' said Thea. 'It's not at all like what you read in *Harry Potter*.'

'I never thought it was,' said Stephanie stiffly. 'It's not like *Frozen* or *Toy Story*, either, whatever Mr Ellis might say.'

'Who?'

'The PSE teacher at school. He thinks the whole of human existence can be summed up by *Toy Story 3*, just about.'

'Good Lord! Maybe I should watch it sometime, then.'

'Don't bother,' smiled Stephanie. 'It's just a film for little kids.'

'This is great. It's helping me think it all through, having somebody to bounce it off. Why don't we just keep doing this, without bothering to drive anywhere? Apart from anything else, I really don't think your father would approve of us going off without him.'

'Okay,' said Stephanie uncertainly. 'Would it be good to take some notes, do you think?'

Thea laughed. 'I'm always intending to do that, but it never really gets very far. Maybe you'll be better at it than me.'

'We can try.' The child gathered together an exercise book and pen, and turned to a fresh page. 'Where do we start?'

Thea stared at the blank paper, her mind as empty as the page. 'I don't know. With Ollie, I suppose.'

Stephanie made a neat heading, underlined, pen poised. They looked at each other and giggled. 'We must put something,' Stephanie urged.

'He was twenty-eight. His mother is from the Middle East somewhere. His father left her with two children and married Lucy, then left *her* and took up with Tessa. There might have been others in between. I get the impression he's not actually married to Tessa.'

'That's about Kevin, not Ollie,' Stephanie pointed out. But she wrote it down anyway.

'Ollie made films for YouTube or whatever it is now.'

'Still YouTube,' said the girl with a roll of her eyes. 'The people in Northleach – what about them? Did they all know him?'

'They knew Kevin. He came to Bobby Latimer's house,

even though she didn't know him or Tessa. And that's odd, when you think about it.'

'How do you spell Latimer?'

Thea was having new thoughts, making new connections. 'Why didn't all this strike me yesterday when I was telling Caz about it?' she muttered. 'She wasn't very interested in the neighbours.'

'Because they weren't *Ollie's* neighbours, were they?' asked Stephanie reasonably. 'Have I got that right?'

'You have, but I can't imagine how.'

'Google maps,' came the succinct reply. 'West End, High Street, East End. Very logical. Bypass. Old turnpike road. I do really want to see it all with my own eyes, though.'

'Well, we're not going today.'

'I realise that,' said Stephanie with a sigh.

Chapter Sixteen

It had been sheer delight to share all the Northleach observations with her stepdaughter. The questions she was required to think about were quite different from those asked by Caz Barkley, even though they were ostensibly aimed at the same final big one – who killed Ollie Sinclair? Caz had been satisfied with the simple fact that everybody in town knew everybody else, and had connections that went back for decades, if not longer. Even the Latimers, fresh from America a mere fifteen years ago – 'At a guess,' said Thea carefully. 'It might be rather less than that' – were thoroughly embedded into local networks. Stephanie wanted details, filling the page of her exercise book with names and ages and probable lines of enquiry. As Drew had been, she was intrigued by the committee, writing it in large letters in the middle of the page. 'That sounds as if it might be illegal,' she suggested. 'Hate speech. What if Ollie reported them, and they all got together to take their revenge on him?'

'Unlikely,' judged Thea, while enjoying the idea enormously.

It had gone on for over an hour. Tim and Drew had wandered into the room, one after the other, and been ignored. The dog tried to interpose itself between Thea and Stephanie, to be pushed rudely away. Only when the flights of fancy began to enter realms of extreme silliness did Thea bring it to a halt. 'Well, that's it,' she said. 'No more for today. Thanks, though – you've been a great help.'

'It was fun,' said Stephanie. 'Now I'm even more sure I want to join the police, like Jessica.' Jessica was Thea's grown-up daughter, recently promoted to the rank of police sergeant and aiming for the CID in another year or so. The stepsisters had become firm friends over Christmas, and Stephanie's ambition had been conceived.

'Could be worse,' said Thea, thinking a bit of variety might be preferable. Her first husband's brother was in the police as well. 'Although maybe you could consider tree surgery or something, as a second string?'

'Very funny,' said Stephanie.

Thea was preoccupied for another hour, niggling away at elusive ideas that arose from chance remarks that she could not precisely recall. Something about Faith-and-Livia, who Stephanie had called 'the witches' for no better reason than that Thea had mentioned that Livia had a long nose. The implication was that they had secrets that they withheld from the people of Northleach – 'It wouldn't be accurate to call it a community,' she told Stephanie. 'I don't think any of them care much for each other' – and that they didn't have very wholesome opinions about the world and its ways. 'They're fascists,' summarised Stephanie with a nod.

'Be careful about applying labels to people,' Thea told her, not for the first time.

When it came to Hunter Lanning, they found remarkably little to write down. 'He seems like the king of the town, and yet I know almost nothing about him,' admitted Thea. 'He's patronising, complacent – all that sort of stuff – but I think he's all talk.'

'But he's big and strong?'

'Yes, but . . .' And Thea could give no foundation for her conviction that the man was no murderer. 'It just seems too *obvious*, somehow. That sounds daft, I know – but I don't believe it could possibly have been him.'

Stephanie was tinkering with a tablet that was the joint property of the whole family, mainly used for checking websites. Drew consulted it every morning about the forthcoming weather. 'Here's Lucy Sinclair, look,' she announced suddenly. 'She's put herself at the top of a page about the history of Northleach. With a picture. Lots of pictures.'

'Let's see.' It was, Thea slowly realised, the website that Lucy had told her about, the one that had resulted in her becoming unpopular with the people of the village. One reason for that might well be that Lucy had given herself top billing as a local historian. A lot of densely packed information filled the page, with photographs of fields and old houses and prints from pre-photographic times. The main theme seemed to be wool and sheep and the arcane details of power struggles between various merchants and the peasantry. 'I'm not reading all this now,' said Thea. 'It looks a bit dull, actually.'

'I thought you liked history.'

'I do. I love it. But this is very badly done. The pictures don't match the text, and the dates are all over the place. Here's a bit about Kett's Rebellion, which was in the sixteenth century, all muddled up with how the church came to be built, with nothing to explain how they connect – if they do at all, which I doubt.'

'Isn't Lucy meant to be a computer wizard?'

'When I knew her before, she was a fixer, a techie. She mended people's computers. I suppose that doesn't mean she's good at websites. They're not at all the same thing.'

'No,' agreed Stephanie, with a little frown. 'Do you think the Northleach people *paid* her to do this?'

'That's a good question.' Thea looked at the child in admiration. 'Fancy you thinking of that.'

'Well – money's not very complicated, is it?' said Stephanie. 'Everybody wants it, so they fight over it, and it's quite often a reason for murdering someone.'

'So it is,' said Thea.

Mother and stepdaughter prepared supper in comparative harmony and Timmy recited his whole poem perfectly as the after-dinner entertainment. Everybody clapped. Then for good measure he gave a brief summary of the state of Iowa in relation to the rest of the country, and how only a minority of Americans could claim to have been there or even know exactly where it was. 'They mostly think it's further west than it is,' he explained.

'I'm impressed,' said Drew, and meant it.

A while later, he asked Thea, 'Are we going down to Northleach tomorrow, then?'

She had not been looking forward to this, and made a face accordingly. 'I'm not sure,' she began. 'I mean – I don't really see a lot of point in going to the actual town. I'd be happier if we went a bit further on, to the Coln Valley. I could show you where I stayed in Barnsley. You never did come to see me when I was there.'

'What about the pub? I thought it was just what we wanted. The Sherborne Arms – is that right?'

She nodded. 'It looks really nice,' she admitted. 'Better than the one in Barnsley, probably. The thing is, I don't want to bump into anybody I've been talking to, and that's quite a lot of people. Higgins is going to think I'm interfering.' She had another thought. 'The incident room was in the pub – they might not be open, because of that.'

'You're making excuses,' he said in surprise. 'What's the problem?'

'It's difficult to explain. Everything feels stuck, but also very delicate. I might say the wrong thing to the wrong person. I'm right out on the edge this time, and there's too much that I don't understand.'

'Oh, I dare say you understand more than you think,' he said, with the merest whiff of accusation. 'I'm still wondering why you wouldn't let that wretched woman stay last night.'

'What? Mainly because I thought it would annoy you, as it happens. Anyway, it must have turned out all right, or we'd have heard by now.'

'Heard if she'd been murdered in her bed, you mean?'

'Something like that,' said Thea lightly, with her fingers secretly crossed.

Nothing had been decided by the time the children were in bed, which Thea experienced as a real failure. The indecision was born of a reluctance to disappoint Drew and Stephanie, balanced against a worry that the police would never forgive her if she interrupted some careful strategy to ensnare the killer. All the police officers she knew constantly stressed the absolute necessity for evidence. It was entirely possible to know full well who had committed the crime, but unless they could prove it strongly enough to withstand the onslaught of clever defence lawyers, it was all a waste of time. Even a confession, caught on tape or signed in blood, was not enough without supporting evidence. As a layperson and an amateur, Thea was not constrained by the many limitations imposed on the police, but even she could not just poke a man in the chest and say '*J'accuse*.'

'Let's watch *This Country*, then,' said Drew. 'There's time for most of the first series.' And before Thea could reply he had clicked and toggled and produced the programme like magic.

It was undeniably Northleach in the very first scene. There was the bus shelter, large as life. But most of the action took place in a modern house that could be anywhere. There were few glimpses of the famous Cotswold stone, or the big church or anything else she recognised. Until towards the end of the series, when there was Kurtan standing in front of a house that was either Lucy's or one close to it. The whole thing was gone in seconds, but it gave Thea a jolt.

There had been little laugh-out-loud comedy to it, as far as she could see. It was actually very bleak and depressing and she wondered what Stephanie would make of it. She asked Drew if his daughter had seen it.

'Don't think so,' he said. 'I doubt if she'd like it.'

'She'd hate it,' said Thea with conviction. 'She'd say that life around here is nothing like that.'

'It is for some people,' said Drew.

'That line, early on, something about the locals having "utter hatred of each other" – that was a bit near the bone, don't you think?'

'You mean because one of them has actually murdered someone in real life and not on the telly?'

'Quite a few times, in fact,' said Thea. 'If you count the whole of the Cotswolds. And that vicar loves *Midsomer Murders*, remember.'

'I think that's quite funny,' said Drew.

'A bit obvious,' said Thea critically. 'And the bit where she lets the hamster die because she forgot about it. When she's babysitting people's pets, as they put it. I hope none of my clients thought that was a reference to me.'

'Not a chance,' said Drew. 'Don't take it so personally.'

'Huh,' said Thea.

'You're not meant to take it seriously, either. It's just a bit of fun.'

'You're right,' she said insincerely. She didn't think the

programme was actually intended to be fun. She thought it was very much darker than Drew would acknowledge. She wondered what the people of Northleach thought about it. Although the village wasn't named, several surrounding ones were, and it was clearly public knowledge that theirs was the chosen spot. At least there hadn't been any mention of drugs, which might have been a step too far for the residents. 'I like the vicar,' she added. 'He's the most realistic person in the whole thing.'

It was late by the time they'd watched every episode, and they scrambled up to bed without any further delay. 'Sunday tomorrow,' said Drew with a relieved sigh. 'And we still don't know what we'll be doing.'

'Sufficient unto the day,' said Thea, hoping he realised she was quoting her father. Her family was rich with sayings, whereas Drew's parents had apparently never coined phrases or bowdlerised existing ones. 'Who knows – you might get three new funerals again.'

At six the following morning, at least one part of Thea's prophecy came true. The phone rang and a nursing home reported a death. 'They want us to come before breakfast,' Drew told Thea. 'Apparently there's a scramble for the room, and they want everything cleared away instantly. It's just like old times.'

Thea was hazy about the details of the mainstream undertaker where Drew had learnt his craft, but she understood that, by comparison, his present operation was considered slow and sloppy. Nursing homes were notorious in wanting their dead removed quickly, and were not always sympathetic towards the Slocombe limitations. Several times Drew had had to recruit families in his support, who willingly resisted the unseemly rush on his behalf. He had grown adept at shaming the care home into admitting that it really wouldn't do any harm to wait a day or two. They all had a room somewhere to accommodate a deceased resident in some degree of dignity.

But this one was adamant. There were special circumstances. And, they threatened, if Drew couldn't do it, they would have to ask someone else. The deceased person in question had expressed a general sort of wish for a natural burial, but nothing was in writing. They had only come to him because he was the closest geographically.

'Is Andrew any better?' Thea asked. 'I forgot to enquire about him yesterday.'

'He's still delicate, but he says he can drive. Not that that's much use. It's carrying and lifting I need him for.'

'This is déjà vu,' she pointed out. 'It's last week all over again. We can't go on like this indefinitely. You'll have to find another person, if he's not better soon.'

'I know. Andrew knows as well. He feels awful about it. But he insists it'll get better before long and he'll be fine.'

'I wonder. It's going on rather a long time. Maybe there's something more serious the matter with him. Either that or he's just being a wimp.'

Drew gave her a very severe look. 'I'll pretend I didn't hear that. More likely there is something more serious wrong with him, that the doctors can't find.'

Thea had experience of people with bad backs, and the capricious nature of their sufferings. Doctors were very often no help at all. 'But you told them you'd come, did you? The nursing home, I mean.'

'I did. Luckily it's like the one last week – a small person, and there's a couple of strong nurses willing to help. The real problem is that it makes me look so amateurish.'

'Make a virtue of it,' said Thea. 'I told you that before.'

'I'll try,' he said meekly.

The phone call and subsequent conversation roused Stephanie, but not Timmy. When Drew was in the bathroom, the child went to ask Thea what was happening. 'He's got a removal,' she said from under the duvet. 'It's a nursing home that won't wait.'

'Mean things.'

'My thoughts exactly. Do you want to snuggle in with me for a bit? We don't have to get up yet.'

At twelve, Stephanie was very close to being too old for such intimacies, but nobody had said so yet. Thea was pleased at the level of acceptance it represented, when one heard such awful stories about stepfamilies. Whilst *snuggle* might be overstating it, they lay comfortably side by side, chatting quietly. Drew pulled an exaggerated expression of envy when he came back to get dressed.

'All right for some,' he said.

'I dreamed about Hepzie catching the murderer,' said Stephanie, when he'd gone. 'She was with a whole lot of little kids, and they were running across a field after him.'

'Did they catch him?'

'I don't know. It never seemed to get anywhere. Like in the *Alice* books – just a lot of running. Probably that's where

261

the dream came from, actually.' Stephanie was profoundly attached to the works of Lewis Carroll.

'Could you see who it was that they were chasing?'

Stephanie laughed. 'You think I dreamed the answer to the murder, so we can just tell the police who to arrest? No, sorry. The person didn't have a face – just straggly hair and big boots.'

'I think I dreamed about small children as well,' Thea remembered. 'A girl. I told you about Millie Latimer, didn't I? I think it might have been her in my dream.'

'The one who knew Ollie,' Stephanie nodded. 'I made a note of her name – and her father's. We didn't really go over her whole family, though.'

There was a reason for that, which Thea did not explain. The slight suspicion that there could have been something unwholesome in Ollie Sinclair's interest in the very young children at a local private school rang inevitable alarm bells – which she had not wanted to repeat to a twelve-year-old. There was a convoluted and unlikely scenario in which the outraged father, learning of something along those lines, had taken it upon himself to remove Ollie from the picture. It seemed very likely that this line of thinking lay behind her dream.

'When will Dad be back?' It was Timmy in the doorway, with rumpled hair and eyes still crusty with sleep.

'Probably in an hour or a bit less,' Thea told him. 'Did you hear him go?'

'No, but I saw the van was gone, from my window. And then I heard you two talking.' He cast a wistful look at the bed. Thea felt a pang of remorse at the way the little boy had been excluded, while knowing it was really nobody's fault. To some extent, over the years, this had been the story of his life. His mother had been struck down when he was still little more than a baby and he had no memory of her as the energetic campaigner she had once been. Lingering in a very much reduced state over the next few years, her image in Timmy's memory was of somebody who read him a lot of stories, went to bed very early and did not always understand things very well. Whilst Thea was entirely acceptable, she would never fully replace his mother – and getting into bed with her would never feel right.

'We'd better get up,' Thea announced. 'I have a feeling it's going to be a busy day.'

The feeling was strengthened when a second phone call came at eight o'clock, ten minutes after Drew finally presented himself for breakfast. 'I don't believe it,' he said. 'It's a conspiracy.'

This time the call was from a GP who had just attended a death at home. And this time there was no special hurry, although the new widow wanted to speak to him that day, to discuss her options for the burial. And if it was all the same to him, could Drew perhaps manage the removal before nightfall? There would be a sturdy nephew on call to help him, if necessary. 'She just *offered*,' marvelled Drew to Thea. 'I didn't even have to ask. The GP just came out with it.' He paused. 'I bet she'd heard through the grapevine from the nursing home or one of last week's funerals that I'm short-handed. That's not going to be good for my image.'

'I told you before, not to worry about that,' Thea

advised. 'Have you ever met this family?'

Drew didn't even have to think. All his clients, whether waiting for their demise or already buried in his field, were engraved on his memory. 'A year ago. He's done well to last as long as he did. They're nice people.'

'You always say that,' Stephanie reminded him.

'Yes, well. People nearly always *are* nice, when somebody dies. It makes them think about their behaviour, and they make more of an effort to be pleasant – when it's too late, you might say.'

Thea cast her mind over the people in Northleach, wondering whether she had only seen them at their best, once Ollie's body had been found. The theory did not hold up very well, she decided.

'When will you go for him?' Thea asked.

'This afternoon, I suppose. I'm to phone the wife at ten o'clock and we can agree a time then.'

'So if we were all to go out for the day, we'd have from about half past ten to mid afternoon?'

'Something like that,' he agreed distractedly.

'Hm,' she said.

'So what are we doing about lunch?' asked Stephanie, pragmatically. 'Are we going to a pub or what?'

'We are,' said Drew. 'I'm still in the mood for spending, after such a busy week. Especially as we've got work for next week now, as well.' As a rough rule of thumb, Drew reckoned to make about five hundred pounds clear on every funeral he performed. With an average of eighteen or twenty a month, the family income was more than adequate. But the sheer unpredictability of it was the main problem, as he regularly pointed out.

Thea and Stephanie were reading each other's minds. *Make something happen!* they were both inwardly shouting. There were people to question, mysteries to be solved, dreams to interpret and here they were in limbo, unable to plan their day. Timmy ate his Cheerios obliviously, and Drew tried to juggle competing priorities. Outside there was no sign of the sun.

'It's not a very nice day,' Thea observed. 'Looks windy.'

'Blustery showers,' Stephanie predicted, having consulted the tablet. 'Just how Hepzie likes it.' It was true – the spaniel went manic when the wind lifted her long ears and made her feel she was flying.

'I'm going to phone Caz,' Thea announced, all of a sudden.

'Half past eight on a Sunday morning?' Drew queried. 'She won't thank you. What are you going to say?'

'I'm going to say we have a whole family sitting here ready and willing to assist the police investigation in any way she can suggest. She might have a long list of ideas.'

'I can't imagine what,' said her husband, with a long-suffering smile. 'And I have to request that you do not include me in your offer. We all know I'm hopeless at that sort of thing.'

'Don't let Maggs hear you say that,' Stephanie protested. 'She can tell a whole lot of stories about how you solved the killing of that woman in the Peaceful Repose field – remember?'

'She exaggerates. And don't pretend you can remember, because you weren't even a year old.'

'And Den says the same. When there was that little girl covered in bees.' Stephanie shivered. 'That was horrible.'

'It was. And he never should have told you about it.'

'I never really heard the details,' said Stephanie.

'Nor did I,' Thea realised. 'It was all before my time.'

'It all began when I got the job with Plants, all those years ago. I was twenty-six or thereabouts. It was a baptism of fire. They teased me mercilessly.'

'Twenty-six!' Thea tried to visualise it. 'And you were a nurse before that?'

'Yes. They called me "Nurse Drew". Some very antediluvian attitudes prevailed amongst some of those men. And my own father wasn't much better.'

'I thought it was the undertaking he didn't like.'

'That was the final straw. He never got over the idea of a male nurse, either. He wanted me to be an accountant. I think he kept expecting me to see sense and mend my ways.'

'Hopeless,' sighed Thea. 'Why are we being so nostalgic, all of a sudden?'

'It was me,' said Stephanie. 'I like hearing these stories. We don't do it often enough.'

'It's a Sunday thing,' said Thea. 'Nothing so evocative as an English Sunday.'

'Not these days,' Drew argued. 'Most things just carry on the same as every other day.'

'Which means I can phone Caz with impunity,' Thea decided.

Chapter Seventeen

It was still not quite nine o'clock when Kate Temperley came to the door. Drew opened it, and cocked his head in half recognition. 'Hello?' he said. 'Haven't I seen you before?'

'You buried my grandfather eight months ago,' she confirmed. 'Sorry if this is outrageously early. It's actually your wife I wanted to see.'

'Okay,' said Drew slowly, unable to hide his bewilderment. 'She's right here.'

Before Drew could call her, Thea came unobtrusively out of the kitchen, assuming the visitor was there on funeral business. 'No – I came to see you,' the woman insisted, when Thea tried to go upstairs. 'My name is Kate Temperley. I'm a staff nurse at the John Radcliffe. I spoke to you on the phone.'

'Did you? What about?' Her mental cogs only then began to connect. 'Oh – about Lucy Sinclair, was it?'

'That's right. It was my uncle who drove her home. Except she wasn't going home, was she? She came here instead. I've been thinking about it ever since he told me. Something's not right,' she finished, clasping her hands together in an attitude of disquiet. 'I know I shouldn't be here. everything's so confidential nowadays, I'm not really allowed to say anything at all. But I can't rest until I talk to someone. We can say I came about my grandad, if anybody asks. A tree for his grave or something.'

'No problem,' said Thea, who regarded data protection laws as the work of the devil. 'Come and sit down somewhere.'

There followed a hesitant story about Lucy Sinclair's collapse on the morning of her scheduled operation. 'She came in very early, as arranged, and we did all the pre-op business. She seemed very stressed, as people usually do. Especially with backs. Brains and backs frighten patients more than anything.'

'Understandably,' said Thea.

'I know. Now I must make it clear that I did not personally witness what happened next, but what I gather – and what it says in her notes – is that she simply lost consciousness about a minute after the first of the sedatives went in, so everyone assumed it was an allergic reaction. But I'm thinking it might have been just psychosomatic.' She put a hand to her mouth. 'I shouldn't say *just*,' she corrected herself. 'But you know what I mean. Extreme emotional overload. Her mind using her body to get out of having the operation.'

Thea regarded the woman pensively. In her early thirties, plump, open-faced and guileless, she seemed to have no ulterior motives in making this visit other than a need to voice her concerns. 'That worries you, does it?' she asked. 'Enough for you to drive over here on your day off?'

'It did when my uncle told me what happened on Friday. I can't stop thinking about it.'

'Oh?' Thea was only then becoming aware of all the questions she had never thought to ask Lucy. About her connection with Vicky, for one. And exactly how she had persuaded Hunter Lanning to drive her to Oxford so early on Wednesday morning.

'She was making phone calls for most of the way, and after the last one, she changed her mind about going home. She made him bring her here instead. He said it was the call that did it. Her voice got all shrill and it was obvious she was scared of something. "I can't go back there now," she told him. "So where do you want me to take you?" he asked her. It took her a minute to decide on Chipping Campden. Then she made him put her down by the church, and said she'd go and have some lunch at a hotel or somewhere. He didn't mind – it was only a bit further for him to drive. But he was worried about just dropping her in the street like that. He's very conscientious.'

'He sounds sweet,' said Thea.

'He's the kindest man in the world. He tried asking her what the problem was, and whether she ought to call the police if she felt threatened, but she said she'd be all right here with you.'

'I made her go home,' said Thea with a grimace. 'I thought she was just being paranoid.'

'When? On Friday?'

'That's right. I did mention it to a police detective, so they've probably been keeping an eye on her. We'd have heard if anything bad had happened. Really, I think you can put your mind at rest about her. It sounds to me as if she'd got herself seriously worked up about the operation, and it all stems from that.'

The nurse tilted her head sceptically. 'It would be easier to think that – but then I started wondering how you come into it. I mean, are you a close friend or what? You didn't drive her in or come to collect her. You wouldn't let her stay the night here. And I'm getting a feeling that you don't even like her very much.'

All good questions, Thea acknowledged. 'She wanted me to guard her house,' she said, anticipating the response that came all too predictably.

'But *why*? What was she afraid of?'

'She said she didn't trust the neighbours. They didn't get on, and she seemed to think they might damage her property somehow. I house-sat for her before, when she lived in Hampnett. Now she's in the middle of Northleach.'

'Where there's been a murder,' said Kate Temperley heavily. 'Of somebody with the same surname as her. So perhaps it's not very surprising that she's scared – don't you think?'

'I was assuming that most people in Northleach are fairly scared,' said Thea. 'There's been so much media coverage of the murder, and so little progress by the police, that they must all be feeling twitchy.'

'But Mrs Sinclair's *related* to him – the boy who was killed. That must make it far worse.'

'He wasn't a boy,' Thea corrected her. 'And he wasn't a blood relation. He was the son of her ex-husband, and it doesn't sound as if she had much to do with him.'

'Is that what she told you?'

'She didn't tell me anything much. Ollie's girlfriend was a lot more forthcoming. Honestly, I know hardly anything useful. I've met her neighbours and a few other people – and Ollie's father. He's the most important one, I suppose.' She was going over it again as she spoke, wondering whether the killer could be anyone she'd met, and whether Lucy Sinclair was justified in feeling so apprehensive. She watched Kate's face as her thoughts swirled. 'Actually, I'm not at all sure why you've come like this. What do you want me to do?'

'I think I want you to understand why I'm so worried about her. Nobody at the hospital is bothered – except over the fact that she wasted a theatre slot, and Mr Mehta was furious. There wasn't time to move everybody up or call someone else in. They're gold dust, you know.'

'Sorry? What are?'

'Chances to have him do your surgery. His waiting list is enormous. Nobody just drops out like she did.'

'She didn't do it on purpose.'

'No,' said Kate Temperley slowly and unconvincingly. 'I don't expect she did.'

It still wasn't entirely clear what she wanted Thea to do, other than simply listen, but there was a dawning inkling that the idea was for her to go to Lucy's house and make sure she was all right. This became increasingly definite, until the woman said so in as many words. 'I mean – *I* can't go, can I? What would I say to her?' was the disarming cry.

Thea understood the irony of the situation. She and Stephanie did want to go to Northleach, but under no circumstances did they want to meet Lucy. At least Thea didn't. All she really wanted was to be in the centre of the action, prepared for anything, standing by for a call from Higgins or Barkley as they followed leads or had sudden insights. Being stuck out in Broad Campden with nothing to do made her seem irrelevant and useless in her own eyes. And the link, of course, was Lucy Sinclair. Lucy was her introduction to the town and its people. Visiting her was the only viable pretext for going there again.

'All right,' she said. 'I'll go down again and make sure she's all right. Probably later this morning.'

'Thank you,' said Kate Temperley. 'That makes me feel a lot better.'

'Good,' said Thea, while wondering at the ease with which the woman had dumped all her worries squarely in the lap of a sadly unreliable house-sitter – who had so meekly accepted them. Kindness must be catching, she thought foolishly.

'We'll go at eleven,' she told everyone. 'You lot can go exploring while I talk to Lucy.' She cringed inwardly at the prospect, so soon after making every effort to avoid the woman. The exercise was already appearing futile, or worse.

'I'm not coming,' said Drew, as if reminding her of an established fact.

'Oh! But there'll be plenty of time for you to remove that man when we get back.'

'That remains to be seen. In my experience, life can become very unpredictable when you're on one of your murder quests. I think you should leave the children and the dog here, and do whatever it is you think you have to, on your own.'

'No – I want to come,' Stephanie protested.

'And me,' said Timmy, with much less certainty.

'Damn it,' said Thea to the room in general. 'When did it all get so complicated?'

'About four days ago, at a guess,' said Drew. 'I'd rather you didn't take anyone with you.'

'Dad! Don't be so mean,' Stephanie reproached him. 'We don't have to take Timmy, but I'm definitely going.' *So there* rang silently through the room.

'Maybe I won't go after all, then,' said Thea. 'I can leave it till tomorrow.' Then she remembered. 'No, I can't. It's the holidays. I've got you two here for two whole weeks.' She gave a melodramatic sigh. 'God help me.'

It was all still up in the air when Thea's phone jiggled with an incoming text.

CAN YOU MEET ME TODAY AWAY FROM NORTHLEACH? I NEED TO TALK TO SOMEONE. BOBBY.

'Well, that's that, then,' said Thea. 'I for one am going to Northleach – or somewhere near it. Now.' She texted a reply without any further discussion.

HOW ABOUT THE HAMPNETT CHURCH AT 11.30? T.

PERFECT. THERE'S NO SERVICE THERE TODAY. BOBBY.

Only then did Thea convey to her family what had been arranged. They all stared at her, wondering how it affected them, each with a difference conclusion.

'What about me?' said Timmy.

'What about Lucy?' said Stephanie.

'What about lunch?' said Drew.

'It's only ten now. I'll make something quickly before I go. Stephanie – you can come with me. You might have to amuse yourself for a bit while I talk to this woman, but we can do some exploring as well. Timmy, you can decide whether to come or go. It's up to you. I'm easy either way.'

'He'll have to go with you,' said Drew. 'I might have to go out before you get back, and he can't stay here on his own.'

'I can, Dad,' said the nine-year-old.

'You can't,' said Drew with utter finality. He looked hard at Thea. 'Why does everything have to be so *dramatic*?' he complained. 'People having secret meetings, playing childish games. Hasn't this woman got a husband? And children? What's the matter with her?'

Thea thought wistfully of the Drew of only two or three days ago, who professed himself eager to hear all the details, to be included and kept informed. That person had disappeared, to be replaced by a tight-mouthed judge,

274

who clearly thought himself considerably more mature and sensible than anyone else in his immediate circle. 'What do husbands and children have to do with anything?' she asked.

'I think you already know the answer to that.'

'Oh, Drew,' she sighed. 'Let's not go through all this again. Isn't it enough that I'm wanted by someone in Northleach? First Lucy, then Caz, now Bobby – they all think I have something to offer. They think I can be useful or sympathetic or . . .' She couldn't think of words for the other ways in which she might be appreciated. Just being on the spot, providing a watching eye or an intelligent insight at a crucial moment. Things she had done before, and which she did not like to boast about. She had gained a strange and not always accurate reputation amongst the Cotswolds villages, which served a purpose of its own that went beyond any present action. A murderer might hesitate, a witness might drop a hint, a suspect might reveal an exculpatory secret – all because it was Thea Slocombe who was on the scene. She was known to be fearless, clever and often illogical. She kept people off balance. Not least her own husband, she admitted to herself.

'It's what she *does*, Dad,' said Stephanie, effortlessly summarising the situation.

Drew and Thea both laughed, the tension instantly defused. Timmy looked confused, while Stephanie squared her shoulders and repeated, 'But what about Lucy? You told the nurse you'd go and see that she was all right.'

Thea also squared her shoulders. 'We can do that as well. I'll peel some potatoes now, and get some mince out

275

of the freezer, and get some lunch going. Drew – you can finish it off. Just mash the potatoes, add some onions and tomatoes and stick it all in the oven. Why am I telling you this?' she interrupted herself wildly. 'You're a grown man. Get your own lunch.' She playfully punched him on the shoulder. 'What am I thinking?'

'I can do it, if you let me stay here,' offered Timmy. 'I know how.'

'He does,' Stephanie confirmed. 'He did it in cooking at school, remember?'

'Stop!' commanded Drew. 'This is getting out of control. I refuse to leave Tim here alone, if I'm called out.'

'So take him with you. Tell the people they'll have to wait. Call Fiona. There are any number of options. Stop being pathetic,' said Thea, already reverting to impatience and something even darker. 'Just listen to yourself.'

'Mr Shipley would have him,' said Stephanie quietly. 'He wants to teach him how to play chess.'

'Cool!' said Timmy, enjoying being at the centre of attention.

Thea and Stephanie drove off at ten-twenty, leaving their menfolk to argue over lunch. 'As if it matters,' grumbled Thea. 'Nobody's going to starve, are they?'

'Poor Dad,' said Stephanie. 'He's probably tired after going out so early this morning.'

'I forgot about that,' Thea admitted. 'It seems ages ago now. So, listen. We'll go to Lucy's first, and just make sure she's all right. I might tell her about the nurse being worried. She didn't tell me not to. We'll only stay a few minutes and then go to Hampnett. It's a lovely church, by the way. There are very unusual decorations all over the walls. All a bit bonkers, really. You can look at them while I talk to Bobby. She might not want you listening in.' Thea had been worrying about the possible direction the talk might take, ever since getting Bobby's text. But she was confident that it would all work out somehow. Things usually did. This time, with Stephanie at her side, it was crucial to be careful and clever and possibly even kind.

'What are we going to say to her?' the young girl asked in the car.

'I don't know. It's going to be a bit embarrassing, I expect. We probably shouldn't explain about the nurse, if we can help it. I'll say I felt bad about Friday, and that you wanted to have a look round Northleach, and I've got a little job to do a mile away, so we thought we should make sure she's all right. Does that sound okay?'

'More or less,' said Stephanie.

The roads were reasonably clear and Thea drove fast until they were passing Sezincote. 'We must come here one day and look round,' she said. 'Isn't the view amazing?' In fact, the view was not at its best under low cloud. It was another disappointing day as far as weather was concerned.

'I'm not sure I really get views,' said Stephanie. 'I mean what are you meant to *look* at? Is it just that we're supposed to get excited because we can see a long way?'

'That's pretty much it, really. There comes a moment in your life when something suddenly clicks and you understand why it's special. I watched Jocelyn's Noel, when he was younger than you, on a day out in Somerset. Near Glastonbury. There's a tor that rises out of flat meadows, and somehow we'd got to a spot where it's framed by trees, and that boy just stood there with his mouth open. Transfixed. It was magic.'

'I must be a slow developer,' sighed Stephanie.

'Not at all. I think I was at least seventeen before it happened to me.'

The last part of the drive was taken up by reminiscences from Thea about the many small villages she had known, close to the A429. 'I have a lot of associations with this road,' she concluded. 'They get stronger every time I come down here.'

'All those people!' Stephanie marvelled. 'You must know nearly everybody in the Cotswolds.'

Thea was reminded of her surprise encounter with Priscilla Heap in Northleach on Friday. 'I do know a lot,' she agreed. 'I bump into them now and then. In fact, I saw one only two days ago. The trouble is, I mostly knew them when something horrible had happened, which means they're not always very friendly towards me.'

'Like Lucy.'

'Oh dear – I suppose that's right. Like Lucy.'

But Lucy Sinclair was surprisingly amiable when she answered their knock, although she did not invite them in and her face looked as if she had not slept for days. Thea glanced up and down the street, feeling awkward and conspicuous. People might think she and Stephanie were Jehovah's Witnesses, she thought wildly. And what did it matter if they did, came a reassuring voice.

'Come to check up on me?' It was said with a smile. 'Well, everything's fine. I was just having a wobble on Friday. Hunter even came to see me yesterday, and gave me some chocolates. I can't imagine why, but it was friendly of him. Hunter never was the problem, really,' she added in a low voice.

There was a note of defiance that Thea found unsettling. It seemed entirely out of character for Lucy to stand in full view of the neighbours, talking to a woman and child on the doorstep. Those who did not conclude they were on a religious mission would probably identify Thea Slocombe, maverick amateur detective and incompetent house-sitter. And the knowledge that Bobby Latimer might be watching from across the street was even more uncomfortable.

'Well . . .' said Lucy, taking hold of the edge of the door. 'Now you've seen me . . .'

It was a clear instruction to go away. Thea and Stephanie looked at each other, their eyes full of questions. In the still grey morning, the sound of singing floated down from the church. 'There's a service on,' said Thea, in foolish surprise.

'It's Sunday,' said Lucy. 'There's one every Sunday here. It's an important church. Quite a lot of people go.'

'Not you?' asked Stephanie boldly.

'Not me,' said Lucy emphatically. 'I have better things to do.'

Stephanie instantly morphed into something not too far from a proselytising Christian. 'Oh, but why not, when it's such a fabulous church, and you live so close? It would be a good way of making friends. And if you've got worries,

279

don't you think it might help?'

Both women stared at the child as if she had stepped out of *The Exorcist*. Thea recalled the vicar from the television sitcom, wondering whether the reality was anything at all similar. 'Stephanie?' she said. 'Where did that come from?'

'Oh – Mr Shipley, mainly,' said the girl easily. 'He thinks we're wrong to forget about the church and what it has to offer.'

'Blimey,' said Thea.

'That's very sweet,' said Lucy, her face much softer. 'What a very nice girl you are. A hundred years ago you'd be saving the souls of the heathen in China or Zanzibar or somewhere.'

'Yes, I might,' smiled Stephanie. 'But none of my family like to hear talk about religion. Not even Dad,' she finished ruefully.

'It worries people,' said Lucy. 'It worries *me*. A lot.'

Nothing was going as Thea had expected. Her assignation with Bobby began to feel both urgent and irrelevant. There was a subtext that she completely failed to understand, but could not bring herself to interrupt. 'Listen,' she said. 'Why don't I leave Stephanie here for a bit, so you two can discuss forgiveness of sins or the transmigration of souls or something, while I go and sort out a little job I've got to do? Would that be possible?'

'Why the hell not?' said Lucy, with a laugh that sounded slightly manic. Stephanie's expression of enthusiasm was almost wounding. Apparently, Thea and Drew had been very remiss in not noticing that the child had religion. A minefield lay ahead, it seemed.

'I'll be back by half past twelve and then we can go for lunch,' she said. 'If that's not too long.' She looked at her watch. 'An hour and a quarter?'

'Sounds perfect,' said Lucy. 'I'll give her a drink.'

As she got back into her car, Thea could hear loud voices in her head, telling her that it was one thing for her to go walking into strange houses and accosting potential murderers, but it was quite unacceptably another to leave her stepdaughter unprotected in the house of a woman she barely knew. But it was in an ordinary street, with people on all sides, and Lucy Sinclair was no murderer.

She drove off to Hampnett, wondering whether Bobby Latimer had been watching her for the past ten minutes, and would be following right behind her.

Chapter Eighteen

Three ancient pathways met in Hampnett. One, the Diamond Way, came directly from Northleach. Timmy's beloved Monarch's Way swirled crazily around, looping and dog-legging up from Chedworth, and after a merry dance around the A40, it proceeded waveringly all the way to Chipping Campden and beyond. Plotting it on a map, you could almost see the fleeing king desperately trying to evade his pursuers. To add to the tangle, there was a bridleway cutting across the fields.

Bobby was sitting on her coat on a patch of grass outside the church. She looked pale and cold. Thea parked her car close by and got out. 'Isn't that grass wet?' she said.

'It is, but I had to sit down. I walked here. It's barely a mile, but I was early and went on a bit.' She shook her head. 'It doesn't matter.'

'Do you want to go in the church?'

'If you like. If there's nobody in there. Tourists come here a lot.'

'I know.' Thea was experiencing strong echoes of her time in Lucy's barn – which was not visible from the centre of the village. She had not been back since, but the whole scene was vividly familiar, despite the fact that there had been snow on the previous occasion. 'It's nice in there, though,' she added weakly.

Bobby followed her, head bowed, saying nothing. Thea chose a pew near the front of the church and ordered the young woman to sit next to her. 'So, what's all this about?' she began, more like a police officer than a counsellor.

'I've had a spat with Artie. A row. A fight. Whatever you want to call it. I had to talk to somebody, but there's no one in town I can trust. They probably all know what he's done, and will be thinking I'm an idiot.'

'So what *has* he done?'

The reply was both predictable and startling. 'He's been sleeping with Faith, from over the road.'

'Gosh!' said Thea, feeling hopelessly English. 'Really?'

'I can see you're trying to imagine it. She's eight years older than him, for the Lord's sake. And thin, and plain and not even all there half the time. It's humiliating.'

'It must be. Gosh!' she said again.

'What about the kids?' Bobby suddenly wailed. 'I can't leave him – I've got nowhere to go, and hardly any money of my own. And Millie – she's such a Daddy's girl. I can't tear them apart. He'd insist on keeping her, and letting me have Buster.' By her tone it was evident that Buster was a poor substitute for his sister.

'I'm not sure . . .' Thea began, feeling helpless. What was she supposed to say? Or do? 'Why me?' she blurted. 'Haven't you got a sister or mother or something? I'm a complete stranger.'

'Because of Ollie,' said Bobby Latimer. 'It's all because of Ollie.'

Thea shivered. The interior of the church was several degrees colder than outside. 'Are you sure you want to tell me?' she said. 'You know I work with the police – sort of. I'm not going to protect anybody if it means withholding information or telling lies.'

'I just want the whole truth to come out,' said Bobby. 'For better or worse. I grew up with secrets, and I know what it's like. It warps you. It makes you mistrust everybody. I don't want that for Millie. Even less for Buster, I guess.' Her eyes suddenly filled. 'Poor Buster. What a mess! I've already made his whole existence into a secret, Lord help me.'

It was all there, behind the flimsiest veil and Thea felt little surprise. The child's dark colouring was impossible to ignore. 'He's Ollie's, isn't he?' she said.

Bobby's tears overflowed. 'Is it that obvious?' she sniffed.

'No, not really. But you've practically said it already. I just took the next step.' She looked directly at the weeping woman. 'Does Artie know?'

'He knows there's a chance, and the older Buster gets, the less doubt there is. Artie's always been very civilised about it. Until now. Ollie never took any interest, never seemed to matter much, to be honest.'

'But something changed?'

284

'Right. He came back – in that house nearly all the time, just down the street. I didn't dare go anywhere in case I bumped into him. The pub, shops – anywhere. I didn't want him to see Buster. It was all I could think about. And then bloody Lucy Sinclair told me about Artie.'

'Hang on. What?'

'A couple of weeks ago now. Said she'd been noticing for a while that he was meeting up with Faith, and they'd go off in her car together. Didn't know whether to tell me but had always thought women should stick together and it would be too awful if I realised later that she'd known about it. I didn't believe her. I mean – *Faith!*'

Thea was sharing the disbelief, at the same time as processing what must have been Bobby's own infidelity two years or so ago. 'And you confronted him?'

'I tried to. He turned it all around, saying it was payback for Ollie, and how did I like it. It all blew up last night, and we were up for hours going over it. He was so *calm*, as if it didn't matter. So I got hysterical and said I was going to leave, and he said just try it, and then it all started again this morning. The kids must have heard some of it. So I texted you, and just walked out of the house. Hours ago.'

Connections and suspicions were firing in Thea's brain, as she constructed a mental network that incorporated all these new revelations. 'Did Artie kill Ollie, then?' she asked baldly. 'Is that what you've brought me here to say?'

Before Bobby could reply, Thea's phone jingled. It was Stephanie, 'Thea?' came a breathless little voice. 'I don't want to stay here any more. Can you come back for me?'

'Why? What's the matter?'

'She's crazy. She's gone upstairs and left me on my own. She's *laughing*. It's horrible.'

'Okay. I'll be five minutes. Maybe make it ten. Soon. Maybe you should go and open the front door, just to be on the safe side. Then you can run outside if you need to. But it doesn't sound as if she's going to do anything to you.'

'She's crazy,' said the girl again. 'Stark raving mad. All I said was that the Quakers aren't too keen on the idea of confession and the easy forgiveness of sins . . .'

'Don't tell me now, Steph. Let me have another minute or two here and then I'll come for you, okay?'

'Be quick, then,' said the child on a stifled sob.

Bobby was waiting, like another forlorn little girl in need of Thea's attention. As soon as the phone call was ended she said, 'I think he might have done. He was so dreadfully jealous, you see.'

'Of you and Ollie, you mean?'

'No. Of *Millie* and Ollie. She adored him, you see. And she wouldn't stop talking about him.'

Thea remembered the scene in the town square, and fitted another piece into the picture. Her immediate feeling was of anger towards the insensitive young man who had allowed the daughter of his former lover to befriend him. Such crassness almost made her feel he deserved to be murdered. 'But nobody deserves to be murdered,' she said aloud, answering her own outrageous thought.

'No,' said Bobby. 'But then, hardly anyone liked Ollie. He really wasn't a nice person.'

'What about Vicky? His girlfriend?'

'What about her? Just another addict he picked up

somewhere.' Bobby actually shrugged the reference away. Vicky was beneath her contempt, it seemed.

'Except she wasn't. An addict, I mean. She's got leukaemia. She might be dying.'

'Rubbish. Who told you that?'

'She did and I believed her. The whole drug story is wrong. All lies. There never were any drugs.'

'Of course there were.' Bobby's eyes flickered in panic. 'There must have been. Everybody said so. Lucy, Kevin, Hunter – all of them.'

'I've got to go,' said Thea.

'But we're not finished.'

'Go home. Be nice to your children. Wait for someone to come. Are you scared of Artie?'

'No. Not at all. That's what's so insane. He's the last person in the world you'd ever think capable of murder.'

Thea was barely listening. It would only take two or three minutes to get to Lucy Sinclair's house. Nothing was going to happen to Stephanie in that time.

Was it?

You had to go out onto the A40, turn right, proceed for a short distance and then left into the western fringe of Northleach. A tractor was in front of her, turning onto the main road, which seemed to Thea to be a personal insult. A lorry came up quickly behind it, blocking Thea's exit, and then two more lorries came from the right. Suddenly there was dense traffic, making her wait for long seconds for a chance to get out of the little road from Hampnett. Almost bursting with frustration, she was tempted to lean on the horn and make everything disappear. Not that they would, of course. But there was already a stream of vehicles coming from her left, piling up behind the oblivious tractor. She was never going to get out at this rate.

The only solution was to turn left instead, go up to the roundabout where the A40 intersected with the A429 and turn right and right again into Northleach from its eastern end. Which took three minutes. Which meant it was at least ten minutes since Stephanie's phone call before she arrived at the house.

The door was open and Thea ran in, expecting to find Stephanie just inside. Instead, there was Lucy, sitting on the stairs, her head in her hands. 'Where is she?' Thea demanded.

'I scared her away. Sorry. It all got too much. She'll be all right. She's just out there somewhere.'

Thea went back to the pavement and looked all round. No sign of a solitary girl. '*Where?*' she demanded of the impossible Lucy. 'What happened? What did you do to her?'

'Other way round, dear. It was all her doing. I might have known, I suppose.'

Taking a deep breath, and telling herself to stay calm, Thea extracted her phone from her pocket and called Stephanie. It was the first time she was glad they'd given the child her own mobile. As she listened to it ring, she wondered briefly how anybody had ever survived without one.

'Hello? Thea?' came the blessed reply on the third ring. 'Where are you?'

'Here. At Lucy's house. Where are *you*?'

'By the church. With a lady.'

'What lady?'

'Here. You can talk to her.' The phone was evidently handed over and a new voice said, 'Mrs Slocombe? This is Priscilla Heap. You should come here as quick as you can.'

'Half a minute,' said Thea, and covered the ground with two seconds to spare.

It was too much to process. An avalanche of revelations and events threatened to overwhelm her sanity. Odd phrases and images kept sparking each other off – Artie and Faith, Bobby and Ollie, Lucy spilling the beans, Stephanie getting religion – *Priscilla Heap* coming to the rescue, of all people. A woman who had known Thea in another village, and seen a little too much of her less admirable side for comfort.

'Sorry!' was all she could pant. 'Oh God, Steph – I am so sorry.'

Stephanie frowned at her. 'Why are *you* sorry? You haven't done anything. It was me. It's all my fault, not yours.'

'I met her running up to the church,' said Priscilla. 'And I thought perhaps I should see if I could help. I had no idea she was yours.' She laughed. 'Although I suppose I could have guessed.'

'I couldn't think where else to go,' said Stephanie.

'But what on earth *happened*?' Thea burst out. 'I was only gone for half an hour.' The church clock chimed twelve-thirty, as if in direct correction of this assertion. 'Well, less than an hour, anyway.'

'I told you. We were talking about Quakers, and that of God in everyone, as Mr Shipley says. It all seemed all right, and I was telling her how Mr Shipley said it was something everyone should keep in mind, even when it was somebody really awful. And she said, "What about murderers?" and I said I expect there was often a reason for it, and Quakers were very keen on prison visiting and redeeming people. Redeeming,' she repeated, savouring the word. 'And then she said was it enough for the person to confess their sins, and I said I thought there might be more to it than that, and they couldn't just go free and think everything was all right, because a person was dead and that was very serious and terrible. And she started laughing and crying and being . . . just crazy. She went upstairs and that was when I phoned you.'

'Echoes of Raskolnikov,' said Priscilla Heap obscurely. Thea and Stephanie looked at her in bewilderment. '*Crime and Punishment*,' she explained. 'It's all in there. Everything you ever need to know about guilt, redemption, the sheer horror behind every murder.' She almost smacked her lips. 'Lovely stuff,' she added.

'Well, it sounds horribly upsetting,' Thea said to the child, shuddering at what Drew was going to say and not really listening to Priscilla. 'And now I suppose we ought to call a doctor or something, and get Lucy seen to. It must be some kind of breakdown.' She took out her phone, but didn't activate it. Priscilla was making small tutting sounds, as if she'd committed some sort of mistake. Thea looked up. 'I think I know who killed Ollie Sinclair,' she said. 'That's why Bobby wanted to see me. I should probably call Caz first and tell her.'

'Take the child home,' Priscilla urged. 'Never mind all the rest of it. It can wait.'

'No!' said Stephanie. 'We should stick to the plan. I'm hungry, and I want to just . . . talk. I'm not upset, exactly. Just – it was too *grown up* for me.'

'You are a very wise child,' said Priscilla. 'I am very pleased to have met you.'

Thea was feeling gauche and out of step. 'How did you happen to be here, anyway?' she asked the woman.

'I came to the church service. I'd stopped to talk to the vicar and was one of the last to leave. It was a splendid service, I must say. First class. One can never be quite sure what to expect these days.' She smiled at Stephanie. 'So you're a Quaker, are you, dear?'

Stephanie shook her head. 'I'm not. But I'm friendly with a man who knows a lot about them. They're called Friends, you know. The Society of Friends. There's a Meeting House where we live. I've never been inside it,' she finished wistfully.

Thea felt reproached, and in turn decided that Drew had been very remiss in not giving more attention to the little chapel and its small group of worshippers. But who could ever have anticipated this turn of events? Wouldn't any parent feel annoyed or offended at their child being indoctrinated without their knowledge? They were going to have to speak to Mr Shipley.

'We can go to the pub and have lasagne,' she said. The whole family was in agreement that by far the best pub meal was lasagne. 'If they do it on a Sunday,' she remembered to add. 'We might have to have roast meat and potatoes.'

'What did Bobby say?' Stephanie asked. 'Did she tell you who killed Ollie?'

'Wait a bit and I'll tell you – some of it, anyway.' She looked at Priscilla. 'Will you join us?'

'Oh, no. I have to get back. I'm walking this afternoon. It's a nature ramble. The hedgerows are just getting interesting, don't you think?'

Thea was distracted by the thorny problem of how much she could safely convey to Stephanie about love affairs and children born with the wrong father and the oddness of the whole story. Not very much, she concluded – which would make things difficult.

The square was almost deserted and had been throughout the conversation. A man was walking a dog along the pavement past the bus shelter, and another was going into a house in the south-west corner, having thrown a few curious glances at the little group. Nobody had been there to rescue Stephanie, except for the providential Priscilla. There was no real safety in a small Cotswolds settlement, as Thea had discovered on previous occasions.

'I'm desperate for the loo,' said Stephanie as if only just noticing the urgency.

'Pub, then. Quick,' said Thea, who had never entirely learnt that even quite small children could control their bladders pretty well when they had to. Her sister Jocelyn had often laughed at the way Thea got into a panic over it with Jessica. But Jocelyn had five children and knew how far she could push them when necessary.

The Sherborne Arms was irritatingly full, but Thea and Stephanie found half a table near the lavatories and staked their claim. 'You go to the Ladies and I'll call Caz,' said Thea. 'Then we'll get some food.'

The phone call was awkward, made at a table already containing two strangers. 'This is impossible,' Thea realised after half a minute. The police detective was listening patiently, but there was no way the necessary words could be uttered in such surroundings. 'Sorry,' she said. 'I chose a bad time – and a bad place. I'll try again in a few minutes.'

'Where are you?'

The pub was noisy. Thea had to shout – or felt she did. On reflection, it was obvious that Caz could hear her far better than the other way around. A whisper would have been quite enough. She named the pub and said she would be there for an hour or so.

'I'll come,' said Detective Sergeant Barkley. 'I think that would be better.'

'I think so too,' said Thea, with a long exhalation of relief. 'It really is a case of "developments" this time.' And she remembered the first time, with Millie Latimer bawling out her grief for Ollie, to a father who seemed more than likely to have been the person who killed him.

Chapter Nineteen

The A429 ran beautifully from Cirencester to Northleach, with barely a kink – although there were undulations as it passed through Fossebridge. The distance could easily be accomplished in ten minutes. Even so, Thea was startled when Caz appeared before the pub kitchen had produced her lunch. 'That was quick!' she gasped. 'Where were you?'

'At the station. There's nowhere to sit. Hello Stephanie.' She took another look. 'Are you all right?'

'We've had rather a morning,' said Thea.

'We can't talk here.' All three eyed the couple at the table accusingly, which was most unfair as they had been there first. Sharing tables was uncomfortably un-British anyway. Nobody could speak freely, and the dilemma as to whether or not to acknowledge the others' existence was seldom properly resolved. Very belatedly, Thea understood that this was the pub that featured in *This Country* – thereby attracting telly addicts who believed there was something magical about putting themselves in a setting that had been immortalised on film. Such a silly business, Thea thought, complacent in her own superiority.

The food then arrived, which made everything even more complicated. But then the inconvenient sharers of the table gave up and decided they'd finished. 'Here you are,' said the man to Caz. 'And welcome.'

'That's good of you, sir. You didn't have to leave. It's not your problem.'

'It never used to get so crowded in here,' said the woman. 'Spoils it, really.'

And they got up to go. Caz and Thea immediately spread themselves out, to deter any newcomers, leaving Stephanie on a chair at one side of the table, while the women occupied a bench against the wall.

'Steph – we're going to talk business for a bit, okay?' said Thea. 'Some of it isn't really suitable for you to hear, so I'll talk quietly. It's going to seem a bit rude, but don't take it personally. Is that all right with you?' Thea smiled. 'At least you're right in the middle of things – like you wanted.'

'That's okay. I can listen to my phone.' She produced the mobile and a miraculous earphone, which she plugged into herself and the gadget, with a smug grin. Then she looked down at her lunch. 'This lasagne's *huge*. I'll never manage all of it.'

Thea laughed. 'Yes you will. Take it slowly.' She turned to Caz. 'Do you want anything? A drink?'

'I suppose I should. It looks bad otherwise. I'll go and get myself something.'

The detective's relaxed demeanour and the inexorable passing of time both made Thea restless. Things could be happening out there, just down the street, which the police ought to know about. It was already nearly an hour since she had left Bobby Latimer – what would she be doing now? Where would she go? Her disclosures had been cut short by Stephanie's phone call, with nothing decided. Had she really been trying to say that her husband was a murderer?

And what about wretched Lucy Sinclair?

At last, after what felt like an endless delay, Caz was sitting close beside her, listening to the report of the Hampnett rendezvous. She asked few questions and made no notes, despite the convolutions of marital infidelity and neighbourly spying.

'So,' Thea summarised, 'Bobby thinks Artie was jealous of Ollie and probably killed him.' It sounded almost ludicrously stark, put like that. And for the first time, the absolute lack of evidence raised its annoying head.

'But didn't he take revenge on her by having an affair of his own?' Caz said. 'Didn't that make it quits? And when did he first know about Ollie and Buster? Sounds as if it was never much of a secret – so why now?'

'Because of Millie. She'd got close to Ollie, who seems to have threatened to replace Artie as her favourite man. He was much nearer the normal age to be her father, after all. And if he's already Buster's dad, then that would make it seem more natural – in the family, so to speak.'

Caz raised an eyebrow at this, and said nothing for a

moment. 'Maybe not from Bobby's viewpoint. It all sounds rather *crowded*, don't you think?'

Thea blinked. 'You're not suggesting it was *her*, are you?' She tried to think. 'It would make some sort of sense, I suppose. She'd have as much motive as Artie, or nearly. But she must have feelings for Ollie, surely – the father of her child and all that?'

'It looks to me as if there are other people with motives that go back a bit further and a bit deeper. I told you, didn't I, that I've been digging into Kevin Sinclair's background? Well, there's quite a lot to dig up. He doesn't come out of it smelling of roses, not by a long way.'

Thea glanced at Stephanie, who was making a very obvious demonstration of not listening to the conversation, eyes focused on nothing as she listened to whatever was on her playlist. The sheer competence of the child was impressive. Thea had never got round to compiling a playlist of her own, or even being entirely sure how it might be done.

'Oh!' she said to Caz's remark. 'Then the plot really does thicken, doesn't it?'

'Did something happen to your daughter?' Caz went on. 'She looked a bit shell-shocked when I came in.'

'Yes, that's a whole other thing you ought to know about, I suppose. I left her at Lucy Sinclair's this morning—' But she got no further than that. They were loudly interrupted by DI Jeremy Higgins marching into the pub and calling 'Barkley!' so loudly that every head turned to stare at him. The man at the bar and some others showed obvious signs of knowing who he was and being excited and intrigued as a result.

Caz stood up and calmly replied, 'Sir?'

'Come with me.'

So she went, with the faintest of rueful grimaces at Thea.

Stephanie looked up, wide-eyed and pulled the plug out of her ear. 'What?' she said, like a deaf person. 'Is she going?'

'Apparently.'

'Did you tell her about Lucy?'

'Sadly, no. I was just about to, when she had to go. I suppose it doesn't much matter. It's not really for her to deal with. We ought to get a doctor or something.' The importance of Lucy Sinclair's vapourings had already receded. 'I expect she was just overwrought because of her operation and everything,' she said vaguely.

'She's crazy,' said Stephanie. 'And crazy people are scary.'

Thea was sitting back, pressing into the wooden bench behind her, trying to sift her thoughts. *Echoes of Raskolnikov* reverberated insistently. She did read *Crime and Punishment* when she was seventeen and had a boyfriend three years older who told her if she didn't read it then, she never would. It had made disappointingly little impression on her. 'I thought Raskolnikov was the man in *Doctor Zhivago*,' she muttered.

'What?' said Stephanie again. She had watched the film with Thea and Drew only a month earlier.

'The Tom Courtenay chap. The one driving the train just before the intermission.'

'Strelnikov,' said Stephanie instantly. 'Nothing like what you just said.'

'Silly me,' said Thea cheerfully. 'What would I do without you?'

'I've finished,' the child announced, having scraped every atom of grilled cheese from the edges of her dish. 'It was yummy.'

'So have I,' Thea noticed, wondering how she had eaten so much while talking so intently to Barkley. 'We should go.'

'Where? What's happening now?'

'I don't know. I have no idea.' They stood in the town square again, pulling up collars against a nasty east wind that had come from nowhere. 'Maybe we should have a look at the church. Isn't that one of the things we came for?'

'I don't really want to now. I think we should go back and see if Lucy's all right.'

'Stephanie Slocombe – you're a much better man than I am,' Thea announced. 'I'd already forgotten about her.'

The girl giggled. A year ago, she would have protested *We're not men!* But now she let it pass. Thea's jokes took some getting used to, but it was great when you did. Nobody else was quite as funny as Thea, once you got the hang of her. 'You can't have really forgotten about her,' she said.

'Well, let's say she slipped my mind for a moment. You think we should go and check on her, then? It's right here, so I suppose we should.'

'Where did Caz go? Is she coming back?'

'Her boss wanted her. I thought we might see something going on out here, but it's as quiet as always.' The only sounds were of voices and laughter in the pub behind them.

The church clock struck half past one, for good measure. 'We've only been here an hour,' said Thea. 'I thought it was a lot more than that.' It amazed her how much could be said, absorbed, understood and imagined in such a short time. 'I get the feeling the whole thing is coming to a head.'

'But where?' asked the child, looking round.

'In a house, maybe. There are quite a lot of them, spread around. I thought I knew who must have killed Ollie, but now I'm not at all sure. And it could be anyone – somebody I've never met or even heard of.'

'I don't think so,' said Stephanie, shivering in the wind. 'Let's not just stand here. I'm freezing.'

'Right. Come on, then. The car's outside Lucy's house, anyway, so we have to go there whether we want to or not.'

'I don't want to, but I think we should,' said Stephanie stoutly.

When did she get so grown-up, wondered Thea, not sure that she altogether liked it.

The door of Lucy's house was wide open as they approached, heading for the spot where Thea's car stood ten yards further down the street. A woman was standing there, looking into the house.

'Who's that?' asked Stephanie, showing an unwarranted confidence that Thea would know.

Except the confidence was entirely warranted. 'I think it's Tessa. Kevin Sinclair's woman. I wonder what she's doing?'

The pavement was so wide that they could have walked past leaving six feet or more of space between themselves and the doorway, and probably escaping notice. Tessa appeared to be calm and there was every reason to leave her to straighten Lucy out in whatever way seemed best. But there were invisible currents criss-crossing the quiet street, with Lucy caught in the meshes. She had known about Artie and Faith and had told Bobby. That alone justified feelings of hatred and revenge towards her. Not only the erring couple but their significant others had reason to blame Lucy for their lives falling apart. It explained, in fact, the need for a house-sitter. This came to Thea in a flash, while she was still a yard away from the door. Details had yet to formulate themselves, but the stark vulnerability of the property was already clear. Now Tessa was here, a woman who had no reason to feel warm towards her partner's former wife. And, for good measure – rather *more* than a good measure, really – a male voice was heard coming up behind them. 'Ah – Mrs Slocombe, if I'm not very much mistaken. Here again, is it? What magnetic charm this dull little village must have for you.'

She turned round slowly. 'Mr Lanning,' she said.

'Guilty as charged,' he said fatuously. But there was an intelligent gleam in his eye. 'And this is . . . ?' he indicated Stephanie with a tilt of his chin.

'My daughter,' said Thea, for economy. She saw no need to elaborate.

The house door was still open, but Tessa had moved a few steps into the hallway. There was no sign of Lucy. Hearing the voices, Tessa turned round. 'The door wasn't locked,' she said.

'I suppose that was me,' said Stephanie. 'Most doors lock themselves, don't they? I mean, when you shut them behind you.'

'It wasn't you. I was here after you,' said Thea.

They all looked at the mechanism; even Thea felt a need to check what she already knew. It was a basic Yale with a metal nub that you slid up or down depending on whether you wanted the lock to engage. For all her apparent paranoia, Lucy had failed to update her security in that respect. Most likely, thought Thea, her fears lay in more subtle directions.

'So where is she?' said Tessa.

'Why do you want her?' asked Thea. Then she looked at Hunter. 'And you – were you coming here as well?'

'Not specifically,' he said unhelpfully.

'It's the drugs,' said Tessa obscurely. 'I wanted to confront her about her lies about the drugs.'

The presence of Stephanie was having a subduing effect on them all. Nobody could clearly speak out about sex or drugs or violent death with a child in their midst. Even Thea felt inhibited, when she wanted quite badly to immerse herself in what felt like an oncoming climax. It only needed Higgins and Caz to come hurtling up, tyres screeching, to complete the picture.

'They've convinced Kevin that his son has never used any hard drugs,' Tessa went on, her tone quite conversational. 'So he's had to think back to where the idea came from – and it was Lucy. Two months ago, she told him quite plainly that his son was injecting heroin and was stealing money, living in a squat and mixing with undesirable characters. But before that – *long* before that, when Ollie was a teenager – she made similar accusations. She turned Kevin against the boy, then and now.'

Thea looked up at the windows over their heads. Lucy was almost certainly inside one of them, and quite probably hearing what was being said. 'But why?' she said.

Tessa sighed. 'Jealousy, we assume. It all came pouring out last night. Poor Kev, he's completely wrecked. Destroyed. If Lucy wanted him to suffer, she's certainly achieved her purpose.'

'Jealousy of what?'

'Kevin having children that weren't hers. She was desperate for her own, but he went for a vasectomy without telling her. Lied about it for a bit. Stupid of him, but she was always difficult to confront, apparently. He only confessed when she was too old for it to matter any more. He says she took it very well, as far as he could tell. Started adopting all those animals, training herself up to work with computers, spending his money on the barn conversion. Ollie and his sister were off making their own lives by then, so her nose wasn't being rubbed in it any more. But then Ollie came back, and Kevin was away in his lorry most of the time, and suddenly they were getting divorced.' She frowned. 'I'm still a bit hazy about what was the final straw.'

Everything had come out in good order, making sense and clearly assumed to be true. There were even credible motives behind the accusations. But Thea's thought processes were still clogged with information that Bobby Latimer had so recently revealed. She still assumed that everyone hated Lucy for their own good reasons, but that none of them linked directly to Ollie Sinclair.

Hunter Lanning had put a large hand on Stephanie's shoulder, and she was trustingly leaning against him.

'This is all a bit rich, eh?' he murmured to her. 'All these people – what are they like?'

It was avuncular, witty, self-confident and entirely benign. Stephanie looked up at him and laughed. Thea felt torn between a conventional panic about middle-aged men and pre-adolescent girls on one side and an instinctive knowledge that there was no harm in the man on the other. Perhaps he was genuinely and extraordinarily open-minded, as he claimed. Perhaps everything was to be tolerated equally. Perhaps that was actually quite a saintly way to be.

'Shall we go for a little walk?' he went on, with a wink at Thea. 'Just down to the end of the street and back. Give these ladies a chance to clear the air. We won't go out of sight,' he promised.

'All right,' said Stephanie, with a look at her stepmother that combined apology with an awareness that she was not meant to be involved too closely with whatever came next.

Which left just Tessa and Thea together on Lucy's doorstep, directly visible to any Latimers who might be in their front room over the road, and obliquely so to people in adjacent houses. Faith and Livia would have to peer sideways through their downstairs windows, or else lean out from upstairs. It could not be assumed that none of this was happening.

'I'm going in,' said Tessa, and did so. Thea was not conscious of any definite decision. She just followed automatically.

'Stephanie was here before lunch – just her and Lucy,' she told Tessa. 'She ran off because she was scared. She said

Lucy was behaving like a madwoman and went upstairs in hysterics. They were talking about forgiveness of sins.'

'Huh!' said Tessa. 'Sounds about right. The kid seems fine again now, anyway. Hunter's the perfect chap to be keeping an eye on her.'

'You know him of course,' Thea remembered.

'Everyone knows Hunter. He's like a king around here.'

'Lucy!' Thea called, more loudly than she'd intended. 'Where are you? We're coming upstairs to find you.'

It was like a perverse game of hide-and-seek. She almost added *Ready or not.*

There was a thud from one of the bedrooms, which sent both women up the stairs at top speed, Thea in front. On the landing there were three closed doors. 'This is her room,' said Thea, and took hold of the doorknob.

'Careful!' said Tessa, her face suddenly pale. 'You don't know what she might do.'

But Thea pushed and the door opened and she went in.

Lucy was standing by a wardrobe, a suitcase on the floor at her feet. 'I dropped it,' she said blankly. 'I forgot it had things in it.'

'Are you going somewhere?' Thea asked. The glittering eyes and rigid mouth all too starkly confirmed Stephanie's diagnosis of insanity.

'Or are you *on* something?' Tessa said. 'You look as high as a kite.'

'That's not drugs,' said Thea slowly, while her heart thundered in her chest. 'That's *guilt.*'

'I guess you're right,' said Tessa, sinking her substantial body onto the side of the bed and staring hard at Lucy. 'You planned it every step of the way, didn't you, you bloody bitch. Just to get at poor old Kev.'

'*Poor old Kev!*' Lucy shrieked with a ghastly grin. 'That man deserves everything he gets. He's ruined five lives at least with his selfishness and carelessness and total lack of responsibility. He had to be *shown*. Somebody had to show him.'

Thea had once before been forced to compare current events with ancient legends. Medea had cropped up before, and here she was again. The woman who killed a man's children in order to teach him a lesson. The final act of a wife with no more weapons in her armoury. 'You killed Ollie,' she said. 'Just to teach Kevin a lesson?'

'Five lives?' Tessa was trying to calculate who they were, caught up with a silly distraction. 'Ollie, Sayida, Annie – who else?'

'Me, you fool.'

'That's only four.'

'Don't forget yourself,' sneered Lucy. 'You might not know it yet, but you were going to be just another one he betrayed, sooner or later.'

'I don't think so. Kevin's no saint, but he's just an ordinary man. It doesn't do to have unrealistic expectations.'

Thea was speechless at this bizarre exchange. A woman had come close to confessing to a deliberate murder of an innocent young man, and her accuser was worrying about irrelevant details. 'Planned?' she managed to say.

Tessa nodded. 'Right from those lies about drugs. She needed to keep Kevin estranged from Ollie right to the end, to make it all the worse for him. Don't you see? If they'd got back together, everything she wanted would be gone. Her whole life has been spent in resentment and jealousy and hating. I know all about you, Lucy Sinclair. Never making any lasting friends, using people, trying to make them fit your own ideas of them, and throwing them aside when they wouldn't play ball. All nice and smiley on the outside, and a total sociopath underneath. Those animals you rescued were a good smokescreen, a perfect foil, giving you their love whether you deserved it or not. And then you killed Ollie,' she tailed off in a whisper. 'For no real reason at all.'

'Yes,' said Lucy. 'I thought it would be easy.'

She turned to Thea. 'I never guessed that you'd be the one to ruin it. I should have done, after the Hampnett business. You were always in the wrong place, saying the wrong thing, refusing to *co-operate*. And after all that, your bloody kid, so wide-eyed and innocent, talking about sin without the slightest idea of what she was saying.' The hysterical laughter erupted without warning. 'That was just so funny. That's the thing about life, you know. It's just one big joke.'

'I have no idea what you mean,' said Thea untruthfully. When she had time to think about it, she supposed it would turn out to be disconcertingly accurate.

'See what I mean?' said Tessa. 'She was even trying to manipulate you. You were intended to be a distraction, a red herring. Instead, you kept asking questions and getting in the way.'

'Like I always do,' sighed Thea. Then her phone pinged

307

with a text and she took it out of her pocket, Stephanie at the forefront of her mind.

Instead it was from Caz Barkley.

FOUND THE MURDER WEAPON

Thea texted right back.

AND I'VE FOUND THE MURDERER

Chapter Twenty

Lucy put up no resistance at all when the police came to the house and listened to the story. Hunter and Stephanie came back; Tessa phoned Kevin and gently reported what had happened; the neighbours all kept away and Thea drove herself and her stepdaughter home.

'Don't go anywhere,' Caz said. 'We'll need a proper statement.'

In the car, Thea tried to keep the conversation safely abstract, but was minimally successful. Stephanie was quiet but composed. The adult world was still a surprising place, full of unanticipated shocks and revelations, which she quickly processed as part of growing up. If this was the reality, she was going to have to accommodate it, and take it in her stride. She already knew that people died when they were young, at the hands of others who were bad or sometimes mad. It fitted with fairy tales and films and old legends. 'I feel lucky, sort of,' she said, as they turned off at Stow to take the short way home.

'Lucky?'

'To be seeing so much that's *real*,' she tried to explain. 'Not just on the tablet or phone. It's the difference between 2D and 3D, if you see what I mean. It makes me feel special.'

'I know exactly what you mean,' said Thea.

Caz did not appear until the next day. The children were outside with Drew, Andrew and Fiona. There appeared to be an earnest conversation going on. Hepzie was with them, wandering aimlessly between the various pairs of legs, sniffing at the walking stick that Andrew leant on.

'She confessed,' said Caz. 'She's not a bit sorry. I felt physically sick. How anyone could do that to a harmless young man . . .'

'What did she do exactly?'

'You probably don't want to know exactly. It was a pruning saw, with jagged teeth. Sharp and very nasty.'

'How did you find it?'

'Fluke. She'd dumped it in a litter bin, pushed down to the bottom. And then a tractor accidentally knocked it over, and the farmer was trying to pick everything up when he found the weapon. He wouldn't normally have done anything about it, but one of his Ukrainian workers was with him and made the connection. It's not easy to dispose of a murder weapon, you know. Almost as tricky as a body.'

'What happened in the hospital, then? Before the

operation? Nurse Kate said she thought it was emotional – stress or something.'

Caz shook her head. 'No idea. It never came up. But stress sounds about right. She just never imagined how it would take her afterwards. She must have done the deed late on Tuesday or the early hours of Wednesday – that's what she says, anyway. Then most likely not slept all that night, before going off to have her surgery. It wasn't anything very major, you know. She fixed it all up with the hospital – you can name your date, pretty much, when you go private. It was meant to be a cast-iron alibi, with the visit to you muddying the waters on Tuesday, and then organising it that Ollie wouldn't be found for days.'

'What? How?'

'Oh, that's still a bit muddled, but she was sure he was going to be on his own, with nobody worrying about him all that week. She'd fixed the girlfriend somehow, which also took care of the mother. But she didn't know Vicky would send her friend to check up on him. Apparently, that was just one more thing that went wrong. Took us a while to figure it out, but Lucy believed Vicky would be otherwise engaged for the relevant days. She wasn't too busy to get poor Ms Shapley to go round to check on Ollie, though.'

Thea went on trying to fit it all together. 'She said Kevin was a menace to women – implied it, anyway. That he ruined lives. But I don't really get it . . .'

'She said that to us, as well. Kevin was an absent father, messed up badly and the kids were never altogether right emotionally. We'd worked that out already. Then he

311

seemed to get his act together when they were teenagers, and was all over them for a bit, trying to make up for the past. But it didn't last. The sister got away, seems to be making a decent life for herself, but Ollie never really got straightened out. Things went wrong for him.'

'But no drugs.'

'Nope. He wasn't at all self-destructive, just a bit hopeless and unlucky. Lost all ambition once he was too old for the competitive stuff, although the films he was making sound pretty good to me. He never quite stopped wishing he could get his parents back together, according to the girlfriend. Immature, probably.'

'What about the Latimers and the women next door?'

'What about them?'

'Well – the affairs and all that. Bobby's youngest is Ollie's child, she told me. And Artie was sleeping with Faith. And Lucy was stirring it all up.' Thea frowned. 'Except, when I thought about it again last night, I wasn't sure it made any sense. I mean – they were all cheerfully together on Wednesday, with no sign of any of that sort of thing.'

'The operative words are "Lucy stirring it all up", I should think. She was addicted to spreading rumours. Telling people that Hunter Lanning was a fascist, for example. He's nothing of the sort. He kept trying to give Lucy another chance to be a proper part of the community, but she always threw it in his face.'

'And then she had the nerve to get him to drive her to Oxford,' said Thea, for whom this detail still rankled. 'After I'd refused.'

312

'He'd already offered, apparently. He's a bit of a fossil, I know, but he's really a nice man.'

'He thinks Northleach is really a community, does he?'

'You think he's wrong?'

'I didn't see much sign of it. They all seem to be at each other's throats, or else breaking up each other's marriages. You know, Bobby Latimer herself said she'd had an affair with Ollie. And Artie admitted to having sex with Faith. That much is true.'

Caz grinned. 'Okay – but isn't that just normal small-town stuff? Take any village and half the kids will be the biological offspring of some other man than their mothers' husbands. If you follow. It's always been the same. Good for the gene pool, presumably.'

'I thought Artie had killed Ollie,' said Thea humbly.

'Well he didn't. And I think we can safely say that the Latimers will weather the storm and all will be fine.'

'And we might never know about Faith and Livia,' sighed Thea.

Later, she tried to give a final account of it all to Drew, but he cut her off. 'Spare me,' he said. 'Just tell me you won't be going to Northleach again for a while. And let me tell you what Fiona suggested today.'

'Go on, then.'

'She's offered to work here, as well as Andrew. There she was, all along, right under our noses, ready and able. From now on, it's Slocombe, Emerson & Emerson. And the first thing we're going to do is get cracking on the new building in the field. It's onwards and upwards for us.'

313

Thea knew better than to cry, *But what about me?* Nor did she mention that she had just received an email from a man in Oddington who was having great difficulty in finding someone to watch over his houseful of animals at the end of June.

REBECCA TOPE is the author of three bestselling crime series, set in the stunning Cotswolds, Lake District and West Country. She lives on a smallholding in rural Herefordshire, where she enjoys the silence and plants a lot of trees, but also manages to travel the world and enjoy civilisation from time to time. Most of her varied experiences and activities find their way into her books, sooner or later.

rebeccatope.com